THE LEONARDO GULAG

Also by Kevin Doherty

Patriots
Villa Normandie
Charlie's War

THE LEONARDO GULAG

A NOVEL

KEVIN DOHERTY

OCEANVIEW PUBLISHING
SARASOTA, FLORIDA

ISBN 978-1-60809-435-6

Published in the United States of America by Oceanview Publishing

Sarasota, Florida

www.oceanviewpub.com

10 9 8 7 6 5 4 3 2

PRINTED IN THE UNITED STATES OF AMERICA

In memory of my mother and father,
Winnie and Willie Doherty

ACKNOWLEDGMENTS

I owe particular thanks to certain people.

To Pat and Bob Gussin, Lee Randall, and the team at Oceanview, who have done such a great job.

To my agent, Leslie Gardner of Artellus, for her wise counsel.

Above all, to Roz, without whom *The Leonardo Gulag* would never have happened.

THE LEONARDO GULAG

PART ONE

CHAPTER 1

1950. Russia

A FREEZING JANUARY night. Snow blows into drifts all around Lobachev Row in this small town north of Moscow. It shrouds the windows of the dom, blocks its doorways, lines the branches of the chestnut and lime trees in the lane. Ice lies thick on the canal. No barges have moved along it for over a month now, though the nearby rail line is kept clear and the occasional goods train still trundles past. At this dead hour, three in the morning, sensible citizens are fast asleep. There is silence but for the distant creak and clank of a snowplow working through the night. There will be extra wages for the driver and whichever street-sweeping gang is following the machine.

But now there is another sound, drawing closer, that of a vehicle engine. Headlights appear. A militia truck is arriving. Brakes squeal as it skids to a halt, raising flurries of snow.

The coarse voices of the militiamen echo in the stairwell of the dom, their boots stamp and scrape, there is the ring of metal striking metal. Doors are pounded, names demanded—some apartments have lately been subdivided, yet again, and their numbering changed. Behind the doors sleepy, frightened voices reply; the men move on.

Three flights up, a young man is woken by the din. He starts upright on the ancient sofa that doubles as his bed. His name is Pasha Kalmenov. He is twenty years old.

In the darkness of the room a shadow flits past. His mother is already awake and on her feet, drawing her shawl about her shoulders and chest. The shawl is black, embroidered with tiny blue cornflowers. Her hair, streaked with gray, tumbles loose over the shawl, her long winter petticoats and shift trail along the floor, issuing soft sounds with each step.

"Please, dear Lord," she mumbles. She crosses herself before the holy icon on the wall and kisses the crucifix in Christ's hand, careful as always not to kiss the face of Jesus since that was what Judas did. "Dear Lord Jesus, protect us. Don't let it be us."

Pasha rubs sleep from his eyes. "Protect us, Mama? Why? Whatever's going on, it's nothing to do with us. We've done nothing wrong."

She shakes her head. "No need to have done anything wrong, Pashenka." She has faith in Christ and she trusts the Father of the Great Soviet People, Josef Vissarionovich Stalin, whose portrait watches over them from the opposite wall, but she has also lived through the purges. She knows about boots stomping on stairs in the middle of the night and doors being thumped. She knows the sound of rifles being readied.

She jumps as a fist pounds the thin door.

"Kalmenov!" a voice bellows.

There is more pounding, from something harder than a fist this time; perhaps a rifle butt. Pasha fears that the door will cave in if they keep this up.

"Pavel Pavlovich Kalmenov—we know you're in there!"

At the sound of his name, Pasha feels something shift in his stomach, as if a great stone has suddenly descended toward his bowels. He searches hurriedly for his clothes in the darkness.

Mama moans, torn between her two saviors, Jesus and Josef Vissarionovich.

"Open the door, Mama," Pasha tells her. "It's a mistake. We'll straighten it out. Don't worry."

The words sound hollow even to him.

Mama tugs her shawl tighter and slides back the bolt. She mumbles another prayer as she does so, having opted for Christ over Josef Vissarionovich.

The sound of the bolt magnifies like a gunshot in the moment of stillness that has fallen. The door bursts open. By the light of their torches Pasha can see that there are four of them, gangling boys no older than himself but made self-important by their uniforms. Their red faces are burning with the cold. Their eyes remind him of the dogs he watches skulking around the meat market: barren and dull, stupid; but dangerous. Their racket must have woken the whole dom. He supposes this is their way, to tell everybody that something is going on and they are in charge of it.

The stone is pushing harder at his bowels.

"Marya Kalmenova?" one of them, a junior sergeant according to his stripes, barks at Mama. "You took your time."

She dips her head. "I apologize, comrade officer. Please excuse the delay. I was asleep."

"Why are you apologizing, Mama? There's nothing to apologize for."

"Where is he?"

"I'm here. You're the ones who should apologize. This is our home. You can't just come pushing in here in the middle of the night, as if we're criminals. What do you want with me?"

Torchlight flashes over Mama's shoulder and falls on Pasha. The sergeant pushes past Mama. He has a pistol in one hand and a rifle slung over his shoulder.

"Pavel Pavlovich Kalmenov, you're to come with us. Get a move on. We'll see who's a criminal."

Mama's hands fly to her cheeks. In the torchlight her eyes shine with tears. "Why him? He's done nothing wrong, comrade."

"Hush, Mama."

"We'll want your passport, Kalmenov. And your propiska."

Every adult citizen has to have an internal passport. The propiska is the residency permit, also obligatory. As Pasha and everyone else knows, Josef Vissarionovich likes to keep a beady eye on his beloved masses, likes to know they are snug and all accounted for in the places where they are meant to be—and preferably in those places only—and that those places are not being infiltrated by criminals, foreigners, gypsies, or other wandering subversives. The sagacious Comrade General Secretary knows best, always has the Soviet people's true interests at heart. He knows all about wandering subversives, having been one himself in his time; and look what that led to.

Without a passport and the right propiska, a person belongs nowhere and is entitled to nothing: no education, no accommodation, no job. In short, no hope. Only arrest and a term behind bars—or worse, much worse, in the gulag. Good reasons to keep the passport and propiska safely close to hand.

Pasha digs in the pockets of his long coat—his late father's coat—finds the green passport with the permit pasted inside and passes it to the sergeant.

The other militiamen are cramming in now. The tiny room is packed. There is ice everywhere from their boots. It glitters in the torchlight. These men, too, are armed to the teeth. What were they expecting—a nest of counter-revolutionaries? Someone switches on the ceiling light, but there has been no electricity all week. There is only the oil lamp, empty and unlit.

A movement catches Pasha's eye. At the edge of the torchlight, old Griboyev, their neighbor whose family shares the kitchen, is peering in: two terrified eyes and a quivering chin thick with stubble.

The eyes take in the guns, the uniformed militiamen, and Pasha and Mama. The old man's wife is whispering for him to come away, tugging at his elbow, but Griboyev stays put. This is too good to miss. His four daughters join him in the doorway.

"Help us, my Lord," Mama is murmuring. She crosses herself over and over.

"Save your breath, Kalmenova," says the sergeant. "God isn't in charge. We took over long ago."

Pasha glances at Josef Vissarionovich. Impossible to guess whether he agrees or not.

The sergeant produces a typewritten form and shakes its folds open. He squints at Pasha's documents by the light of his torch and compares them with the form. Pasha realizes it is an arrest warrant. The stone descends deeper in his gut.

The passport and propiska disappear into the sergeant's pocket. He secures the flap.

"Wait—I need those," objects Pasha. "Give them back."

"You won't need them for a while. I'm saving you the inconvenience of worrying about their safety. How did you get out of military service? Who did you bribe?"

"Do we look like we can afford bribes? I'm a student, I'm exempt. It says so right there."

Other torches are sweeping the room. Someone whistles softly, one long, falling note. The walls are covered with sheets of Pasha's drawings. More are strewn on the floor, over the table, on the windowsill, even among his blankets and bedding. They spill from his portfolio case.

Someone chases the Griboyevs away. The only sounds are Mama's sniffles and the rustle of sheets of paper being seized and examined.

"Where'd he get all this paper?" one of the militiamen is complaining. "How does he afford it? Is he even allowed all this?"

The sergeant pokes among the drawings, using the barrel of his pistol to swivel the pages toward him. Pasha sees the look that comes over the man's face, the same look he sees in the face of everyone who beholds his artistic ability. It is the look that is in old man Griboyev's glittering eyes when he sidles over from next door to watch Pasha at work.

The sergeant raises his gaze from the scattered pages and looks directly at Pasha. Torchlight reflects from the sea of paper. Pasha would like to capture that play of light on the man's face. He will try from memory, he will go within himself and find it once this present confusion is over and the militiamen have gone. For confusion it surely is; and they will go away when they know that.

Surely.

But the sergeant puts an end to any such hope. He slaps the warrant down on the arm of the sofa.

"Sign this."

"What is it?"

"Acknowledgment of the legal and proper means of your arrest. Says we've done it by the book. Says we didn't intimidate you or beat you, you're coming with us willingly. Says you loved the whole experience."

"Arrest?" cries Mama. "Not my Pashenka! We're honest citizens here. His father gave his life, he was a hero and a martyr in the Great Patriotic War. This is a terrible mistake!"

"Mama—enough!"

She tries to rush forward, arms outstretched to embrace Pasha, as if she can wrench him from the jaws of this decision that neither of them understands and that has been made in some unknown place by someone that neither of them even knew existed.

Her path is blocked. A militiaman holds her back.

"Come with you where?" says Pasha.

"Militia station."

"Why? What law have I broken? I have a right to know."

"So now you're a lawyer? Sign the damned thing."

Someone pushes a fountain pen into Pasha's right hand. It is a cheap Soyuz, a type he would never trust. Ink splutters over the warrant.

"Clumsy bastard," says the militiaman who provided the pen. He seizes Pasha's hand and twists it back, clear of the warrant. The sergeant's pistol chops down hard on the man's arm. The militiaman wails and drops Pasha's hand. More ink splatters from the pen.

The sergeant bends down to Pasha.

"Nobody harmed you. He didn't hurt you. Agreed?"

Pasha stares at him, baffled. What kind of arrest is this, in which the prisoner is first mocked and manhandled but is then protected? As if the insults and bullying come naturally, instinctively, but the protection is by order of a higher authority and has to be considered consciously and remembered just in time. As if there will be trouble otherwise.

"No one harmed me. I loved the whole experience."

"Very good, Kalmenov. You're learning. All you have to do is cooperate."

"All you have to do is go to hell."

The sergeant chuckles. He takes a corner of blanket and dabs the blobs of ink dry. Pasha transfers the pen to his left hand and signs the warrant. Mama whimpers again.

They allow him a visit to the communal toilet in the courtyard before they set off. Two of the militiamen stand guard outside. They make him keep the door open.

In the truck the sergeant rides in the cab beside the driver. Pasha sits in the back surrounded by the other militiamen, including the one with the injured arm. All of them cling to the leather straps hanging from the metal roof. Even so, with every heave of the vehicle as it bounces into potholes camouflaged by snow, they are tossed up and down and from side to side so that they can never be still for more than a few seconds at a time.

The truck has no heating system. One tiny bulb mounted on the bulkhead is the only source of illumination; it changes the flushed faces of the militiamen to a sickly green, making them pale versions of the truck's paintwork.

The journey takes forever. Pasha cannot see out, so never knows where he is. Yet there is a militia station not far from the dom; a few minutes would have brought them there. He listens to the keening of the wind, the drone of the engine, the rattle of the restraint chains fixed to the metal side walls of the truck. The sergeant has spared him the chains—another part of the mystery: to be arrested but not in chains, which is the picture Pasha carries in his mind of arrested prisoners.

At his feet lies the bag into which Mama bundled some clothes for him. The bag already had a few sheets of his drawings and several partly filled sketch pads. He grips its top and keeps his gaze fixed on it, because he is wondering now if his instinct was wrong—he does not want to look at his captors or meet their gaze, he no longer wants to draw any of this nightmare. He does not want to go to the special place within himself for any part of this. It would be a desecration, as wrong as spitting on Mama's holy icon. He wants to be safely back home, to wake and discover that a nightmare is truly all this episode has been, and to embark on a day as uneventful as yesterday and the days before it.

This is all he wants.

* * *

At last, the drone of the engine begins to fall. He feels the truck slowing. The brakes squeal, the vehicle sways suddenly, turns a tight corner and halts. Its engine continues to run.

He hears a tremendous cacophony of noise from outside: sudden piercing squeals and crashes as of great unoiled doors sliding back and forth, a multitude of voices shouting commands, deafening screeches that are high pitched but resonant in timbre, like moving metal plates being pressed against other metal plates with great force.

Over everything is the steady roar of what sounds like an enormous furnace, its volume rising and falling in a constant rhythm. He cannot imagine what furnace could be so huge. Or where he is that he can hear such a sound.

Every now and then arises a terrible shriek that raises the hairs on the back of his neck. It sounds louder each time, closer. It lasts for ten or fifteen seconds, then dies, but soon returns.

All this tumult booms and reverberates as if occurring in a giant enclosed chamber.

The truck moves forward again. Stops. The engine shuts down, its vibration ceases.

They have arrived. But wherever they are, it is no militia station.

CHAPTER 2

Twelve years earlier

PASHA IS EIGHT years old. He is in his classroom in School Number 2, on Armory Lane. There are pencils and crayons and sheets of paper on every child's desk because the art lesson is underway.

Like all the class, Pasha is busily drawing. He draws with his left hand. He holds the pencil perfectly, controls it perfectly. Autumn sunlight slants through the tall windows and falls across the page as his picture takes shape.

The children are enjoying themselves; the room is lively with chatter and laughter. Pasha is the only one who is silent, lips pressed together in concentration, every atom in his small body dedicated to his task.

There is a special place within him where he goes when he is drawing. A good place. He is there now.

On the wall is a picture of a man in military uniform. Pasha knows the man's name. Everyone knows it. Everyone loves him. He has smiling eyes and is hoisting aloft a happy, rosy-cheeked child. Each morning before lessons, Pasha and his classmates chant the words beneath the picture in unison:

"Thank you, dear Comrade Stalin, for our wonderful childhood!"

As they chant, they hold little flags emblazoned with the red star and the hammer and sickle, exactly like the flag the child in the picture is waving.

Pasha's teacher has the whole class to supervise, so she moves diligently from desk to desk, child to child, bending close to offer encouragement here, a suggestion there. Praising, always praising.

But her gaze constantly returns to Pasha and she keeps coming back to his desk; she cannot help herself. Little Pasha is the only child for whom she has no suggestions. Has never had any suggestions. It has been a month now since he joined her class. His previous teacher told her what to expect and now she sees it for herself, day after day. When she watches this child draw, she feels as awed as she would by the performance of an athlete or the daring of a circus star. She knows she is witnessing a miracle.

The other children labor over flat, scrawled figures with dot eyes and misshapen, misplaced stick limbs, but Pasha, with his pale, perceptive gaze and the hand of an angel, records faithfully what he or his imagination actually sees. Line, form, color, light and shade, shimmering movement—all these bring the page to life before her, with people as real as those who pass along Armory Lane. All correctly formed. Not mimicking the heavy figures of noble Soviet workers and soldiers in the posters and statues he and the other children see everywhere, nor like the cheerful simplified figures in the classroom's illustrated books, but observations of real men, women, and children.

Pasha is oblivious to her excitement. He is oblivious to everything except the page before him. Sometimes he closes his eyes to see things more clearly.

The teacher takes some of his drawings home with her to show her husband. He smiles indulgently and shakes his head: someone else has done these, not a child but a talented adult, someone with a true gift.

He says this. Then he sees the expression on his wife's face and hears the determination in her voice.

"Pasha is a prodigy," she says. "A Mozart in art. His crayons and pencils are his clavier."

"Very prettily put. Is he from an artistic family?"

"No, they're simple working people, ordinary citizens. They don't even have any proper pictures on their walls, just a holy icon and a portrait of Comrade Stalin."

"Covering their options, then." He gives her a long look. "You've been to see them?"

"His mother's a street sweeper, his father's in the Army and rarely home. I've spoken to the mother. She doesn't understand what a gift the boy has. It will all be lost."

He cocks an eyebrow. He knows his wife. "You're planning something. What are you planning?"

She has a contact in Moscow, a giant hulk of a man called Sergei Vladimirovich Lysenko. He is a full professor, an elected member of the Academy of Arts and a leading light in the Artists' Union. She sends him some of Pasha's drawings and eventually, despite his skepticism, he journeys all the way from Moscow to see this apparent prodigy for himself.

Sergei Lysenko has a hedge of beard and a cascade of thick flowing hair that make him the very image of Karl Marx, and a temperament that is dour and laconic. He wears a tan-colored suit and cape. He smokes nonstop, not Russian cigarettes but a type that Pasha's mother has never seen before, with foreign writing on the carton; and he lights them with a gold lighter. Not only that, but he arrives by motor car. The children playing in the lane outside Lobachev Row cluster around and stare at it.

Pasha's mother stands in the corner of the tiny apartment, unsure what to expect from this visitor, just as she is unsure what is expected of her or her Pashenka.

Pasha, sitting quietly with his pencils and paper, is thinking that this man is the largest and bulkiest person he has ever seen. He is accustomed only to skinny people.

Sergei Lysenko wrinkles his nose at the smell of cabbage drifting into the apartment from the communal kitchen. He lights a cigarette as he examines his surroundings. He sees a single upright wooden chair, the old sofa on which Pasha is sitting, a small table, little else. On one wall is the usual portrait of Josef Vissarionovich. On the opposite wall is an icon of Christ in gilt and lurid colors. Sergei Lysenko detects no artistic merit in either picture.

"Draw something," he commands Pasha in a voice that rumbles like one of the goods trains passing behind the dom. His hand sweeps lazily through the air, leaving a trail of tobacco smoke. "Draw whatever you like—anything."

So Pasha draws Sergei Lysenko himself, this towering stranger with his beard and his heavy eyes. The likeness is perfect, even to the tobacco-stained teeth.

The schoolteacher hides her smile.

"Tch," says Sergei Lysenko, shaken by what he sees. He does not meet the teacher's questioning gaze.

Further drawings follow. This time the professor specifies what he wants, one drawing after another: the view across the canal from the apartment window; Pasha's mother with her hands folded nervously together; the eager schoolteacher; the lime and chestnut trees in the lane; the grubby children playing beneath them and clambering through their bare branches.

Pasha never fails. It is as if the drawings are there within the paper all along and all he has to do is release them.

At last, addressing only Pasha's teacher, the professor announces his decision.

"In the interests of furthering the artistic and cultural flowering of the USSR, I am willing to take this boy under my wing and coach him. He will be provided with all the materials he will need throughout his apprenticeship. For his part, he must be prepared to work hard and loyally for the honor and glory of the proletariat and the USSR."

He delivers this as if even his words are a gift.

"Comrade Professor!" The teacher raises her hands in delight, clasps them together.

Marya Kalmenova's gaze flicks back and forth from the schoolteacher to this stranger with his fine clothes and cultured Moscow accent and clouds of aromatic tobacco smoke. A trip to the moon would make as much sense to her as the things she is hearing.

But there is one point that she manages to seize on. She thinks about how, as she sweeps the streets, she scavenges and saves scraps of cardboard and paper to bring home for her Pashenka. She thinks about the money she already spends on pencils and crayons.

Hard enough to afford food and clothing.

She blinks in the cloud of tobacco smoke. Christ and Comrade Stalin have watched the proceedings. Is that an encouraging twinkle in Josef Vissarionovich's kindly eyes?

"You say I don't have to pay anything for this?"

The teacher smiles, openly this time, and shakes her head. "Not a kopeck."

Unnoticed by any of them, Pasha has been quietly drawing again. Now he finishes, grabs paper and pencil, and, barely pausing to ask Mama's permission and bow farewell to his visitors, makes good his escape and dashes outside to join his friends and draw the amazing motor car.

The schoolteacher picks up the sketch he has left behind. There they are, standing together in one tableau, the three adults who have set the course of his future for him. A course that none of them could possibly predict.

He has captured them all to the life.

* * *

So begins the program of development that defines Pasha's childhood and early adulthood. Every Saturday morning in spring, summer, and autumn, for as many months of the year as the water of the canal flows freely, he packs his satchel, kisses Mama goodbye, and follows the dusty footpath to the canal. He hurries past the scary old woman that Mama says is not right in the head and who sits by her shed in all weather and seasons, even the depth of winter, with lines of used clothing for sale. He looks away because, like all the children of Lobachev Row, he knows she has the evil eye.

At the canal he clambers aboard a barge transporting sawn timber south to Moscow. For the rest of his life the sweet fragrance of fresh-cut wood will summon up these mornings.

His studies are hard. He learns that instinct and his God-given gift on their own are not enough—they must be trained. Sergei Lysenko, his beard and flowing hair more grizzled as each year passes, grumbles and tut-tuts at his efforts—"Draw as if your life depends on it" is his constant command. He leads Pasha through the city, in spring, when the squares and boulevards are busy with conscientious citizens, the subbotniki—Saturday people—who, on top of their ordinary weekday employment, give their weekend labor without payment to clear garbage, to clean and repaint buildings and wash windows and mend pavements, to help with Moscow's unending construction work. They are building the socialist dream, the workers' paradise, with their bare hands. This is what they will tell their children and their children's children.

Sergei shows Pasha how to make sketch notes at high speed—of the gangs of subbotniki at work, of the flight of wild geese over the Moskva, of any subject that involves movement. He grumbles and scowls as Pasha works these rapid sketches into finished drawings, pointing out where his attempts go wrong.

"Use your eyes, Pavel Pavlovich. See what's right in front of you—really *see*. Take these geese. A single goose never flies the way it does when it's part of a formation. The air resistance is different."

He pushes the sheet aside, finds another, makes more criticisms, until Pasha feels like a solitary wild bird struggling in vain against the resisting air and crashing to earth.

"Movement is a river," Sergei declares. "Miss one part of the flow and it never comes back. Do you hear? Are you listening?"

"Yes, Comrade Professor. I'm listening. I'm always listening."

"Now work on."

So Pasha does, not only in his time with Sergei but also every waking hour not taken up by his education and ideological training.

Then comes war with Hitler's Germany.

"We'll see if your big Sergei survives," says Mama, her face grim. "We'll see if any of us survive."

In the event all three of them do. But Pasha's father does not. Mama dyes all her outer garments black—sparing only the tender blue cornflowers on the black shawl that was a gift from Pasha's father on their wedding day.

"The Lord gave and the Lord has taken away," she sighs. "Blessed be the name of the Lord."

She crosses herself, lights the little candle under Christ's holy icon, prays. When she weeps, her tears dry to little rings of salt on her black garments.

This then is Pasha's life. A modest life, and simple, not much to it. Dominated by his art, his craft. But it is enough of a life. As long as he can settle down with pencil and paper to make his drawings, this little life of his, simple and narrow in its scope, is all he has ever wanted.

CHAPTER 3

After the dimness of the truck, the ocean of light into which Pasha is pushed is blinding. As his eyes adjust, he looks around.

He is in a railway station. It is a vast cavern of brick and concrete and marble. High, curved ceilings arch over the platforms. At first, he thinks these gleaming ceilings are made of white marble but then he sees that they are glass, covered on the outside with snow. They reflect and intensify the fierce floodlight beams shining beneath them. Tall metal arms tower over the rail tracks, bearing lamps; all the lamps are showing red.

He begins to understand the confusion of noise he heard in the truck. A colossal steam locomotive is arriving at the nearest platform. It must be four times the height of the workers, both men and women, who swarm around it. Some of them carry oilcans, ready to begin work. Even before it stops, others start to scrub with yard brushes at its mechanical parts, the cylinders and water tanks and pistons all visible as if it is a gross black insect and these are its exoskeleton. Each wheel is taller than the man or woman who labors at it. Steel crankshafts and connecting arms as long as a human body link the wheels. A snow scoop at the front leads to steps on which two men are already climbing; they have brushes and cloths with which they begin to clean the front lamps.

More workers clamber up to the footplate along the side of the boiler; others take outsize spanners to the smoke door at the front. Clouds of steam spurt from the chimney on top and from outlets along the side. The steam engulfs the workers, then evaporates so that they reappear for a moment, then it swallows them again. At intervals the whistle blares. It is the shriek that made the hairs stand up on the back of Pasha's neck. The acrid sting of steam assaults his nostrils; he feels particles of soot in his nose and mouth.

The locomotive shunts forward to the soot-blackened buffers at the end of the platform. Pasha recognizes the screeches he heard, of metal on metal as the brakes are applied and the wheels grind against the rails. The workers close in again and begin to knock away the ice clinging to the locomotive's underbelly.

His gaze shifts to the closed wooden wagons ranged behind the tender. They are cattle wagons. Here further teams are busy. These workers wear high rubber galoshes. They move in pairs from wagon to wagon, throwing open the sliding doors as they climb aboard, so that the runners squeal and the doors crash against the stops. They lug heavy fire hoses with which they wash each wagon out, sending a brown stream splashing down to the track below. The stench of excrement and urine reaches Pasha.

He has stepped into a vision of hell.

Someone grips his shoulder. It is the militia sergeant.

"Hurry up, Kalmenov. Get moving."

"Why have you brought me here? You said a militia station. Where are we?"

"You're in Moscow. This is the Yaroslavsky railway station."

Pasha stares at him. Trains from Yaroslavsky go north; only north.

"Why are we here?"

"You're going on an outing. Keep moving."

There is activity off to Pasha's left. On the far side of the concourse a number of trucks are waiting. Some are militia vehicles like his, others are Red Army trucks. The latter have already begun to unload their human cargo. A group of these people is coming in his direction. They are men and women of all ages. They shuffle along in single file, their wrists chained and bleeding. All of them have injuries; he sees bloodied faces and torn clothing. He remembers how a rifle butt was used on his apartment door; butts may have been used here, too, but on heads and bodies. Armed soldiers pace back and forth alongside these prisoners, urging them forward with oaths and insults.

"Who are they?" he asks the sergeant.

"They've been arrested. They're going on an outing, too."

"I've been arrested but I'm not in chains."

"I can fix that if you like."

"Why are they in chains?"

"That's up to the officer in charge. They're politicals. Dissidents, troublemakers. Politicals are dangerous, they disrupt and corrupt. The Red Army gets to handle them. Don't concern yourself with them, you won't be mixing with them. You're going to the same destination but you'll be with your own kind."

"Who are my kind?"

"Over there."

Pasha follows the sergeant's gaze. The militia trucks have now opened their doors. The occupants are climbing out and looking about themselves anxiously. Like him, they have been rounded up in ones and twos rather than the larger numbers in which the politicals have been delivered. Also like him, they appear to be uninjured.

"What makes them my kind? Where are we going from here—what destination?"

No answer. But the truth has begun to sink in anyway. He looks again at the locomotive. He has heard of monsters like this but never knew if they really existed or were merely the stuff of myth and legend. And propaganda. Now he knows. He is looking at one of the most powerful railway engines in the world, built for the most forbidding climatic conditions in the Soviet Union—meaning the worst anywhere on earth.

The sergeant's words play over. Same destination as the politicals. Everyone knows where politicals end up. Everyone knows where the agitators and awkward ones are sent. They are sent where they cannot disrupt or corrupt.

The sergeant prods him toward the locomotive and the wooden wagons.

"You'll enjoy the ride."

The ride to the bleakest reaches of the USSR. The ride to the gulag.

CHAPTER 4

THE TRAIN HAS been underway for two or three hours when daylight finally comes. It leaks into the wagon through chinks and knotholes in the walls of wooden planking, sending thin fingers of light quivering across the darkness. People press their faces to the cracks, peering out in hope of discovering where they are. They learn nothing; there are no convenient signboards with town or city names, no feature or landmark they can recognize. There is only snow for them to see. The vast emptiness of Russia rolls past, its endless plains and heavy skies bleak and incomprehensible, its dark pine forests the only witnesses to the train's passage.

"I can tell we're being taken north," someone asserts. "I saw where the sun was rising. I saw that, at least."

North. As Pasha knew. He cannot be the only person thinking about the gulag and this rail line that is taking them there—a line said to have the corpse of a slave worker beneath every sleeper, the remains of the men and women who built it, the uneasy dead that he and these others are passing above. A railroad of the dead.

The thunder of the locomotive pounds through his brain and body. It feels like he will never be free of it. In the dim light he counts the people in the wagon. Twenty including himself. Then there are the politicals. He counted them, too, on the platform, abandoning the task when he reached a hundred and twenty. They were being crowded into only two wagons. The twenty in this wagon will be enough to generate warmth but not so many as to be intolerable. In each of the politicals' wagons there are at least three times as many in the same space. They will be crammed shoulder to shoulder for however long this journey takes.

Someone has planned things this way.

There is something else. He and the other non-politicals were given blankets and extra clothing as they boarded—greatcoats, fur hats, heavy gloves. He is now wearing the extra coat over his father's coat. They were also given food—a portion of bread, strips of dried meat, a small square of cheese, a wooden drinking cup. There is a barrel of water for them to share. The water is already turning to ice but there is an ice pick on a hook above the barrel. So they will not freeze to death on the journey, or starve or die of thirst.

But the politicals boarded without blankets, additional clothing, or food. At most, all they have is water—so someone has also decided who can be allowed to freeze and starve and grow weak, even die, and who is to be kept alive.

The question is not why some may be allowed to die. The question is why efforts are being made to keep some alive.

And then there is the question of why he, Pavel Pavlovich Kalmenov, who has done no wrong—none that he knows of—is here at all.

* * *

One restless man seems to be the exception to the oppressive apathy in the wagon. He is about thirty years old, with a thin face, a long nose, and a little black beard that is thick on his chin but skimpy on his cheeks. He is tall and lanky, easily the tallest person among them. He is carrying a small cardboard suitcase. He moves about the wagon, speaking quietly with individuals here and there. Each time he begins one of these conversations he removes his shapka, his fur hat, revealing receding hair, and bows politely to the other person. He keeps his head bowed to their level as he speaks and listens. From time to time he slips off a glove to warm his bony fingers with his breath. Few people want to say more than a few words to him. Some decline to talk at all. He smiles an ironic little smile, puts the shapka on again, and moves on.

In due course he reaches Pasha and crouches beside him. The case goes on the floor, off comes the hat. He makes his little bow. His dark eyes are friendly enough, but watchful.

"Greetings, comrade. I'm Viktor." It is an easygoing introduction, with neither patronymic nor family name offered.

Pasha returns the informality. "Pavel. But Pasha will do."

"Well, I'm pleased to meet you, Pasha." Viktor adopts the familiar form of "you" without bothering to ask permission. His casual air suggests he is accustomed to this way of doing things.

"Too bad about the circumstances," he adds. He smiles wistfully. "The accommodation could be better."

His Moscow accent reminds Pasha of Sergei's. It is a confident, educated voice, a relaxed drawl. Not an ordinary worker's voice like Pasha's.

Pasha offers no reply. He will not risk making criticisms to a stranger.

But Viktor seems unperturbed by his reticence and shows no inclination to move on.

"So, tell me, Pasha, what did you do? Forgive my curiosity. As good socialists, we should be interested in our fellow citizens."

Not too interested, thinks Pasha. He notices that several of the people standing nearby are watching and listening. He will answer this pushy Viktor, but he will be careful.

"I didn't do anything. It's a mistake. They'll correct matters when they realize."

Viktor grins. "I didn't mean that. All I meant was what kind of work did you do, what was your job?"

Pasha notices the past tense. "Oh. No job."

"Student, then? Higher institute?"

Pasha nods.

The train lurches as it passes over a set of points. The watchers dash to their peepholes. The eavesdroppers are thrown against each other and become busy with apologies. They lose interest in the conversation.

"And your main subject, Pasha? Your specialism?"

"Fine Art Studies."

"Excellent choice." Viktor nods slowly, as if waiting to see if Pasha will say more. But Pasha keeps his lips firmly closed and after a few moments Viktor takes the hint. He places his hands on his knees, getting ready to stand up.

At once Pasha feels guilty. He is being impolite, even unkind, to this man, odd though the man may be.

"And you?" he says quickly. "What's your work?"

"Well, I *was* working in the Office of the Municipal Surveyor for Moscow district as a draftsman—surveying buildings, drawing up plans, that kind of thing. All over and done with now, of course. Gone forever."

"Why do you say that?"

Viktor turns his sharp gaze on him. "Surely you know where we're going. You know where we'll end up. We're in a sealed train. You know what that means, don't you?"

"It's a mistake, like I said."

Viktor's smile has a bitter twist. "Of course, Pasha."

Nearby, a girl is trying to fill her cup at the water barrel. Ice has formed, making the task awkward. Viktor watches.

"To tell you the truth, Pasha, what really mattered to me was what I chose to do in my own time, not what I had to do for a living. I consider myself an artist. Art was my real life. I've had exhibitions of my work. They wrote about me in *Izvestia*. Does that sound boastful? It's not meant that way. I've nothing to boast about, not where we're headed."

He has stopped watching the girl. He is looking at the floor and his voice has trailed away. He sighs.

"But what about you, my young comrade? Has your work ever been placed on public display? For all to see?"

Pasha shakes his head.

"Still, you must be a good artist, Pasha. Someone knows that. Mark my words—someone somewhere knows that."

He picks up his case, stands up, pulls his hat on and slips away before Pasha can ask what he means.

* * *

There are latrine buckets in a corner of the wagon. Someone rigs blankets around them for privacy. Pasha wonders if the politicals have been allowed the privilege of buckets. Remembering the wagons that had to be hosed out in Yaroslavsky station, he reckons not.

* * *

The finger of light he has been observing moves closer to where he is sitting. Finally, it reaches him. He looks around. No one is paying him any heed. He opens his bag, keeping his movements small and close, unhurried, so as not to attract attention. He takes out a sketch pad and leafs slowly through the drawings. Sorrow fills him as he turns the pages. They show another world, another life. Was that life really his? How beautiful that little life was.

After a few minutes he closes the pad and puts it away. The sorrow has become a stifling pain in his chest.

There is a movement beside him.

"Wait, may I see?"

Viktor has returned. He gestures at the sketch pad.

Pasha considers. What harm can it do? He retrieves the pad and passes it over.

Viktor looks through the pad without speaking. He does not skip any pages but studies each one closely. Occasionally his long fingers tug at his beard. There is no crooked smile this time. This is a different Viktor.

"And those?" he says, indicating the other sketch pads.

Pasha passes them to him. Again, Viktor takes his time.

"The loose sheets? What are they?"

Pasha pulls a couple out. Viktor studies these even more closely, lifting them into the little patch of light and examining them from all angles. Sometimes he glances at Pasha. Pasha lowers his gaze.

"These are silverpoint, aren't they?"

Pasha nods.

Viktor clears his throat. "You can use silverpoint."

This is not a question. Pasha nods again.

Viktor returns the sheets, pulls his hat and gloves on, picks up his case, and straightens up to his full height.

"You really are a very good artist, Pasha. I said you were. I wasn't wrong."

* * *

The daylight ends and it is dark again in the wagon. Pasha does not have a watch and does not want to ask anyone the time, but the return of darkness means they must have been traveling for six or seven hours. He eats sparingly because he does not know how long he must make the food last.

Not far from him a woman is weeping softly, a low, desolate sound, like a funeral dirge, that worms its way into his head. The temperature continues to fall. He huddles into his blankets. His feet are cold. His boots are not good enough. Eventually he falls into an uneasy half sleep.

Gulag. Without meaning to, without wanting to, he fits the word to the rhythm of the clacking wheels of the wagon and the woman's sobs. So there is no reprieve to be had, no escape, not even in sleep.

* * *

Something wakes him—a loud, piercing noise that sets his teeth on edge. It is the sound he heard back in Moscow, in the railway station: the shriek of metal grinding against metal. The wagon rocks back and forth. The locomotive is braking. The train is stopping. Anxiety ripples through the wagon. Here and there voices murmur.

"We're stopping."

"Yes, yes—but where?"

The train comes to a complete halt. Nothing happens. Pasha waits. It is surely too soon for their destination. Everyone waits. Nothing. No sound except explosions of steam from the locomotive.

Anxiety is replaced by fear. It hovers over them in the darkness. No one speaks now; no one moves. Their little world has stopped spinning; it hangs suspended, waiting.

Suddenly, there are shouted commands outside. The voices draw closer. Footsteps can be heard, the crunch of boots in deep snow. Rattles and loud clangs announce that the padlocks are being unlocked and the bolts drawn back on the door of the wagon. It is a moment of high terror. The cries of the weeping woman mount to a shrill pitch.

The door crashes open. Freezing air floods in. Pasha sees a panorama of black sky, an immensity of blackness densely strewn with stars as bright and sharp as diamonds. It is beautiful. It is God's sky, his universe. It might be the last thing Pasha will see.

Then torchlight beams shine into the wagon, blinding him, and the ethereal vision is lost.

"Out!" shout the soldiers. "Leave your belongings!"

The prisoners scramble down from the wagon, limbs stiff with cold and inactivity. They look around fearfully. They are in the middle of nowhere—no station, not even a platform, no lights anywhere in the landscape, only the dark shadows of a pine forest all around, trees heavy with snow.

Pasha sees now that the soldiers are not militiamen. They are Red Army. They must have taken over from the militia back in Yaroslavsky station. Like their comrades who shepherded the politicals, they are armed with the new Kalashnikov submachine guns, said to be the world's best. Pasha catches his breath. This is the moment when the bullets will fly; this is the place, where there is no one to tell the tale.

He hears Mama, hears one of her familiar refrains: "Jesus will always be there for you, Pasha. Remember—he'll be there when you need him."

So where is Jesus now?

But perhaps Jesus has stepped in after all, for there are no bullets. All that happens is that two prisoners are sent back into the wagon to fetch the latrine buckets and empty them by the track.

Pasha tries to stop shaking, hunching into his coats and blankets even though he knows the problem is not the cold alone. It is relief as much as fear. It is the aftermath of fear.

He hears the sound of someone being sick. He looks around. Steam is rising from the snow.

The buckets are frozen solid. The men upend them and wait while a soldier brings a shovel of burning coals from the locomotive with which to thaw the contents.

Afterwards the prisoners are allowed a few minutes in which to move about, under the gaze of their armed guard. Pasha looks along the track, toward the wagons carrying the politicals. Nothing is happening there. The politicals are being kept locked up. No fresh air for them, no slopping out, no stretching of cramped limbs.

Viktor is at his side again.

"I was afraid our number was up just then," he whispers. "Still, it was useful. People talk when they think it's the end. You see the small man over there? Quick, before they switch off the torches. Elderly chap in spectacles? Gold medal winner, USSR Academy of Arts in Moscow. Over to your right, the gray-haired woman? Honorary member of the Academy in Leningrad. Not even those two escaped this. The rest of us are a bit less distinguished but still good at what we do. We may even be some of the very best. Just listen to this."

Viktor's gaze rests briefly on various individuals in turn as he lists them. Pasha only just manages to keep pace with his rushed accounts.

"There's a woman who creates pictures for children's storybooks. The woman behind her is an architect. The bearded fellow is a costume designer from the Bolshoi. Beside him is someone who specializes in drawing all sorts of animals. The man over there paints portraits of children. And then there's that pretty girl." He is referring to the girl who was at the water barrel. "She makes maps for atlases. Counting you and me and the academicians, that's half of us."

"And?"

"Why have we been arrested, Pasha? You want to know, I want to know, we all do. You shouldn't be here, you said. We all think we shouldn't be here. So I've been trying to work out if we have something in common. And I've found it. It's just as I thought all along."

Pasha waits.

"We're artists, Pasha. We're all artists!"

"What do they want with a wagonload of artists?"

Viktor shrugs. "They've rounded up some of the best, and I think that's what landed us here. Just as I said, someone knows how good you are."

He stops and stares at Pasha, waiting for a response. But Pasha can only wonder what to make of such a strange idea that explains nothing. And what to say to this strange man who has proposed it.

They are hustled back into the wagon. The door crashes shut. The bolts are flung in place, the padlocks rattle. Pasha and Viktor and the others are in darkness again.

CHAPTER 5

Windsor, England

"BIT GRAY TODAY, sir. Bit murky."

The policeman glances briefly skyward at the fog that shrouds the turrets and crenellations of Windsor Castle, touches his helmet deferentially, and smiles at the man who is passing his gatehouse.

The civilian inclines his head slightly in response, a restrained movement that registers the social gulf between them. Must maintain the proper order.

"Indeed so, officer. Be worse in town, I fear."

Windsor is quiet this wintry morning. Town, meaning London, will also be quiet. A good day to be getting on with things.

The civilian's heels click confidently on the cobbles as he makes his way downhill, the sound maintaining a pleasing counterpoint with the tap of his furled umbrella. The briefcase he is carrying, a stout, boxy affair in expensive full-grain leather, hefty with its weighty contents, swings in rhythm with each step.

This is a man of contradictions. He abhors excess and showiness, yet he is a man on whom postwar clothes rationing has had no impact. His shoes are handmade for him by a little man in St James's Street, as they have been since his Cambridge days. His suit, a charcoal pinstripe, was made by another little man, this one in Savile Row, as was today's elegant camel outer coat. In keeping with his ascetic principles, there is only one other suit in his wardrobe—but the cost of today's ensemble would be enough to feed and house the policeman's family for many months.

The man's looks are compelling rather than handsome; perhaps there is something a little predatory in the long, narrow face, the aquiline nose. He is impeccably groomed, the cheeks and long upper lip close shaven, his hair beneath the trilby compressed and pomaded into perfect waves. Though he has barely entered his forties, those careful waves are beginning to be touched by their first hints of silver. The silver adds distinction. He knows that women are attracted to him, perhaps because of his wit and obvious intelligence, perhaps because of his aristocratic connections, vague and distant though they are. Or perhaps it is his growing reputation as a historian and critic of fine art that draws them.

Whatever the reason, they must lust in vain. Anthony Frederick Blunt prefers the rough caress of a drill sergeant or the sweet body of a youthful equerry. And there are plenty of opportunities for both in Windsor, this garrison town and Home Counties retreat of the British royal household. That such encounters are illegal in prudish England and punishable by imprisonment serves only to make them all the more exciting for him; as does their flouting of class divisions.

To hell then with the proper order.

At the railway station he buys a copy of this morning's *Times* and tucks it under his arm. He glances back at the castle on its hill of rock. The royal ensign hangs listlessly above the weathered stonework, barely visible through the creeping fog. In London it will not be gray, that fog; it will be a filthy yellow, loaded with the effluent of thousands of chimneys and factories. He will feel it in his lungs for days afterwards.

But he has his publisher to see. A relaxed lunch—though, as ever, he will consume no alcohol. Excitingly, there is his book to discuss.

Not a dreary catalogue this time but, at last, his own modest little effort, on Nicolas Poussin, doyen of French Baroque. A modest effort indeed, but a start to his longed-for literary career.

After lunch he will not return to Windsor. He will repair to the Courtauld Institute of Art, of which he is director, in Home House on Portman Square, where he has his little flat on the top floor. It is spartan, that little refuge of his, as bare and cold and empty as a monk's cell, with its worn linoleum and not a single creature comfort in sight—but there are windows to paradise in the pictures with which it is hung, all borrowed from the Courtauld collection.

Before he does any of these things, however, he has one other commission to fulfill—in its own way as important as anything else to his sense of self, his definition of who he is. For, over the years, Anthony Frederick Blunt has shared with his friends in the Union of Soviet Socialist Republics enough operational documents and classified papers detailing the secrets of his country's government and intelligence services to fill a small removals van.

But, always of late, he hears the hounds at his heels, the hounds of the security services, hears them drumming ever closer, feels the wind of the snapping of their jaws.

All part of the glorious game, of course, all part of the romance—at the beginning. But a decade is a long time to play the game. A long time to run free, even for him, the great pretender. It is a long time to listen out for that baying and yelping. Sooner or later the hounds will find the scent. They will close on him. No spy runs free forever.

So now is the time for his final flourish, his last hurrah. It is not to do with intelligence or security, since he no longer has access to that world; the hounds have seen to that. It is not to do with great matters of state—and so much the better for that, for it stands high above the grubby world of politics.

No, what he has set in motion is something far more elegant. Like the man who conceived it, it has style, panache, éclat. It is timeless. It is something the dullard hounds will never expect. And it is something that only Anthony Frederick Blunt, Surveyor of the King's Pictures, could pull off.

He smiles to himself. The ensign on the castle means his employer, King George VI—shy, stammering Bertie who never expected to be king—is in residence.

"Oh, Bertie, if only you knew," Blunt says now, with only the deserted platform to hear him. "My dear chap, if only."

* * *

He has the first-class compartment to himself.

He never usually travels first class. It goes against his grain and his upbringing—children of penniless clergymen do not go first class. But his Muscovy friends insist; it is more discreet, they tell him.

He supposes they have a point. And in any case, they pay the fare. It is the only pecuniary consideration he accepts from them. Or ever will accept. A man must have honor or he has nothing.

"For what shall it profit a man, if he shall gain the whole world, and lose his own soul?"

The clergyman taught the son well.

As the train approaches London, a well-dressed man of roughly Blunt's own age enters the compartment. He settles himself facing their direction of travel, as Blunt has done. On the seat between them is Blunt's briefcase. By coincidence, the stranger has an identical case. He places it beside Blunt's.

The two men nod a greeting, then, like well-bred Englishmen, they bury their noses in their newspapers and completely ignore each other for the rest of the journey.

When the train draws into Paddington station, Blunt rises to his feet, retrieves his trilby and umbrella from the luggage rack, and picks up the wrong briefcase. The other man appears not to notice.

The train stops. Blunt opens the door, gathers the skirts of his outer coat to keep it clear of the sooty coachwork, and steps down to the platform.

He knows that, behind him, his traveling companion will take possession of the weighty briefcase he has left behind.

Blunt smiles again. Oldest trick in the book but it still works.

Already the air around him is tinged with yellow. Already he feels his weedy lungs constricting in protest. Never mind; still a day with many rewards in store. He tips the trilby to a rakish angle and raps his umbrella on the flags of the platform to set his pace. Then he marches cheerfully away, heels clicking, empty briefcase swinging by his side.

The first consignment has been delivered. In the months to come, he will deliver many more.

Ah, such a glorious game.

CHAPTER 6

Kuntsevo, southwest of Moscow

JOSEF VISSARIONOVICH DZHUGASHVILI is short in stature. His chest is narrow, his legs are scrawny, his physique is a far cry from those of the swashbuckling Hollywood heroes he so admires and whose movies he spends half the night watching. These physical limitations may explain why he enjoys Charlie Chaplin movies as well. He has hazel eyes and a swarthy complexion that is typical of his Georgian heritage, the Soviet Socialist Republic of Georgia being a place of good wine and sunshine—although there is no hospitality in the soul of Josef Vissarionovich Dzhugashvili and in his eyes no sunshine, only suspicion, however much the official portraits suggest otherwise. Anger him, and the eyes flash amber like a jungle cat's, a deadly warning sign.

His thick hair is swept straight back from his forehead, at first impression a masculine, no-nonsense style. But look again, for there is vanity in the delicately turned points to which his luxuriant gypsy moustache stretches above his wide mouth. He sees to it that the wart over his right eyebrow and the bad skin scarred by childhood smallpox are smoothed away in all those portraits.

On special occasions and at ceremonial events he wears his white uniform jacket in order to stand out from the drab people around him. The rest of the time he favors a plain military tunic or an ordinary peasant shirt fastened at the neck with two buttons, pulls his cap well down, and tucks his breeches into high boots, like a proper man of the people ready for action in the streets.

Those boots, like all his footwear, have cleverly built-up heels, adding an extra couple of centimeters to his height. When sitting, he holds himself ramrod straight, never slouches. Standing or sitting, he is careful not to let his withered left arm and its permanent slight bend be noticed.

He is choosy who appears in photographs with him and where they stand, so that they never steal the scene. In any case, there is no telling who might have to be airbrushed from the photograph at some future time, having been airbrushed from life itself. Josef Vissarionovich's photographers know the rules.

Dzhugashvili is his birth name. It is an awkward, stumbling Georgian name. A village peasant's name, fine enough for a man of the people, but it gets in the way in the wider world. How can a hero, a demigod, be called Dzhugashvili?

Besides which, a man should be more than his birth. And if he has led a bloody revolution and now rules an entire empire, one that sprawls across half a continent, then he is entitled to take whatever name he wishes. One that is easy on the tongue. Certainly something distinctive and memorable—and simple for the masses, of course.

And that is what he has done, this Dzhugashvili of nondescript origin, son of a drunkard shoemaker and a cleaning woman. Not once, but many times, he has taken a new nom de guerre as he schemed and murdered his way to the top.

But one name has stuck, the one he personally favors most, the one that identifies him as the man of steel: Josef Vissarionovich Dzhugashvili is Josef Stalin.

* * *

He gazes out on the snow-smothered woods of Kuntsevo in the first light of morning. Hidden somewhere among the birches and pines are the antiaircraft cannon and a force of three hundred heavily armed elite troops that guard him here at his country retreat.

Despite these reassuring measures, he has not slept well. He never sleeps well. Not because of his conscience—he has none—but because of the thoughts that scurry around inside his skull like cornered rats. They never stop. This morning they are about Churchill and Roosevelt, about how they sneered at him at Yalta, about the looks they threw one another behind his back. Patronizing bastards, waving their Cuban cigars and mouthing praise for his Georgian brandy. They might as well have patted him on the head like a good little peasant boy, their very own serf. Nyak, nyak, nyak, their chitter-chatter about music and literature and painting and fancy-this and fancy-that. Like a pair of old women chittering over their needlework. *What a fine building, this Livadia palace, General Secretary—what style would you say it is?* Nyak, nyak. *Gorgeous furniture—is it Queen Somebody-or-other? These tapestries, are they French, are they Russian?* Nyak, nyak.

How could he know these things? He was raised by peasants, not dukes and lords. He never grew up in a palace, like Churchill. His father's money went on vodka, not on Harvard professors like Roosevelt's.

The encounter he is remembering was over four years ago. But a grudge is a grudge. No one holds a grudge better than a Georgian, and no Georgian does it better than Josef Vissarionovich. That Roosevelt is long dead and that Churchill, suffering the inconvenience of democracy, is out of office—these considerations are neither here nor there.

The moustache twitches as another thought scurries forward for his attention. This one is more gratifying. It is about the hard bargain the wily peasant boy drove at Yalta, so that in the end he got everything he wanted: the Eastern territories, his buffer zones, even a new German state. Not to mention his share of Berlin. Hah—Berlin! His Red Army brought him more of Hitler's looted art and jewels and gold than Churchill or Roosevelt could ever have dreamed possible. First he crushed the Nazi like a cockroach, then he helped himself to his treasure chest, right beneath Churchill's and Roosevelt's privileged noses.

And now there is more to come. The peasant boy has not yet finished. Now comes the turn of the Englishman in Windsor Castle, the one who calls himself king. The peasant boy will rob him blind.

And the best of it is, the English king will never even know.

CHAPTER 7

ON THE THIRD morning, the train carrying Pasha and the other prisoners arrives at the very end of the rail line. No soaring arched ceilings here, no broad concourse. Only a snow-covered wooden platform and a rusting set of buffers.

The padlocks are removed from the wagon and the bolts drawn back. The doors crash open.

"Welcome to sunny Vorkuta," barks a Red Army man. "Out of the wagon! Take your belongings."

Viktor groans. "Vorkuta. I knew it."

The prisoners climb down to the platform, moving slowly however much the soldiers bellow, reluctant to leave what has now become familiar and trusted territory. Even a cattle wagon can feel safe. Now they are afraid of what will come next. They blink at the daylight. Dawn has only just arrived, but this far north that means it is already midmorning.

"Daylight doesn't last long, this time of year," says Viktor. "Two or three hours maybe."

Once out of the wagon, Pasha realizes how cold he has become. A great shiver runs through his body. It is like being encased suddenly in ice. Viktor is feeling it, too. His face is purple and raw. Frost glitters in his patchy beard.

"Twenty-five below zero, Pasha, that's my guess. Maybe lower. We're well inside the Arctic Circle."

The skin on Pasha's face has tightened and feels as if it is being pricked by thousands of tiny needles. His nostrils hurt. He realizes that the moisture in them is turning to ice. He tries breathing through his mouth but the immediate stab of pain in his throat puts an end to that.

Beside him, Viktor is cursing under his breath.

Vorkuta. They all know the name. Every citizen knows it, every adult, every child. They are in the evil heart of the gulag, Josef Vissarionovich's network of labor and penal camps. No one knows how many camps there are. Some people claim there are hundreds. The gulag stretches from the White Sea to the plains of central Asia, but it is most notorious for its presence here, deep in the Arctic Circle.

Every camp in the gulag has its particular product, its output or purpose, the reason it was established. It might be a massive construction project—a dam, a canal, a railway—it might exist for the extraction of precious metals, valuable minerals, or the production of timber. Vorkuta's product is coal. Kick the snow away, as Pasha is doing at the edge of the rail platform, and beneath it there is coal. There is coal everywhere. Vorkuta *is* coal. Coal is mined deep below the permafrost, and its stony slag and filthy black dust lie in heaps and long, low banks all around them, breaking through the crust of snow wherever Pasha looks.

Viktor is shaking his head forlornly. "What have we done to deserve this, Pasha?"

There is such sadness in his eyes that Pasha has to look away.

* * *

They are taken north from the railhead on two open-backed trucks. The land all around is flat and featureless, buried in snow, but Pasha glimpses a mountain range far away to the east, only just visible through the frosty haze.

"The Urals," says Viktor. "Be grateful we're not crossing them."

The weather, calm until now, suddenly deteriorates. Within seconds the mountains have disappeared. A bitter wind drives icy snow and hail into the faces of prisoners and soldiers alike. When they reach what passes for the town itself, the trucks bounce over hard-packed snow along a wide street. Dirty hillocks of scraped snow marbled with coal dust lie on either side. There are few people in the street to see the prisoners. Those who are there, heavily swaddled in furs and scarves, hurry along with their heads down against the weather, paying the trucks and their occupants little heed, as if new arrivals are no novelty.

All the buildings look hastily thrown together. There are banners with Party insignia everywhere—the red star, the hammer and sickle—and enthusiastic slogans: "Coal is our bread!" "Glory to the heroic miners of Vorkuta!" Pasha catches sight of a building with a sign proclaiming it to be a hospital and, in another open space, a low block that claims, bizarrely, to be a people's swimming pool.

Not all the buildings are occupied or in use. Some have been abandoned. Or perhaps were never brought into use. The reason can be seen in their twisted walls and fallen doorways: the foundations have been deformed by the frozen climate. But others are raised above the ground on piles or steel stilts.

"To keep them clear of the permafrost," explains Viktor. "The builders learned their lesson after their first attempts. Am I right, comrade?"

The question is addressed to the woman he pointed out to Pasha on the train as an architect. She responds with a gloomy nod.

All the buildings seem to have been dropped into place at random, with long gaps and empty spaces between them. Rubbish and weeds poke through the snow in the gaps, together with the inevitable heaps and slugs of slag and coal dust. Webs of electrical cables, bowed with snow, stretch overhead between the buildings, along with sewage and utility pipes, which cannot be installed below ground.

Pasha has a vague feeling that the landscape is missing something. It takes him a while to figure out what. It is trees. There are no trees anywhere, only tough, dry brush coated in the ubiquitous coal dust and snow.

They pass along Engels Street, then Lenin Street, which opens into a wide square—and here is the great man himself, peaked cap in one hand, other hand thrust into the pocket of the familiar greatcoat, glowering down at them from his stone pedestal, oblivious to his covering of snow.

Viktor nudges Pasha. "Are you a Party member, Pasha?"

"No."

"But a Young Pioneer in your time, of course. And now a loyal Komsomol member, I bet. Yes?"

"Loyal? I hope so."

"Good for you. Just like me at your age." Viktor pauses. "You know those academicians from Moscow and Leningrad? They're both full Party members. Solid as rocks, full members in the highest standing."

"So?"

"So no one's safe."

As they leave the main part of the town, the wide streets peter out and become a single lane of scraped and flattened snow. Pasha senses that there is only frozen soil now beneath the snow rather than a paved surface. The municipal buildings give way to clusters of shacks sheathed in tar paper and corrugated iron. Unlike the official buildings in the town, the shacks cling tightly together in untidy groups. Narrow alleyways zigzag between them.

"Workers' homes," says Viktor. "Probably put up by the workers themselves."

"Workers? You mean politicals? Criminals?"

"Neither. These workers are here by their own choice—so-called hero workers. They see it as their patriotic duty to conquer the frozen north. Some even bring their families. The hospital and swimming pool—if they exist in more than signage—are for them. There are shops and stores, bars, a school, even a whorehouse. Whether the workers survive their stint here is a gamble. They go down the mines alongside the blatnoi, common criminals. If the work doesn't kill them, there's every chance the blatnoi gangs will."

Pasha sees a long hut with a school sign above it. He sees other huts with wind-torn and faded posters illustrating vegetables and cuts of meat. He wonders how desperate someone must be to take the sort of gamble that coming here amounts to. And to make their family part of it.

The truck rattles on, leaving the shanties behind. The lane fades to nothing and the snow chains on the trucks' tires bite into deeper snow. The snow stops but a cutting wind is still howling, whipping snow from the ground and spinning it in every direction. Showers of hail start and stop, then start up again.

Something is slowly emerging from the misty horizon. Pasha wipes snow from his eyes and watches as it gradually comes into focus.

It is high fencing made of steel and barbed wire—not one run of fencing but two runs set parallel. They stretch as far as the eye can see, fading into the mist, interrupted by wooden watchtowers. Snow encrusts the roofs of the watchtowers and the rolls of wire along the tops of the fences. In every watchtower a sentry with a Kalashnikov looks down at the trucks as they pass. This time there is no doubt which part of Vorkuta they have reached. The gap between the parallel runs of fencing is a death strip. There will be no free workers behind the barbed wire.

"Fifty-eight territory," says Viktor. "Article Fifty-eight of the Criminal Code deals with treason—the definitions of which are many, varied, and imaginative. And remarkably flexible. They can be made to apply to just about anything, any offense. Fifty-eight is the number that'll put you in that place."

Pasha considers this. So these are the compounds where political dissidents, blatnoi, and other troublemakers and so-called enemies of the people are kept—the forced laborers, slaves in other words, who constitute the main workforce of the mines, the ones the free workers labor alongside.

There are rows of snow-covered wooden barracks, single story, all identical, their planking weathered to gray. These are clearly the prisoners' accommodations. But in contrast with the haphazard tar paper shacks, these are organized in perfectly parallel rows.

Again, Viktor explains. "By law all buildings and prisoner areas in labor camps have to be constructed and laid out to a square or rectangular plan. Right angles only, nothing irregular. It minimizes blind spots, making for better surveillance."

"There were politicals on our train," says Pasha quietly. "I suppose they'll be destined for here."

"The people in chains? Yes, they'll end up here."

"They had no food, no blankets. They were never allowed out of their wagons. Some could be dead by now."

"They might be the lucky ones."

In the distance, far beyond the barracks area, strange constructions rise above the colorless landscape like black skeletons. Pasha recognizes them from photographs of mining machinery he has seen in newspapers or magazines. They are the winding wheels and headframes and conveyor belts that mark the locations of the mines.

Beside them loom mountains of coal, their flanks white with snow, their peaks black where new loads of coal are being added. All around these workings swarm figures pushing wheelbarrows, swinging sledgehammers and picks, wielding shovels. The racket of their activities and the clanks and rattles of the winches and other machinery meld into a rumble that resembles thunder except it is continuous rather than intermittent.

Motionless figures watch over the workers. There is something about those still figures. They stand upright, not bending to any labor. Then one of them moves, takes a few paces, then returns. Pasha makes out the stubby barrel of a Kalashnikov. He sees the same silhouette in all the upright figures.

"Behold the proletariat's proud economic miracle," says Viktor, who has also been watching the sinister figures.

They reach the limits of the mining camp and pass the last sentry. The fencing with its death strip and watchtowers slips away. The noise of the mine workings fades to nothing. Ahead of them the frozen wasteland goes on forever—blank, empty, and silent.

All trace of human habitation is behind them now. They see more plainly than ever where they are—desolate Arctic tundra, nothing but snow all the way to an invisible horizon, the vista unbroken but for one thing, a long curving shadow on the snowy landscape that cuts directly across their path. When they reach it, it turns out to be a dip where the ground falls away by ten or twelve meters, only rising back to its original level after another fifty meters or so.

The trucks pause briefly at the edge. It is as if a long slice has been scooped out from the land. The sunken area is perfectly flat, stretching away on both sides. To the right it shows evidence of vehicle use, its snowy surface churned and ridged in the middle.

"Ice road," says Viktor. "Frozen river. They're going to take us further north by driving along it. There are no real roads up here, only ice roads like this one. They don't exist in summer."

"Ice roads? Are they safe?"

"Safe enough, most of the year, provided the ice is solid and the driver knows what he's doing. We'll soon find out if ours does."

The trucks tilt at an alarming angle as they descend to the ice road, gears whining. The snow beyond the churned-up section in the middle is virgin and smooth. The trucks hold to the center, carving their way through the ridges of snow and ice. Pasha and Viktor's truck is in the lead. Pasha looks back at the other vehicle. Previously it had stayed close to them, following at a distance of a few meters. Now its driver has let it fall back to about two hundred meters behind them.

"Why is he doing that?"

"The surface moves as we pass along it—it ripples. That makes waves in the unfrozen water below the ice. So we have to travel slowly, to minimize the effect. Two trucks close together would make more ripples—and the ripples would conflict. That could crack the ice. The other thing is that we might hit a thin patch and go through. Rivers don't always freeze evenly. So the other driver will stick to our route for as long as we show it to be safe—but he'll keep his distance in case we hit trouble."

Pasha shudders. "You seem to know a lot about this place. How come?"

Viktor does not reply.

The ice road is never straight but meanders back and forth, sometimes almost doubling back on itself. The land on either side—actually the banks of the frozen river—is always about ten meters above them.

The daylight fades. The trucks' headlights come on. Pasha is colder than ever, despite his coats and blankets and the fact that down here they are protected from the worst of the wind, which he can hear howling on the exposed land above. He is covered in snow and thick clumps of frozen hail. He shakes off as much as he can and pulls his blankets closer. Viktor has not spoken since his explanation of the ice road. His eyes have been closed, but Pasha suspects he has not been asleep.

Suddenly, both trucks sound their horns. The long notes blare mournfully into the darkness. Up ahead, still distant as yet, floodlights blaze into life somewhere on the land above them, creating an island of light in the darkness. The trucks leave the ice road and climb toward the lights. The gap between the vehicles closes as they return to solid ground. Pasha makes out a number of low buildings. They turn out to be wooden huts, similar to those in the mining camp. These, however, look newly built, their boarding not yet gray and weathered. They are raised above the ground on piles, like the buildings in Vorkuta.

There are lights in the huts, illuminating their windows and casting a yellow glow. Puffs of smoke ascend from the huts, to be snatched away by the wind. Were it not for the barbed wire and death strip, identical to those at the mining camp, the scene could be almost homely.

Alerted by the trucks' horns, a number of figures emerge. They are armed with Kalashnikovs and rifles. Searchlights burst into life, even brighter and harsher than the floodlights, and sweep from side to side before focusing their beams on the approaching trucks.

Not so homely now, the scene.

CHAPTER 8

THE FLOODLIGHTS MAKE the camp compound as bright as day. The prisoners are hurried out of the trucks, lined up, and counted. Twelve men, eight women. Their names are checked against a list. The list also records home addresses, and these, too, are checked. Pasha learns that Viktor's family name is Cherviakov. He is from Moscow's Presnenski district, an area that Pasha knows from his wanderings through the city. It adjoins the Arbat and is home to some of the capital's elite—high-ranking government employees and specialist workers such as lawyers and scientists.

He listens to where other prisoners have come from, as many as he can overhear. There are other Russians like him and Viktor, but he recognizes the names of towns and cities in Ukraine and Byelorussia, and of places that he thinks may even be in Estonia and Latvia. In which case some of his travel companions had already been transported long distances before being boarded on the train in Moscow.

The Red Army escort has departed, but he counts ten guards in the compound—one for every two prisoners. This ratio is even higher if he includes the sentries who have now taken up position in the watchtowers. The guards in the compound carry rifles; those in the watchtowers are armed with Kalashnikovs. Four of the guards are women. They are as hard-faced as the men, are dressed in identical uniform jackets, trousers, and boots, and are heavily bundled up in greatcoats and fur shapkas.

Viktor draws Pasha's attention to the blue flashes on the guards' uniforms.

"NKVD," he whispers. "They run the gulag."

Pasha feels chilled by more than the climate. He is now firmly in the hands of Josef Vissarionovich's jailers and executioners.

He struggles to make sense of what is happening. Clearly, nothing is random. That efficient list with its thorough details was already in the possession of the guards before the prisoners arrived. It did not come here with them. So how long has it been here, awaiting their arrival? When was it made? His name was added to a list and that list was sent here in anticipation of his arrival while he lived his life quite unknowing.

Someone has conceived, planned, and coordinated all this. They possessed or were able to obtain the knowledge needed to single out twenty people, by whatever criteria, from millions of citizens across several different republics. They had the authority to mobilize militia in separate administrative oblasts to make the arrests at a range of times across several time zones. They commanded the resources to put in hand the feat of logistics that has brought these once-scattered twenty together here, now, in the same place at the same time, irrespective of their starting points.

Someone *willed* all these things. Many minds worked to bring them about, but it had to be a single mind, a single will, that set them in motion.

Whose mind, whose will?

He turns his thoughts to Viktor's theory. What use to anyone are a few artists? Pencils and paintbrushes cannot dig wealth or natural resources or precious ores from the frozen wastes of Arctic Russia. He remembers the Lenin statue in Vorkuta. "Everything is connected to everything else," the Father of Socialism once observed.

What are the connections here? Pasha cannot find them.

* * *

The prisoners are separated by gender and marched to their respective wash houses and latrine blocks. Pasha, Viktor, and the other men are told to strip and are allowed three minutes to use the toilets and showers. The toilets are holes in planks over a pit. Boxes of delousing powder are distributed. The prisoners are ordered to apply the powder liberally. When the choking clouds have dissipated, two male guards shave the men's heads and faces; the prisoners are not allowed to handle the razors themselves.

Pasha catches his reflection in a window. At first he does not recognize himself. Viktor comes up beside him. They stand there, staring, until a guard shouts at them to move on.

The clothing that the prisoners shed is taken away to be burned, as well as any extra clothing they brought. Pasha's long outer coat, his only memento of his father, is gone. The prisoners are allowed to keep the heavy greatcoats, fur hats, and gloves they were given in Yaroslavsky station and are provided with further new clothing—new to them, that is, for all these garments are well worn. Pasha takes the pile of clothes a guard thrusts at him. He goes to a bench to sort through it and get dressed. Viktor joins him.

"We're putting on dead men's clothes," he says. "But better than being the dead men who gave them up."

Each man receives one pair of leather work boots, two sets of long underwear, two pairs of long knitted wool socks, two shirts, two undershirts, two uniforms of jacket and trousers. According to Viktor, all are standard gulag issue. The uniforms and shirts have broad horizontal stripes of gray and a dull shade of red. At least everything has been laundered and, as he points out, there are no signs of lice.

"Not yet anyway."

Sizes are a matter of chance. Nothing fits. The men compare and trade whatever they can with one another until the guards run out of patience and put an end to the exchanges.

When all the prisoners reassemble in the compound, Pasha finds that the female prisoners have also had their heads shaved and are dressed the same as the men.

"All part of the process of depersonalization," says Viktor. "We're just zeks now. You're lucky they let you keep your sketch pads and drawings. They've taken my suitcase and everything in it. This is our future, this scrape of ice where the world ends. Say hello to the rest of your life, Pasha."

"You don't know that, Viktor. You don't know how long we'll be here. It might only be until they fix whatever error they've made. You don't know."

It is the wrong thing to say. Viktor's eyes blaze.

"I know more than you think, Pasha. It's nothing to do with any error. They haven't even made a pretense at legal process. There's been no trial for us, no sentence passed. No sentence means no end to our imprisonment until they say so. They make the law and they choose the rules.

"You asked how I know about the gulag. I know because my father did seven years in Norilsk, far side of those Ural Mountains. He was sent to the mines. In his case, he did have a sentence—to start with. It was five years. But it took them another two to find his release papers. An administrative error, they said." He shakes his head. "There are no errors, my friend. There are victims but never errors. My father was a judge in the Supreme Court. He was ordered to convict certain people of crimes they hadn't committed—people who'd fallen out of favor, who'd become inconvenient. He refused. They used Article Fifty-eight on him. Our whole family should have been punished for his crime, but my father pleaded—he abased himself—and an exception was made. We were allowed to stay on in our apartment. The disappearance of his release papers may have been the price they made him pay for that. By the time he returned from the gulag, my mother was dead. He might as well have been dead, too—he was broken; he lived only another year. There's disease in our country, Pasha—it's rife, in the very air we breathe. Sooner or later it catches up with all of us. It caught up with me and you. Our luck ran out. Nothing to do with errors. We'll be here for as long as they want us to be. We may as well get used to that."

* * *

Later, as the prisoners are being led around the floodlit compound, Pasha notices Viktor talking with someone. It takes him a moment to identify the person as female. Then he sees it is the girl who was at the water barrel on the train. Viktor sees Pasha looking and smiles his sad, crooked smile.

Some way behind Viktor and the girl, a man seems to be watching them. He is stocky and powerfully built, like a wrestler. Pasha sees the scowl on his face, but there are plenty of reasons for a person to scowl here. For that matter, he may merely be staring in the general direction of Viktor and the girl, not watching them at all.

Pasha thinks no more about him.

* * *

There are separate dormitory huts for men and women. The prisoners are told that these huts will not be locked, day or night. A row of narrow bunks, two bunks high, occupies one side of the men's dormitory. The remaining floor space is taken up by crudely made wooden tables and chairs. There is a portrait of Stalin on the wall. He is at his most affable, his honest workingman's pipe clenched between his teeth.

"Josef Vissarionovich seems pleased to see us," says Viktor.

"Why won't the dormitory huts be locked at night?" Pasha wonders aloud. "What kind of prison camp fails to do that?"

The prisoners are allowed to select their own bunks. Pasha and Viktor stick together. Others form similar alliances. The exception is the scowling man. He takes himself off to a pair of bunks by himself, forcing the elderly Moscow academician—the odd man out as a result—to do the same.

Next the prisoners are taken to the camp's dining hut. Each of them is issued with a wooden bowl and wooden spoon. They are told these items will not be replaced if lost or broken. Food will not be served unless the individual has a bowl and spoon.

There is another portrait of Stalin on the wall and a large sign above the serving hatch. The sign reads: "He who does not work, neither shall he eat."

Viktor eyes the sign. "Lenin's words. He said that."

Pasha shrugs. "Lenin said a lot of things."

The prisoners are lined up at the kitchen hatch and told they have fifteen minutes, including serving time, to eat their meal. This is watery cabbage shchi, hard bread, a single potato, and some strips of dried meat. They are promised a piece of fruit three times a week. There will be three meals each day. No more than fifteen minutes will be allotted to each meal.

Viktor does the calculation as he and Pasha eat.

"Twenty prisoners, fifteen minutes. Say four of us are served each minute. That gives the last person in line ten minutes to eat. Five minutes if only two of us are served each minute. If some of us slow the line down by arguing over the size of the portions or anything else, then those at the end might not get served—they won't eat. It forces us to keep each other in check." He smiles wryly. "Group pressure as a control mechanism—they're clever bastards."

Pasha has been examining the contents of his bowl. "I don't need ten minutes for this. A dog deserves better."

Viktor chuckles. "Trust me, you'll welcome it soon enough. Three meals a day? In the gulag? We're being treated like tsars."

Pasha stares intently at him, looking for evidence of irony in the remark. He finds none.

After the meal, the prisoners are shown the hut in which they will work, but are allowed to see it only from the outside.

"What is our work anyway?" Viktor asks a guard.

"You'll find out," comes the reply.

"So, we'll be working indoors?"

"You saw the hut."

"Why do you want artists?"

"You'll find out. Now shut up."

Certain parts of the camp are off limits to the prisoners. These include the barn where the camp's trucks are kept and maintained, and the huts that house the guards' and the commandant's quarters. If the commandant wishes to speak privately in his office with any prisoner, that individual will be escorted there under guard. So far there has been no sign of the commandant.

To the prisoners' surprise there are heating stoves in all the huts, including the work hut, where two chimneys are visible above the crust of snow on the roof. Even the dormitory huts are heated. It will still be necessary to sleep fully clothed, but the stoves will be a help. And with the mining camp within reach, there should be no shortage of coal.

In the men's hut the prisoners cluster gratefully around their stove, making the most of its warmth. But to Pasha, the stoves are another puzzle.

"Why are we being allowed to keep warm?"

Viktor shrugs. "It's what I told you—we're here because we're artists. And all of us *are* artists, by the way—I found out in the end. We can't do our kind of work in gloves and greatcoats; it's not like mining coal. Also, no one's laid a finger on any of us. They boss us about but that's all. Same reason—injured artists wouldn't be much use. Compare our treatment with the condition the politicals were in. But don't get carried away—they'll still shoot us stone dead if they have to."

"Unless we starve to death first."

"We won't starve. I'm not saying the food is good, only that it's better than it might be—and better than in other camps. Same reason again—they can starve ordinary zeks and just replace them, but it's not so easy to replace us. Makes no sense to starve us or let us go blind or develop scurvy. I told you, Pasha—they're clever, they know what they're doing. What I can't figure out is what they want us to *do* as artists. They've gone to a lot of trouble and it won't be just to get their portraits done. Do you have any ideas?"

Pasha shakes his head. He is pondering the point about injured artists being no use. It fits with the odd manner of his own arrest—the avoidance of violence, the fact that he was never chained, so that his wrists suffered no damage.

Viktor borrows one of Pasha's pencils, climbs up to his own bunk, and begins drawing something on the wall. It is a grid of intersecting vertical and horizontal lines.

"A calendar," he explains. "I want to count every day of my life these bastards take from me. I want to know when it's spring in Moscow. I want to know when the tulips are out in the Alexandrovsky Garden." For a moment his face looks as if it will crumple, then he forces a laugh. "Trouble is, I don't know how much wall I'll need."

At that moment the door of the hut is flung open and two guards appear. Pasha, Viktor, and the others are ordered back out to the compound. The female prisoners are already there. Once again, all twenty are lined up. The guards stand facing them, rifles cradled in their arms, but issue no orders.

"What now?" mutters Viktor.

A klaxon begins to scream. A second joins in. The wails echo across the landscape. The searchlights explode into life. They sweep the compound, momentarily blinding the prisoners, then wash over the killing zone and from there to the open tundra. The glare of light on the white snow hurts Pasha's eyes. Tonight, the land is deserted, but anyone out there—a fleeing prisoner—would have nowhere to hide, no cover of any kind.

The Kalashnikovs in the watchtowers roar. Pasha jumps in alarm. He looks up at the two nearest towers and sees a blaze of muzzle flashes. The klaxons still scream. Puffs of snow burst from the tundra, line after line of little explosions, as the bullets strike.

After a full minute of this, a whistle blows and the guns cease firing, as abruptly as they began. The searchlights are extinguished. The klaxons wind down.

Now the guards break their silence, but only to order the prisoners back to the dormitory huts. Pasha's ears are ringing; he can hardly hear what the guards are saying. Like everyone else he walks unsteadily. There is no conversation among the prisoners. The smell of gunpowder hangs in the air. Clouds of gunsmoke drift down from the watchtowers.

No explanation is given by any of the guards. None is needed. The point of the demonstration could not be clearer: anyone foolish enough to be out there on the tundra would be cut to ribbons.

"Stone dead, comrade," Viktor reminds Pasha, who has to look directly at him in order to make out his words. "Still wondering why they don't need to lock us up at night?"

Pasha lies down on his bunk. He runs his fingers over the unpainted wood and inhales the fragrance of cut timber. He closes his eyes and at once he is again the small boy on the barge, on his way to Moscow. Pine woods glide slowly past. In the fields he sees the kolkhozniki, the farm peasants, who lift their heads from their sowing and plowing on the vast hectares of the collective farms and stretch their backs for a few moments. He remembers the colors of spring and summer in the fields, melting to gold and russet before autumn dies and winter blows all the colors away. Then the city rises before him: Gorky Park where he hurries after Sergei Lysenko; the Alexandrovsky Garden for which Viktor yearns; the Tretyakov Gallery, where his neck aches from staring up at the paintings.

"We own all these paintings," Sergei is telling him. "This is the people's art gallery now. This is how things should be, this is what the Revolution was about."

Eight-year-old Pasha has never seen so many pictures before. He never even imagined there were places like this.

"Who lives here?" he asks.

"What? Who *lives* here? Nobody lives here. No one lives in an art gallery."

"So this whole big place is only for these pictures? Not people?"

"Of course not. Tch—the very idea."

"A dom where nobody is allowed to live? Then what good was the Revolution?"

When he opens his eyes, the memories are swept away and here he still is, in this desert of ice where not even a tree grows. Here he is, surrounded by guns and by killers who will use them without hesitation.

What good indeed was the Revolution?

Above him, Viktor has resumed work on his calendar. Pasha listens to the steady scratch-scratching of the pencil. At first the sound reminds him of the soft scratch of a silverpoint stylus. Then the shadows come creeping into his mind and he imagines it is the sound of his heart being broken open and peeled apart, flake by flake.

CHAPTER 9

It is the following morning, their first full day in the camp, after a night in which Pasha did not sleep. Nor did Viktor; Pasha heard him tossing and turning. He doubts if anyone fared any better.

All of them are in the work hut, watched over by yet another portrait of Stalin.

"No getting away from him," says Viktor.

With its two stoves, the hut is comfortably warm. Outer clothing is piled in a corner. Outside the world is still dark, but this room is brilliantly lit. The lighting is electric. It burns strong and steady, powered by the camp's generator.

Each prisoner sits at an individual work table, like rows of students. They were allowed to choose their tables, just as they chose their bunks. Pasha and Viktor sit next to each other. The pretty girl is on Viktor's other side. She does not seem to have teamed up with any of the other female prisoners. Beyond her is the scowling man, his expression still sullen. Pasha saw him talking with her during the morning meal—although all the talk seemed to be on his part.

The work tables are well carpentered. Like the bunks and the huts, they appear newly made, as if everything has been built or installed specifically for the camp's present inmates—suggesting that the camp has not been used before.

And here at last are the first clues that Viktor may be right, that this has something to do with the fact that all the prisoners are artists.

On each table is a drawing board. The boards are new and of the best quality, better than the one Pasha used in the Artists' Union, superior even to Sergei's. Trays beside each board hold a comprehensive range of drawing equipment: pens, pencils, crayons, chalks, sable brushes in a range of sizes, jars of ink. There is a neat stack of cartridge paper. Two oddities are a microscope and a stand-mounted magnifier fitted with its own light. Another strange feature is the small metal plate affixed to each table, stamped with a three-digit number. The numbers are not sequential but random.

Four guards are moving about the room. They are placing a single sheet of stiff card on each table, as if they are scholastic invigilators distributing exam papers.

A guard reaches Pasha's table and places one of the sheets before him. Pasha stares at it in bewilderment. It is not, after all, just a sheet of card. It is a photographic print. It shows two drawings. He recognizes them immediately.

"Leonardo," he says under his breath. The drawings in the print are by Leonardo da Vinci. Pasha is looking at Leonardo's work. Here in Josef Vissarionovich's gulag.

He closes his eyes and, just as happened last night, time slips from him and he is in Moscow, in the Artists' Union, watching as Sergei sets half a dozen large books on the table with a thump.

"So you like Leonardo's work," Sergei is saying. He uses the artist's first name, as if he and this long-dead foreign genius are personal friends. "You think Mona Lisa is beautiful. And she is. Well, these drawings are by Leonardo as well. Hundreds of them. Here's true genius for you. Look."

He goes from book to book, flips through drawing after drawing. Pasha's eyes devour everything.

"Leonardo used every drawing technique known in his day. Chalk, pen and ink, charcoal, silverpoint—he was master of them all. And now it's time for you to understand how he employed them. You'll copy many of these beautiful drawings—again and again. And then you'll start over. By the time I've finished with you, Pavel Pavlovich, you'll be almost as good as Leonardo. Almost. Don't get above yourself."

In the weeks that followed, Pasha saw who the author was of the books on Leonardo. It was Sergei himself.

He opens his eyes. They were closed for a blink, nothing more. He is back in the work hut. The guard has moved on, but here is the photographic print, still on the work table. It is small enough that Pasha's hand would cover it. The quality is superb. It has been made on heavy paper, in full color, and is a reproduction of a buff-colored page with two drawings on it, the profiles of two ugly old men. The definition of every detail is crisp and sharp, better than he has ever seen before. He feels an almost physical itch in his fingers as he studies it.

His reverie is interrupted.

"Pay attention, prisoners!" calls a shrill voice at the front of the room, so high pitched it could almost be a child's. Pasha looks up in its direction. Nineteen other prisoners look up with him.

The voice belongs not to a child but to a man. He is fat; he does not look like he has ever had to settle for the kind of diet being doled out to the prisoners. His almond-shaped eyes suggest Mongolian ancestry. His skin is dark. His mouth is small and wet. The earpieces of his fur shapka are raised, showing that the stubble on his shaven head is as dark as that on his fleshy cheeks.

One of the hut's stoves is immediately behind him, but still he is wrapped in a heavy floor-length black shuba, the traditional fur coat, beneath which his feet are invisible. He shows no inclination to remove or even unlace the huge garment. The raised flaps of the shapka are his only concession to being indoors.

Igor Borisovich Bolotsov is the camp commandant. His name was announced this morning. And he plainly does not like the cold.

"Prisoners, you have been brought here to do important work in the service of the Soviet proletariat. I will now tell you what that work is and how you will begin it today."

He pauses, produces a large handkerchief and wipes his nose. The only sound is the crackle of the stoves.

"You have each been given a photograph. There are four different photographs and five copies of each one. The Soviet Union's most advanced photographic techniques—therefore the most advanced in the world—have been used to produce these photographs. They are the most accurate possible reproductions of certain drawings. They show at actual size the pages on which the drawings were made. What you will do is copy those drawings. That is what you have been brought here to do. That is what your work will be."

The prisoners stare at one another in astonishment. Is this truly all that is required of them? Only to draw? No backbreaking labor in the brutal temperatures outside this warm hut? No descent into the bowels of the earth to tear at a rock face?

There is no time to wonder further, for Bolotsov is carrying on with his address, occasionally glancing at a sheet of paper on which he has prepared some notes.

"All artists copy. It is part of your training. Some of you may recognize these drawings. This does not matter. All that matters is how well you copy them. Your copy must be identical to the original in every way. The two must be indistinguishable. You will reproduce everything—even smudges, blots of ink, finger marks. If there is writing on your page of drawings, you will reproduce it. You will not understand the writing or what it says. That is unimportant.

You will copy it exactly. That is all that matters—to copy everything exactly.

"You will work as quickly or as slowly as you need. You may make as many attempts as you like, in order to obtain the best result. You have been provided with magnifying equipment so that you can check your work in detail. There is therefore no excuse for substandard work."

As Bolotsov pauses to dab at his nose, Pasha raises his print for Viktor to see. Viktor reciprocates. There is movement throughout the room and the soft hum of voices whispering as prisoners use the moment to show their prints to one another. Only the pretty girl and the scowling man keep their prints to themselves. Every photograph Pasha glimpses is of Leonardo's drawings.

"In some cases," resumes Bolotsov, "the pages on which the original drawings were made have other drawings or writing on their reverse. This produces faint shadows where these show through on the drawings you are copying. You must reproduce those, too. Some of the original drawings used chalk. The chalk has become blurred or rubbed through careless handling. Your work must reproduce this.

"The only exceptions are as follows. The types of paper on which the original drawings were made were manufactured in a different way from modern paper. This produces a line texture and a finish to ink washes that you cannot reproduce. Second, some of the original pages were tinted with color. Disregard this—the paper on which you will work is white. Further, over time, the pages of the original drawings have become discolored with age. And because they have not always been handled carefully, they have suffered varying degrees of damage. These characteristics do not matter at this stage."

Pasha notes that phrase, "at this stage." How many stages will there be? Over how long?

"You have been provided with the very best drawing equipment. None of the drawings uses pencil, but you have pencils if you prefer to practice that way. Everything else is consistent with the equipment, inks, and chalks used in the original drawings. The most eminent experts have confirmed this. But it is up to each of you to decide which implements and materials are required for the drawing you are copying. You are artists, this is your field. You will put your utmost talent to work. If you do not, this will be evident and you will fail."

A pause to let the notion of failure strike home. He does not elaborate on what the consequences of failure might be. He wipes his nose again, which is now red, checks his notes, and decides he has said everything he set out to say. He crumples the page and tosses it into the stove.

"You will begin your work now."

Pasha adjusts the guides on the drawing board to suit his left-handedness. Viktor was right. They are here because of their artistic abilities—though why these drawings must be copied is still a mystery.

He looks down again at the print. Then he closes his eyes once more. This time it is not memories that steal upon him. Gradually an old, familiar feeling begins. It is a good feeling, the feeling that comes when he enters his special place. The camp, the guards, Bolotsov, Viktor—everything disappears. He sees every mark, every stroke of the pen that Leonardo is making. He feels them in his own fingers, knows how the pen is navigating the page, how Leonardo's line defines and breathes life into the space it encompasses, creating something where there was nothing. He feels the sweep of the brush as the wash is applied, watches how the soft sable moves swiftly from right to left, up and down. He sees the splashes when the brush is overloaded, hears the tiny sound of every drip of ink that falls, unregarded, for although these drawings will have genius, they are not intended as that. Perfection is not sought even though perfection is present—Leonardo cannot help but produce perfection.

Everything is resolved now. Behind closed eyelids, Pasha sees it all.

He opens his eyes.

Under the gaze of Josef Vissarionovich, he begins to draw.

CHAPTER 10

He draws all day. They all do.

Afterwards they are told to write the three-digit number of their work table on the back of every sheet they used. They will continue to work at the same table each day and use the same number.

Pasha watches as the guards collect everyone's drawings. Some prisoners worked their way through many sheets, representing their many attempts. He used only three. He knows his work is good, but he does not know if he should allow himself to be pleased by that.

The evening meal is much the same as yesterday's. A couple of carrots have replaced the potato.

"So this is what it's like to be treated like tsars, Viktor. Tell me, have you ever dined in Restaurant Praga?"

Viktor looks up in surprise. He wipes his lips. "That fancy place in the Arbat? Yes, many times. Have you been there?"

"Only on the outside looking in."

"Ah." Viktor regards him thoughtfully for a moment. "It's nothing special," he adds quietly.

After the meal, the prisoners are at liberty to walk in the compound or return to their dormitories. Pasha and Viktor explore the camp perimeter, where a path has been cleared through the snow. Others are taking the same route, in twos and threes. Guards patrol with the prisoners, and the sentries monitor everything from the watchtowers.

"This is why they wanted artists," says Viktor. "We're here to become forgers. Nowhere better than the gulag for that—there's nowhere on earth more secret."

Pasha is watching the ground ahead of him where others have trodden already. There are patches where the snow is compacting to ice. Its sheen in the floodlights puts him in mind of the ice the militiamen dragged into his home when they arrested him. He thinks of Mama, sitting alone in Lobachev Row, worrying about him. Has she been told what has become of him? Does she know where he is?

He brings his attention back to what Viktor is saying. Forgery. Could such a thing really be feasible? There would be so many difficulties to overcome.

"There'd be a long way to go before our copies could be any use as forgeries," he tells Viktor. "Bolotsov mentioned shadows showing through on some of the pages we're copying. That's because Leonardo often used both sides of his paper, especially for his anatomical work. Paper was expensive, it was made by hand, he didn't waste it. Also, sometimes he scribbled notes on the backs of drawings as things came to mind—they might be meaningful ideas or they might only be trivial reminders to himself. We consider his drawings priceless, but to him they were often nothing more than practice exercises. He didn't have posterity in mind, so why not jot down a shopping list or an idea for his next invention? Obviously, one reason we can't read his writing is because it's Italian—medieval Italian at that—but it's also because he often wrote backwards."

"I bow to your knowledge."

"The most difficult thing of all is that some forgeries would have to be done back to back. Pages with drawings on only one side, they'd be hard—but double-sided pages . . . can you imagine? The positioning of every detail on each side of the page, every single line and piece of shading, they'd all have to be precise, with everything aligning perfectly. Just think how hard that would be."

Viktor nods slowly as he takes this in. "But if Leonardo's paper was handmade, why are we being given ordinary cartridge paper?"

A guard is approaching. Pasha waits until he passes.

"The cartridge paper might just be for practice. To produce convincing forgeries, they'd have to replicate Leonardo's paper."

"How could they do that?"

"No idea. But they'd know what they're trying to match because clearly they have the originals."

"Then we'd have to copy the drawings all over again on the replica paper."

"There's no other way. And the paper would have to be worn and frayed because Bolotsov is right about something else—Leonardo's drawings aren't only old, they've also taken some punishment. After his death they were bound into books, then taken apart again—sometimes several times. That's the reason for the torn corners and other flaws we can see in the photographic prints. One more thing—some of the paper would have to be tinted to colors that match Leonardo's originals. And for silverpoint work, he applied a prepared ground to the page. That would have to be reproduced, too."

"Well, you're the one who knows about silverpoint. How many drawings are there?"

"I don't know. They're scattered across collections around the world. But I don't think any are in the Soviet Union."

They continue walking, neither of them speaking, as they digest all this. Viktor waits until they complete another circuit.

"If they have the originals, why do they need forgeries?"

"Maybe to sell them as originals."

"There couldn't be many potential buyers. Would a deal be for money or for something else, such as political favors? Either way, that would mean someone with power or high rank—or both."

"A black marketeer or government official."

"They're the sort that know how to be careful. They wouldn't be easy to fool. They'd want solid proof of the authenticity of what they're buying. How would the seller arrange that?"

Pasha is shaking his head. "I don't know."

"You seem to know everything else about these drawings."

"You know a lot about the gulag, I know a little about Leonardo. What does either of us know about forged art?"

"Most of all, I'd like to know who's behind this. Someone big, that's for sure—it's not for the glory of the proletariat, whatever Bolotsov says. Look at the whole setup. Who can take over a chunk of the gulag and set up militia arrests, transportation, a complete prison camp? Not to mention enlisting the services of the NKVD. That's not all, either—if the originals aren't in the Soviet Union, then they're being brought from the West for us to copy them. And maybe the forgeries are destined to be sold in the West. So tell me—who can do all that?"

The controlling will, thinks Pasha. Whoever that is.

Once more he shakes his head, at a loss, and returns to watching the icy ground.

CHAPTER 11

In the ensuing days the prisoners work again and again on the same prints, copying the drawings repeatedly.

To begin with, the same four sets of drawings are copied by the same groups of prisoners many times over. Then the sets are rotated between the groups. It becomes apparent that the intention is for all the drawings to be copied by all the prisoners.

In time new sets of drawings are introduced and the process starts all over again. This continues as additional drawings are introduced. Days become weeks. All the prisoners' attempts are always collected; none is ever discarded or destroyed.

"This is a factory," says Pasha. "It's just that we're cranking out art instead of nuts and bolts."

Viktor disagrees. "Making nuts and bolts is honest labor. There's nothing honest here."

Pasha wonders how many drawings they will have to do. He wonders who is keeping track of all this output. Commandant Bolotsov, certainly; but his cannot be the controlling will.

Although Pasha and Viktor keep their speculation about forgery to themselves, it does not take long for other prisoners to reach the same conclusion. But not all of them. For some, the realization that they are not to be worked to death in the mines validates their trust in the system that raised, educated, trained, and governs them in every aspect of their lives.

These are men and women who have always believed in that system. Most of them have never known anything else. Only the two academicians, the oldest among them, have experienced what went before—the reign of the tsars—and they can attest to what a disaster that was. Now, despite the initial terror of their arrests, these believers are prepared to believe with equal conviction in the system's legitimacy in imprisoning them. That act, too, they are convinced, must be right—simply because the system is always right. They must be in the wrong; hence their incarceration. The system is for the best, always. Everything it does is rational and legitimate. Always. Their faith remains solid and unshaken. They can no more reject the system than they could stop breathing air. Such is the unassailability of what Josef Vissarionovich has built.

The architect is one such true believer. Pasha and Viktor come upon a discussion between her and other prisoners during an evening walk.

"I believe our work is for a high purpose," she is saying. "It will be used to showcase the technical skills of Soviet artists. Artists of all kinds, from all disciplines. That's why we've been chosen—we're a cross section of disciplines."

The man from the Bolshoi is skeptical. "But why copy drawings by Leonardo da Vinci, or any other degenerate bourgeois foreign artist, to achieve that? Why copy at all? Why not showcase original Soviet creative work? I've designed costumes for some of the world's greatest ballet productions, and my work has received the highest praise. Why must I copy centuries-old designs for some trivial courtly masquerade that no one has heard of or cares about?"

"Comrade, our work will be shown to the world—to the West," explains the architect patiently. "Copies of art that the West considers the best of its kind, however degenerate, allow a direct comparison that even the cultural illiterates of the West can understand."

"But—"

"She's right," chips in an engineer from Donetsk. His specialty is drawing complex machinery. "Soviet Social Realism is a radical and advanced art form. It's difficult for regressive Westerners to grasp. We have to make it easier for them to appreciate socialist creative achievement. We do that by speaking to them initially in their own terms, in their own visual language. Then we can guide them toward the progressive plane of Social Realism."

Viktor moves closer to the little group, his head bowed to their level in his usual respectful way.

"Excuse me, comrades," he says politely. "Can any of you help with something that's been troubling me? I know I must have been guilty of certain crimes, and no doubt that's part of the reason why I've been chosen for this work. It's my opportunity to make amends. But I've been unable to figure out what my actual crimes are. So may I ask—do all of you know what your crimes are?"

"I haven't identified mine yet," admits the engineer. "But that's because I haven't succeeded in cleansing my thinking of deviationism and dogmatism."

The architect nods her approval of this analysis.

"I see," says Viktor. "So my failings are what make me unable to see what my failings are. My dialectical limitations stop me from perceiving my dialectical limitations. Is that it?"

"Naturally."

The pretty girl has also been watching and listening. She puts a suggestion of her own to the engineer: "You mean, like a fool who can't see he's a fool precisely because he's a fool?"

The engineer frowns. "I wouldn't put it like that."

She smiles, turns, and walks away toward her dormitory hut.

"Wait!" calls Viktor. He hurries after her, bending down to her and talking rapidly, his long arms gesticulating. Pasha looks around. The scowling man is watching again.

Later that evening, Pasha asks Viktor about the man.

"Who is he? He's always watching you and the girl."

Viktor grins. "What girl?"

"You know exactly what girl. The one you were talking to. The one you're always trying to talk to. The one who's not interested in you."

Viktor is indignant. "Who says she's not interested? She's called Irina, my nosy comrade. She's Ukrainian."

"And the man?"

"He's Ukrainian, too. He reckons that gives him a special connection with Irina. He's been pestering her since the two of them boarded the train that brought them to Moscow. He's after more than friendship from her. Irina wants nothing to do with him. He has a certain difficulty with that."

"Maybe with you, too, as a result."

Viktor shrugs. "He's best ignored."

It turns out that the Ukrainian has difficulty with others as well. And with his own hot temper. He and the engineer from Donetsk come to blows in the dining hut over an accidental spillage of the Ukrainian's food. They have to be separated by the guards.

"In any other camp they'd let them fight until one of them kills the other," says Viktor. "Then they'd shoot the survivor."

* * *

That night the weather turns even colder, with sudden squalls of icy sleet and snow, and hail like sharp stones. When there is no wind, frozen clouds of exhaled breath hang in the air like smoke, marking the path of the prisoners as they hurry between huts. When Viktor spits, it becomes a pellet of ice even before it lands in the snow.

"Minus thirty or worse," he says. "Dangerous."

It is not a night for walking. Muscles and limbs refuse to coordinate properly in such temperatures. After the evening meal, the prisoners go straight to the dormitory huts, where they can be warm. Pasha settles down to draw the scene in his hut: prisoners talking together or resting on their bunks, some of them reading books they managed to keep when their possessions were confiscated. It is a peaceful scene if its context could be overlooked.

Soon he is lost in his work. His gaze probes each face, each fold of clothing, each limb. His pencil follows what he sees and senses. He is in the page, in the drawing, in the mystery that is his gift.

Outside, far away across the tundra, the wolves begin howling. Their cacophony sounds simultaneously human and alien, like lost souls pleading to be released from hell.

A sudden scream surmounts their din. It is close, in the compound right outside the hut. There is no doubt that this scream is human.

Viktor is the first outside. Pasha follows. They see a figure pressed against the inner run of fencing. It is the engineer. His body is facing directly into the fencing but his head is turned sharply to the left as if somehow fixed in that position. His gloved hands grip the barbed wire. He seems oblivious to the risk of the wire piercing the gloves.

For a moment he is quiet, but it is only so that he can draw breath. He begins to scream again. There are words now, but poorly articulated, as if the movement of his mouth is restricted: "My face! Help me, for God's sake!"

His stance, so close against the fence, never alters.

Other figures have appeared: guards and, to Pasha's surprise, Bolotsov himself, who is rarely seen after the end of the workday.

"Stay back!"

The bellow is from the guard sergeant. He raises his rifle. Other guards join him, leveling their weapons at Pasha and the others. Up above, the sentries watch with interest.

The engineer's screams have diminished to a sob. His stance against the fence has not changed. The sergeant seizes the man's shapka and tugs at it. The engineer screams again, but the fur cap comes off smoothly. His shaven head remains locked in place.

The sergeant and Bolotsov confer, their words inaudible. The engineer continues to whimper. Bolotsov produces a handkerchief and dabs at his nose. The discussion ends. The commandant hastens back to the warmth of his quarters.

The sergeant turns to the prisoners.

"Get back to your huts. There's nothing for any of you here. Back to your huts and stay there."

"What do you think happened?" Pasha asks Viktor as they cross the compound.

Viktor kicks snow off his boots on the steps up to the doorway. "My guess? He fell against the fence. His face connected with the steel upright and stuck fast. In these temperatures it happens instantly. Moisture on the skin. If the shapka's earpiece had been between him and the upright, he wouldn't have had a problem."

"So how do they free him?"

"I don't see that they can. Warm water's no good—the water will freeze as soon as it hits the metal, making the situation worse. Half his face would rip away. Boiling water would scald him—and then freeze just the same. Either way, he's unlikely to survive, even with medical attention."

As he finishes speaking, they hear a scream. A single shot rings out. The scream stops abruptly.

"Medical attention won't be necessary," concludes Viktor.

Outside, all becomes quiet but for the distant howling of the wolves. At the other end of the hut, the Ukrainian is climbing into his bunk. For once, something close to a smile flickers across his face. Pasha looks away, quickly, for fear the man should catch him watching.

By morning, the engineer's body has been removed but shreds of facial flesh and skin remain attached to the fence. They have shriveled into frozen brown threads that wave in the wind.

"Zygomaticus minor and major, levator labii superioris," recites Pasha to himself, naming the muscles from which the shreds might have been torn. It is a way of trying to neutralize their horror by reducing them to scientific specimens, like one of Leonardo's anatomical studies.

Sergei's voice rumbles through his mind.

"Study death to understand life," the big professor is saying through a cloud of cigarette smoke.

He has brought Pasha to the mortuary of the medical faculty of Moscow State University. On the slab before them lies a naked cadaver, its flesh waxy and slack. Sergei lifts one of the arms, from which the skin has been peeled back.

"This is all we are, Pavel Pavlovich—bits of meat strung together on a few bones. But God's no fool—it all works. Study it well."

Pasha hurries past the fence. Eventually the wind carries away the last traces of the engineer. The bloodied snow is buried beneath fresh drifts.

In the days that follow, Leonardo's drawings of weaponry, engines of war, pulleys, and mechanical apparatus, previously the engineer's preserve, begin to come Pasha's way. When he works on them, the dark gossamer of the engineer's flayed skin floats into his vision again.

Something else troubles him. It nags until one sleepless night he opens the sketch pad in which he was drawing on the evening of the engineer's death. The floodlights in the compound always remain on through the night; their light shines through the hut's windows so that the dormitory is never completely dark. He angles the pad toward the light and turns to the sketch he was making that evening. He looks at it for a long time, and at the places in the hut where he and the others were sitting or resting.

Eventually he puts the pad away and tries again to get to sleep. But he cannot. The sketch will not let him.

* * *

Despite the engineer's death, the true believers continue to believe. One day Viktor finds himself behind the architect as they line up for the midday meal.

"Too bad about your friend the engineer," he tells her. "Is that also part of how our leaders plan to showcase Soviet creativity—by shooting us?"

She turns her back on him, takes her bowl of watery soup, and hurries off to a table.

"Don't taunt," Pasha admonishes Viktor. "Things are bad enough for all of us without that. It's not her fault."

"That she's an idiot?"

"That she's a loyal socialist."

"You told me once that you were loyal, Pasha. Remember?"

Pasha sighs. "I did."

That evening, Viktor decides to wash one of his uniforms. Pasha helps him spread it out to dry beside the dormitory stove.

"What about you, Viktor? Do you believe in socialism? You've never said one way or the other."

"Haven't I?" Viktor chuckles softly, then sees that Pasha is serious. "It's an interesting question. You mean despite what's being done to us?"

"Do you believe in the workers' struggle? Is the gulag part of that? You said we're not here for the glory of the proletariat."

"What's brought this on?" Viktor glances at the portrait of Stalin. "Is Josef Vissarionovich getting to you?"

Pasha picks up a pencil and sketches a cornflower floret, its points long and elegant. He thinks about Mama and her trust in Josef Vissarionovich, about her hard work every day, never slacking, no excuses. He thinks also about his father, who gave his life to protect the socialist dream, and about the millions of Soviet citizens who place their faith in that dream—even the free workers in Vorkuta with all their madness, even the likes of the architect and the engineer. Perhaps madness can be just another form of dedication to a cause. Josef Vissarionovich can put every infirmity to use.

"Viktor, do you think imprisoning us here makes for a better world?"

"Of course not."

"Or the way your father the honest judge was treated—did that support the workers' struggle?"

Viktor's face darkens. He pauses for a moment, staring at the damp uniform. "I didn't tell you everything about my father. I said he was a broken man, and that's true. The fact is, he was so broken that he took his pistol and blew his brains out. He went into his study as if it was a day like any other, closed the door, sat down at his desk, and . . ."

He plucks at a sleeve of the uniform and straightens it out. There was no need; the sleeve was already straight.

"I have two sisters. They were there that day, we all heard the shot, but I got to him first. I had to keep them away. You want to know about socialism? Socialism is a lie, Pasha. Everything in it is a lie. Bolotsov's line about serving the Soviet proletariat—just one more lie. Our country is drowning in lies, we can't breathe for them. It was lies that killed my father. He refused to be part of them, but they were too numerous and too powerful, and in the end, he gave up. Just gave up. The lies were too much for him. They brought him down, like a shot animal." He raises his gaze from the uniform. "Now you tell me, Pasha—what's this conversation really about? What's really on your mind?"

Pasha shrugs. "I'm not sure. What are we left with when everything's a lie? Maybe that's what it's about. Maybe that's what I want to know."

* * *

Every month, the copies of Leonardo's work made by the prisoners are packed into wooden crates that are sealed and taken away from the camp in one of the trucks. Armed guards ride with them.

As time passes, the copies run into the hundreds. During every waking moment Pasha carries in his mind the drawing on which he is working. He stands in line for his food, he bolts it down, he talks with Viktor; but the drawings never leave him. They are there in his mind at night as he searches for sleep and they are the first things that pour into his consciousness when he wakes in the morning. He lives within each drawing and it lives within him.

All of them lies.

CHAPTER 12

WITH THE EXCEPTION of the Ukrainian, friendships form among the prisoners. Individuals fall into the habit of taking meals with the same person or walking with them in the evenings. Sometimes a shared background brings them together. Or a shared resentment. There is a young woman from Latvia, diminutive and bird-like, who feels like an outsider alongside the Russians and others from longer-standing Soviet republics than hers. There is an Estonian man who feels the same. Neither of their countries came willingly into the Soviet fold, so it is no surprise that they are more comfortable in each other's company than with anyone else.

The female academician from Leningrad and the gold medal winner of the Academy of Arts in Moscow have enough in common for them to be drawn to each other. The Muscovite is happy to have a companion after his cold-shoulder treatment by the Ukrainian, while the woman from Leningrad is glad to be with someone of her own caste.

As Viktor notes, there are ironies in some of the allegiances. The Latvian and the Estonian can only converse in Russian, the lingua franca forced on them by the oppressor they both despise. The two academicians feel superior to everyone else, but each also holds their academy to be superior to the other's; so they argue nonstop.

Friendships fluctuate just as they would outside the gulag. Some ebb and fade, new ones replace them. Viktor follows the changes as he drifts between people in the dining hut or on the evening walk, listening and watching.

But it seems to Pasha there is one thing that his friend's sharp gaze misses.

"I have a question for you," he tells Viktor. They have been through the weekly shower, have been shaved and are dressing in the wash house. No one is nearby to hear them.

Viktor scratches the stubble on his head. "More political philosophy?"

"Nothing about politics. What if the Ukrainian had something to do with what happened to the engineer?"

"Why would you think that?"

"They were both absent from our hut that evening."

"So what?"

"Do you remember how bad the weather was? Where were they? What was keeping them out in such conditions? What if there was more trouble between them, ending up with the Ukrainian knocking the engineer against the fence? It could have been deliberate or an accident."

"No, Pasha. The sentries would have seen. They'd have raised the alarm."

"But if they didn't see? Bear in mind the weather. All I'm saying is that they weren't with the rest of us, and the Ukrainian didn't show up when we heard the scream and went to see what was wrong. Everyone else was there, men and women alike. But he only reappeared later."

"How do you know who was or wasn't in the hut? Who says the Ukrainian wasn't?"

"I was drawing us. He's not in my drawing. I'm certain he wasn't there."

"It proves nothing. Listen, Pasha, he's dangerous. Take care he never hears you saying any of this."

"Maybe you're the one who needs to be careful."

* * *

Some of the relationships run deeper than friendship. People are only human, even in the gulag.

Irina is the cartographer who produces the maps for atlases. Viktor's persistence with her eventually wins the day and they become lovers.

The Estonian, a big man, has a fine bass singing voice. He sings softly in his own language to the little Latvian woman; his songs have mournful melodies that swoop and fall as if they are ending but then strengthen and return, like memories. He has to explain the lyrics to her in Russian. Pasha overhears some of this. The songs are about the beauty of his homeland and about loss and betrayal—betrayal by a loved one, loss of freedom.

Between arguments, the two academicians hold hands like adolescents. They whisper together and cast haughty glances at the other prisoners.

The woman who creates the pictures for children's storybooks and a Byelorussian who draws animals sit leg to leg at meals, lock eyes, and show no desire to speak to anyone but each other.

Not all the relationships are straightforward. The costume designer from the Bolshoi, a handsome man in his forties, finds Pasha alone one evening. They walk together and chat. He tries to kiss Pasha on the lips. On hearing Pasha's anguished account afterwards, Viktor laughs at his embarrassment until Pasha is laughing, too. In due course the Bolshoi designer finds his soul mate in the young man who paints children's portraits. The other prisoners, unlike the rigid society they have come from, have no problem with their relationship. The designer bears Pasha no ill will.

There are no rules forbidding sexual relationships between the prisoners. The guards are indifferent. But there is no privacy for lovers. The Russian Arctic is not the place for outdoor trysts, so the only option is the bunks in the dormitories. No one pays any heed to these couplings, which anyway are brief and not that frequent—the prisoners' meager rations ensure limited energy.

These liaisons disregard marriages and all other relationships that existed in the world outside. That world is gone. Wives and husbands are gone, children are gone. No one knows when—or even whether—that world will return, not even the truest of the true believers.

The guards have their own liaisons. Given the disparity in numbers between the sexes, the women have the advantage in range of choice. One of them, a little round-faced Kazakh woman, seems to have at least three lovers, judging from the fumblings—admittedly fully clad—behind the wash house and dining hut that are observed by various prisoners. The fumblings are only preliminaries. The Kazakh and her sisterly comrades soon evolve better arrangements. Their dormitory hut has enough unoccupied bunks to serve the needs of all. This is evident from the noises the prisoners hear when they pass within earshot.

Pasha stays away from his part of the men's hut when Viktor and Irina use Viktor's bunk. He makes no complaint about this. He is happy that Viktor is happy. And he likes Irina, who hugs him and kisses him on the cheek each morning when she joins them in the dining hut. She is petite and slender, with green eyes that her lack of hair emphasizes. Her small breasts press against Pasha through the rough camp uniform when she embraces him. Something stirs then. She is unaware of her effect on him. He wonders if he might be falling in love with her himself. Even thinking it makes him feel he is betraying Viktor. He does not allow himself to think about Irina during the night.

One evening he finds Viktor pacing back and forth in the hut. He looks miserable, his head down, his shoulders slumped. There are times when even resilient Viktor's spirits sink low; clearly this is one of those times. Pasha sits down on his bunk and resumes work on the sketch he has been working on—a portrait of Bolotsov. He lets Viktor continue pacing for a while. Then:

"Strange how things work out, Viktor."

Viktor stops pacing. "What things?"

Pasha is shading the folds of the commandant's long shuba. "So much has been taken from us—our freedom, our families, the lives we had. We're dragged all the way to this hell on earth, fenced in like farm animals, kept alive no better than how they're kept alive, and for much the same reason—purely for the value of what we produce. But then consider who's here for you, Viktor."

"Irina."

Pasha continues drawing. "So what would you change?"

Viktor snorts. "Would I choose not to have been arrested since that would mean not meeting Irina? That's what you're asking. Of course not. No. Never in a million years."

"There you are. Strange how things work out."

Viktor raises his chin. His shoulders square. "Clever Pasha. How wise you're becoming, my young comrade."

"I'm learning."

The following morning, Pasha comes upon Irina in the dining hut.

"Viktor told me what you said, Pasha. Thank you. You're a good friend."

"He's not as tough as he pretends, Irina. Don't hurt him."

The green eyes smile. She kisses his cheek. "Never in a million years."

CHAPTER 13

VIKTOR TRIES TO befriend the guards. He never really succeeds, but he does gather some information.

"It's almost as bad here for them as for us," he reports to Pasha and Irina. "They didn't volunteer for this posting. They knew nothing about what our work would be. They're told only what we're told, and at the same time, not before. They're not allowed leisure time in Vorkuta—not even Bolotsov. No contact with outsiders. No alcohol. Their families know they're in the gulag but not where. There's no compassionate leave. The train from Moscow comes to Vorkuta once a week, so mail is only weekly. All mail is read and censored by Bolotsov. The Red Army has nothing to do with this camp except transporting us here, bringing visitors, and delivering supplies."

Pasha thinks about the controlling will, the controlling mind. "Someone's keeping a very tight lid on what's going on here."

The following evening, the snow is too heavy for walking. The three of them keep to the men's dormitory hut. At one end of the room, the Bolshoi costume designer is recounting a story about a prima ballerina and her lovers. In another corner, the big Estonian is quietly serenading his lover. Beside the stove, Irina is mending one of her boots. The sole has split and she has been allowed some horse glue with which to repair it. She heats the glue on the stove.

"Our train journey here," says Pasha. "People were always trying to figure out where we were."

"We were on the only rail line to Vorkuta," says Irina. "Actually, it's the only overland route of any kind that comes here."

While the glue is softening, she draws the outline of Russia and the adjoining republics on a floorboard.

"Here's Lvov, down in Ukraine. It's where I come from. I worked in Moscow and had residency there but I went home to my parents as often as I could. I was arrested during one of those visits, so that's where my first train journey started. And here's Moscow, where I was transferred to the big train." She draws a line across the board, north and then northeast: "This is the rail line." She adds a patch of shading to the east of the final stretch: "This is the Urals." Her pencil returns to the end of the rail line: "Vorkuta." Finally, she places a cross north of Vorkuta: "And here's where we are right now."

Pasha stares at the floorboard. It is like looking down at himself as the train thunders along. It is like looking down at all of them here in the camp. His fingernail inscribes a line from the camp due south to intersect the rail line, running west of Vorkuta.

"How far is this distance?"

Irina applies the glue in the few seconds before it hardens.

"Maybe eighty kilometers," she says. "Maybe ninety."

Viktor has been following the exchange. "Thinking of making a break for it, Pasha? Even if they don't shoot you down in the first hundred meters, you'd never survive out on the tundra."

"I know."

After a few days, Irina's sketch fades, scuffed by passing feet. But the crude map lingers in Pasha's mind.

* * *

Irina is the practical type. Each week the prisoners are allowed a few sheets of cartridge paper for their own use, a concession granted by Bolotsov only because it supports their artistic skills. Irina searches for a flat stone on an evening walk and uses it to prise a nail from a loose board. With the point of the nail she scores and cuts some of her paper into small rectangles, all the same size. She tells a guard that her other boot needs repair, and obtains more horse glue. She glues the paper rectangles together so that they are triple thickness. The glue also stiffens them when it hardens. She smooths their edges and rounded corners with the sandpaper used for shaping silver-point rods.

"What are you up to?" asks Viktor.

"Making playing cards. I can't laminate or coat them, so they're not perfect, but good socialists work with what they have. And we're all good socialists here, aren't we?"

"None better."

"So we'll manage."

For the backs of the cards she draws a design based on a tall, square-shaped tower of some kind.

"The Korniakt Tower in my beautiful Lvov," she explains to Pasha.

For the court cards she persuades him to draw Viktor for the king, her for the queen, and himself for the jack. He puts Stalin's face inside the ace.

"You'll be shot," warns Viktor.

"I could make him the joker."

No one laughs.

* * *

At five each morning the prisoners are woken by the guards on night shift. They have fifteen minutes in which to perform whatever ablutions they choose to do before the morning meal. Take too long and they miss the meal.

One morning Pasha is on his way to the latrine block when he hears voices behind the hut.

"Call it a day, Russki."

There is no mistaking that growl. It belongs to the Ukrainian.

"She's not your property. She makes her own decisions."

This is Viktor's voice.

Pasha steps behind the hut. It is long before daybreak, and although the floodlights are on as usual, the shadows behind the hut are deep after the glare in the compound. It takes a moment for his eyes to adjust.

The Ukrainian has Viktor backed up against the wall and is holding a knife to his throat. His strength far exceeds Viktor's. Viktor is unable to free himself.

Pasha does not take time to think. He kicks as hard as he can between the Ukrainian's legs. It is a clumsy blow. The Ukrainian's heavy coat makes him miss the man's genitals. The Ukrainian roars more in fury than pain. He releases Viktor and rounds on Pasha. The knife blade flashes. But as he lunges, the scene is suddenly flooded with light. A searchlight has come on in the nearest watchtower. The rule of right angles, thinks Pasha; unlike what may have been the case on the night of the engineer's death, a sentry has seen what is happening.

A shot rings out, deafeningly loud—a single shot, from a rifle rather than a Kalashnikov, and from immediately behind Pasha. The Ukrainian stops in his tracks and rocks back, surprise in his eyes. He looks down at his chest, where beneath his open coat a dark stain is spreading over the stripes of his uniform. He sinks to his knees. His surprise turns to a glare of hatred directed at the guard sergeant behind Pasha who fired the shot, then he falls forward, facedown in the snow, and lies very still.

The sergeant shoves Pasha out of the way. He bends down and pockets the knife. He turns the Ukrainian over with his foot, lowers the rifle, and fires another shot, this time directly into the man's face. Debris and blood spray over the snow. The sergeant glances up at the watchtower and signals with a raised hand. He turns to Pasha and Viktor.

"Don't go thinking I shot him to save you," he tells them. "I've had my eye on this one. He's given trouble before. This time he went too far—he had a weapon. Possession of a weapon is punishable by death. Consider him punished."

A sideways nod of his head orders Pasha and Viktor to be on their way. They are glad to comply.

* * *

One morning Pasha begins to itch. First his chest, then his back, his legs. The itch is maddening. No amount of scratching does any good. Other prisoners are suffering in the same way. The Estonian roars like a wild animal and claws at his skin as if he would rip it off.

"Lice," says Viktor, and curses.

"Body lice, to be exact," adds Irina as she examines the creatures. "They're the ones that are really dangerous. They can carry typhus."

Within the day it is clear that everyone in the camp is infected. The lice make no distinction between prisoners and guards. Even Bolotsov has them. Some can be seen crawling in the fur shuba.

"They're good socialist lice if our respected commandant has them," says Viktor. "No barriers of class or rank."

The creatures are everywhere. They are in every seam of every piece of clothing, they dig themselves out of sight deep in blankets and bedding, they even marshal themselves along the edges of bunk boards, like reserve military formations awaiting the order to advance.

The showering and delousing are now done twice weekly. Apart from eyebrows, all the prisoners' body hair is shaved off, including pubic. This is a hazardous undertaking, but no one argues: anything to combat the infestation.

Viktor's strategy is to bury articles of clothing in the snow, leaving only a corner clear. The lice congregate there to escape the cold, and he scrapes them off and dumps them in the snow.

"The lazy man's way," declares Irina.

"What's wrong with that?"

"It doesn't get rid of the eggs."

"I'll deal with them when they hatch."

"Lazy. Ineffective."

Some prisoners spread their garments on dormitory stoves and listen with satisfaction to the cracking noises as the lice and eggs explode. Others pass a candle flame over the seams of their clothing. Pasha follows Irina's method—he searches his clothes and bedding every evening, and crushes the vermin between his fingernails in little pools of blood or tosses both adults and eggs into the stove.

But the lice will not be defeated. They are too numerous and breed too quickly. In the end they are just something else that keeps Pasha awake at night.

* * *

One day a guard enters the work hut and goes directly to the young Latvian woman. He speaks briefly to her. She looks uncertain, turns toward her Estonian lover, who, like everyone else in the room, is watching. But the guard places his hand on her shoulder, turning her away from the Estonian, and speaks again. He is more insistent this time.

She bows her head, then stands up from her work. The guard escorts her from the hut. The prisoners watch mutely as she leaves.

After half an hour, she is escorted back. She is pale. Her face is blank. She looks at no one, meets no one's gaze, least of all that of the Estonian. She returns to her table and docilely resumes her work.

That evening she walks by herself. She pushes the Estonian away when he goes to her. When other women, including Irina, approach her, she shakes her head, remains tight lipped, and sends them away, too. She keeps to herself in the days that follow. The big Estonian is distraught. His eyes fill with tears. He no longer sings.

Some days later, a guard singles out another prisoner, this time the woman who illustrates children's books. A week later, it is the turn of another of the younger women.

"Bolotsov," whispers Viktor to Pasha. "The bastard."

Irina overhears but says nothing.

It happens every few days. Always only with the younger women. It becomes a pattern, one of the rhythms of life in the camp. On returning to the hut, the woman that Bolotsov has sent for may be calm or she may be sobbing. She may be holding her head high in defiance or hanging it in shame or sorrow. Each woman has her own individual way.

The day comes when Irina is the one chosen by Bolotsov. Viktor watches her as she departs from the work hut and when she returns. She does not meet his gaze.

Pasha watches Viktor. Viktor's face is unreadable.

CHAPTER 14

WHEN SUMMER COMES, the snow retreats and there are warm days when the prisoners and guards can go without their greatcoats. Bolotsov remains cocooned in his fur shuba.

When Pasha crosses the compound in the morning, the sky he glimpses is a luminous blue, far deeper than at home or in Moscow. For a brief time there are magical nights when the sun never sets. The light then is unlike any he has seen before, golden and soft, as if honey has been poured over the world.

There is beauty here after all. A delicate beauty: turquoise and copper-colored mosses and lichen underfoot, and sprinkles of tiny Arctic flowers in yellow, pink, and white that look impossibly fragile. A shy beauty.

The price Pasha pays for the sight is a yet more piercing sense of what has been taken from him. So he does the only thing he can to cling to such beauty—he draws it. He obtains permission to take brushes and inks from the work hut so that he can apply delicate washes of color to the sketches. He has to go deep inside himself, to that special place, to find these drawings of his own, it is so long since he has created from nature instead of copying Leonardo.

But he succeeds. And as he works, he feels as if his soul has freed itself from the gulag, taken wing, and soared far beyond the watchtowers and into the infinite Arctic sky.

He draws Viktor and Irina and other couples, including the Estonian and the Latvian, who have found their way into each other's hearts again despite Bolotsov. Or perhaps all the more deeply because of him.

He draws the Estonian when the man agrees to sing for all the prisoners one evening. Pasha understands then that song is the Estonian's way of reaching for freedom.

Sometimes he draws the prisoners as anonymous groups when his purpose is to capture only shape and the urgency of movement, just as Sergei taught him, but sometimes he makes deliberate individual likenesses: bodies and limbs in flux or the expression in a fleeting glance.

He draws the guards. Like some prisoners, he trades these portraits for extra food; but he does not involve himself in the commerce for obscene drawings that arises.

As he traces the gentle contours of Irina's smile, he is reminded of Leonardo's Mona Lisa.

The land is in thaw during these few weeks of summer. The water locked in the permafrost is released, and he observes the sparkle of ponds and lakes on the tundra. Mosquitoes and midges hover above them in dense black clouds. Sometimes the insects descend on the camp en masse in an explosion of noise and black waves. The mosquitoes and horseflies are knuckle sized, the horseflies glittering in black and yellow armor. When thick clusters of the insects attack, their numbers would choke a man. Pasha withdraws indoors.

The richness of insect life attracts migrating birds—duck and teal and other species. He draws as many as he can, coloring these sketches, too.

In July the ice road melts. Trucks coming to the camp from Vorkuta must now hobble over the tundra, making long detours to avoid marshy areas. When they misread the terrain, tracked snowplows have to haul them out.

Reindeer gather nervously at the riverbank to drink and forage. Sometimes the wolves come as well, sometimes with their pups, in search of prey. The reindeer scatter.

One day a solitary straggler is attacked. It is weak and old—there is no need for the wolves to chase it. The pack closes on the animal from behind and each side, gnashing and biting until it collapses to the ground. It makes no sound, as if it accepts its fate. It is still alive as they tear its belly open and rip out its intestines. It lifts its head to witness its own death, paralyzed and helpless.

No reindeer returns to help it. They are prey animals. Prey animals do not defend their helpless fellows. The animal brought down is the animal that saves the rest of the herd.

Pasha draws all these things. There is horror here as well as beauty.

He watches white-fronted geese passing overhead, listens to their hoarse clacking, watches the lazy beat of their wings, and thinks of Sergei.

* * *

Commandant Bolotsov keeps a very close eye on the prisoners' work. It now includes drawings that have to be done by silverpoint.

"Who better than you, Pasha?" says Viktor.

Evidently Bolotsov agrees. He spends more time at Pasha's work table than at any other. Pasha is never aware of his arrival in advance. He is far away within that day's drawing. He does not smell the fur shuba as Bolotsov approaches, does not hear it swish along the floor, and the commandant always sneaks up from behind so that he can observe better. Pasha is oblivious until, as he sits back to rest for a moment, the commandant's hand descends on his shoulder and he is wrenched back to reality.

After these encounters, he thinks of his teacher in the little school on Armory Lane. He remembers how she, too, was always drawn to his desk. He thinks about how that was the start of everything. But how could anyone have known that then?

These are times when he also ponders what Viktor said to him that first day, on the train: “You must be a good artist, Pasha. Someone somewhere knows that.”

But who?

* * *

In every season, at night, as he stands outside or lies in his bunk, he hears the wolves. Their howls are the eeriest, loneliest sound he has ever heard, long doleful cries that echo across the empty tundra, sometimes a solitary wail, sometimes a chorus. The sound comes from different directions as a lone animal calls out and is answered or as a pack warns other packs away. There are intermittent hollow silences in which the wind has its say, then the howls begin again. They are more insistent when the moon is full. They tell him that the vast tundra is never truly empty.

He discovers a place beside the dining hut where he can look at the night sky without the floodlights shining directly in his eyes. He is still visible to the guards on patrol and in the watchtowers—the rule of right angles again—so they tolerate him doing this. He goes there on sleepless nights and watches the moon and stars, studying their paths across the sky as the night wears on. Ursa Major and Ursa Minor are crystal clear and will always be visible regardless of season, but he also has a perfect view of the other constellations nearest the North Pole—far clearer than he ever saw them when he learned their names and locations in his Young Pioneer days. He needs no telescope to follow them, particularly the brightest star of all, the North Star.

When he looks at them now, they remind him of the moment of beauty and terror on the train when the door of the wagon crashed open and the glory of the night was revealed. He remembers his fear and Mama's promise that Jesus would always be there. And one night, at last, he prays with her as if they are standing together before her holy icon. This is the night when he returns to the question he posed Viktor, one that in his heart he knew even then was really addressed to himself: "What are we left with when everything's a lie?"

He knows the answer now. It has taken these long months to bring him to it, but he knows now that he has a choice. He can be left with nothing; or he can be left with God.

* * *

One evening Irina joins him. The moon is new and the stars have the sky to themselves, jewels on a bed of purple silk.

"So quiet," he says. "No wolves tonight."

"Viktor says you're plotting your escape when you stand out here. He says you're more than half crazy and you don't care about the guns and the searchlights. He says you're thinking about that map I drew. Is that what you're doing, Pasha—planning to take your chance, make a break for it?"

He shakes his head. "Who doesn't have ideas like that? Not tonight, though. That's not what I'm thinking tonight."

"Then what are you thinking?"

He shrugs. "How insignificant we are."

"Does that include Bolotsov?"

"He's the most insignificant of all."

"How do you make that out?"

"The last shall be first and the first last."

"Ah, you read the Bible."

"I used to."

"Me, too, to keep my father happy. I liked to tease him. Petrov the Pilgrim I called him. He's probably praying for me at this very moment. Nice of him, but a waste of time."

"You don't share his faith?"

"Not any longer. When I look at the bad things that happen in this world—including here—how could I?"

"It's the bad things that make me believe."

"How so, Pasha?"

"Because there has to be a judgment."

"I see. Well, if there are degrees of damnation, then come your Judgment Day, Bolotsov won't be the most damned."

"So who will be?"

"Stalin." She turns to leave, but pauses. "Do you really think a person could outrun the guns? Do you?"

"No," he says firmly. "Making a break for it is a dream, Irina, that's all. A fantasy. It's a dream for which I don't even have to be asleep."

She sighs. "I know about that kind of dream. I dream, too—that kind and the sleeping kind. The most cruel is the sleeping dream where I'm home in Lvov and everything is just the way it used to be. I'm in my little bed beside the stove. I'll warm some milk for buckwheat kasha. I just need a minute more because I'm so snug in my bed—then I'll get up, I promise, and I'll still be in time to make breakfast for my mother and father and me. Later, I'll go out and meet some friends. In the dream I always know which friends they'll be—different ones each time, but I see them as clear as day." She sighs again. "When I actually do wake up, at first I can't understand where I am. Then I remember. I remember everything—Bolotsov, everything. That's the worst time, Pasha, when it all comes back to me." She shivers. "That's when I think risking the guns might be better."

"You'd never outrun them."

"That's what I'd be counting on."

* * *

Two of the younger women fall pregnant. One is the illustrator of children's books; the other is the architect, the true believer, who argued that the purpose of the work here is to showcase Soviet artists.

The commandant notices the architect's rounded belly during one of her visits to him. He orders the female guards to examine her and the other women. The book illustrator's condition comes to light as well. He orders both pregnancies to be terminated. The procedures are performed by a female guard. She uses a kitchen skewer.

Either baby may have been the commandant's. Possibly both. No one knows, not even the mothers, since both have lovers. The rumor circulates that the aborted fetuses have been incinerated in the stove in Bolotsov's quarters.

The commandant continues sending for the two women just as frequently as before and with no respite for recovery after their surgery.

* * *

Winter returns, signaling the passing of the prisoners' first year in the camp.

Now there are days when the sun never wrests itself free of the horizon. The season brings the magical spectacle of the Northern Lights, which Pasha has heard of but never seen. He is mesmerized. The phenomenon comes and goes for weeks on end, on some nights lasting only minutes, on others hours. Sometimes it is completely soundless, sometimes the crackle of electricity fizzes in the air.

He draws and paints the unearthly sheets and waves of color but is never satisfied with the results. He wonders how Leonardo would have done it, thinks of his drawings of floods and storms, and keeps experimenting.

Winter also brings the feared burani. These are the Arctic blizzards, killers that arise without warning and obliterate everything in seconds. The sky disappears, the camp and its huts disappear, there is no earth or horizon, only a sudden blinding white fog that descends with unbelievable speed.

Anyone caught outside in a buran must fling themselves to the ground and crawl for cover or wait for the danger to pass over them, hoping they do not freeze to death or suffocate, for the change in air pressure can be so sudden and savage that it drives breath from lungs. Hail slashes like blades, the wind screams, sweeps up ice and rocks, turning them into missiles that could split skulls.

One evening the prisoners are trapped in the dining hut while a buran rages. The whole hut shakes when the wind strikes. Air is sucked from the stove; the flames extinguish; the coals clatter as they are sucked up the metal flue.

"We're here until this is over," says Viktor. "People have been carried away by a buran and its vacuum. Swept up like empty scraps of clothing. Sometimes their bodies are found kilometers away—they might be beaten to a pulp, every bone broken, or they might not have a mark on them. Sometimes only parts of them are found. Sometimes no trace of them is ever seen again."

Pasha shudders. The gulag has many ways to feed its appetite for bones.

* * *

Having lost her unborn child, the architect loses her mind as well. She talks to herself and cackles with laughter for no reason. She becomes foul mouthed. Her lover, a botanist, never lets her wander about unaccompanied. He whispers reassurance as if she is a child. He takes her to his bunk and keeps her there all night in his arms.

She still does good work, and Bolotsov enjoys the passion she now exhibits. Her visits to his office are longer and more frequent.

It spares Irina and the other women. The architect is like a prey animal sacrificed to save the rest of the herd, thinks Pasha.

* * *

So life goes on.

The work goes on.

Then come the executions.

CHAPTER 15

Sergei Lysenko's beard and hair are no longer merely grizzled; they have turned white. The permanent stoop that has developed in his spine has reduced him from the towering figure he once was. Flesh has melted from his bones as if a sickness is eating at him. His fine clothes are too big for his frame; their quality is still apparent but they are uncared for. His head hangs forward, his gaze is wary. When he smokes, his hand shakes as it operates the gold lighter, making the flame waver so that he has to chase it with the end of the cigarette.

There are two prominent marks on his head, one beside each eye, on the temple before his hairline. Strangers sometimes stare at them, but his fellow members of the Artists' Union are too discreet to do so. He has long ago ceased worrying what the members make of the marks, whether they wonder what caused them, or what tales are told about them.

The marks are circular, each just under a centimeter in diameter. The skin has thickened and risen in angry welts, shiny and red. They are burn scars, caused by the white-hot steel rods that were put to his head. He was warned that the next application of the rods would be directly into each eye.

A name or two, he was assured; that was all that was necessary to avoid this calamity. Besides, it was his socialist duty to help. Those in whose hands he had found himself were reasonable men: even one name would do the job for them. Provided it was a good one.

So he gave them the best.

A sickness is indeed eating at him. It has eaten at him for over a year now. But it is not a sickness that any doctor can ease. The sickness is in Sergei Lysenko's soul.

Across the Soviet Union the same demand, accompanied by similar methods of persuasion, was made of other teachers and experts—even of senior academicians in Moscow and Leningrad. All did their socialist duty, just like Sergei. The wise ones yielded quickly.

There is something else that Sergei must do as part of his particular bargain. Once a month he leaves the Artists' Union and walks to Dzerzhinski Square, where he enters the massive ochre building behind the statue of Iron Feliks, the founder of the secret police, the Cheka, predecessor of the NKVD. It is for Feliks Dzerzhinski that the square is named.

The Lubyanka is a place that prudent citizens prefer to hurry past, eyes lowered, conversation drying up—if they must come near it at all. Sergei does not have that choice. Two armed uniformed guards take him to the staircase not reserved for senior officials, where two more men await him.

These two are wearing ordinary dark suits, but he assumes they, too, are armed. They do not speak to him, nor does he speak to them. They escort him to the floor beneath the clock on the front of the building and deliver him to the room that is always kept ready for him and in which he will spend the day.

The corridor that leads to the room, like all the corridors in the building, is long, and Sergei can no longer walk fast, so the men, who are young and fit, have to adjust their pace.

The room is so large that four doors give into it. All have glass panels at eye level. The men station themselves outside the room. By moving from door to door they can observe Sergei wherever he is in the room.

Two workmen in white boiler suits are in the room. So are the wooden crates, four each month. They have come a long way for his attention. On his nod—no words spoken—the men unseal and open the crates. They don clean white cotton gloves and unpack the hundreds of sheets of cartridge paper within. He watches to ensure there is no clumsiness. Each crate contains the copies that have been made of the drawing reproduced in a particular photographic print—many copies, made by many hands.

The workmen place the sheets in their correct groupings on the trestle tables along the window side of the room. The tables are covered with white linen cloths. Tall lamps have been placed at intervals along the run of tables should Sergei wish to supplement the natural light from the windows; and in any case, regardless of season, he will be here long after nightfall. The room is also lit by crystal chandeliers. On the tables there are magnifying glasses, jeweler's loupes, microscopes, and stand-mounted magnifiers.

Their task done, the workmen withdraw. Sergei pulls on a pair of white cotton gloves. On a separate table at one end of the room are set out the original drawings, Leonardo's drawings, from which the photographic prints were made—each month, four different drawings. At the other end of the room, as far away as possible from the drawings, is a large glass ashtray. Throughout the day Sergei goes to that table to smoke. He removes his gloves to do so. He does not smoke anywhere else in the room. He does not smoke when he handles the copies of the drawings, though he sometimes stands individual sheets on an easel in order to view them at a distance as he smokes.

Above all, he does not smoke when he handles the original Leonardo drawings, nor anywhere near them. And he handles them as little as possible, bringing the copies to them for comparison rather than the other way around.

In the middle of the day, a hot meal of fish and vegetable ukha or beet and cabbage borscht is delivered to him, or, in warmer months, potato and egg salad and light soup.

When his work is finally done, he signals his dark-suited guardians that he is ready to leave. He has examined every sheet in minute detail for its degree of faithfulness to its original and has determined which copies are of an acceptable standard and which ones fall short.

When he has been escorted out of the building, his guardians return to the room. They, too, don clean white gloves. Earlier they kept an eye on Sergei and he kept an eye on the workmen; now the two keep an eye on each other. One of them turns over each sheet that failed to satisfy Sergei and reads out the three-digit number written on its reverse. The other writes the numbers in a notebook. They switch roles and check what each has said and written. Then they pack everything away.

In the course of the year in which Sergei has been performing this monthly duty, the aggregate performance of each artist has been monitored and scored across the range of different drawings they have copied. Meticulous records have been kept.

The results are mixed, as was expected. Some artists have done well across all the drawings; some have done well on certain drawings but fallen a little short on others; some have fallen short more often than . . . well, more often than is good for them. So that now, with a full year of output available, half of the artists have been judged to have fallen short too often. Far too often.

As judged by Sergei Lysenko. Making more turmoil for his soul.

* * *

In Josef Vissarionovich's sprawling empire, all supply, service, and manufacturing facilities, of whatever kind and in whatever industrial sector, come under the control of an appropriate state ministry. Otherwise, how would he know that his loyal citizens are being provided for? Not to mention watching who is plotting what and who is not fulfilling his Five-Year Plan.

Paper mills have their place in the scheme of things. Generally speaking, they are under the control of the Ministry of Timber, Paper, and Wood Processing.

But only generally speaking.

Sequestered deep in pine woods not far from Leningrad there is a very special paper mill. This mill is different from all the others. For a start, it is what is known as a closed facility—meaning that it is surrounded by security fencing, barbed wire, watchtowers, and armed guards to a level as good as might be found in any gulag camp.

The security is not to imprison those who work in the mill and run it—though it is no bad thing to remind them that imprisonment can easily be arranged. The primary purpose of this facility's security is to keep out those who have no business there.

In addition, this paper mill is not overseen by the dull ministerial bureaucrats of wood pulp and pine oil. It has a grander parentage. It is part of the Ministry of Finance, for it produces the wide range of specialist papers that are used for the country's banknotes, postage stamps, internal passports, and propiski, and all the myriad of paper-based paraphernalia, forms, and certificates that a busy and forward-looking state requires.

Consequently, no other mill in the Soviet empire—nor any academic institution or research establishment—knows as much as this discreet place does about paper of all kinds and their manufacturing processes, both modern and not-so-modern, whether based on wood or rag, whether handmade or mass produced, how sized, how pressed and dried.

And no one man in the whole of the Union of Soviet Socialist Republics knows as much about these things and more besides as does the mill's chief materials technician.

Who, like Sergei Lysenko, one day over a year ago found himself in the hands of smiling men who had clout enough to breeze into his facility, past all its layers of security, and offer him the opportunity to do his socialist duty and put his expertise to work in the same cause as the one for which Sergei Lysenko was enlisted.

And, like Sergei, the chief materials technician has the burn scars to prove it.

CHAPTER 16

BOLOTSOV IS SITTING comfortably on the daybed in his office, the daybed that serves him well for purposes other than rest.

But on this occasion he is alone. The morning is bitterly cold, with the usual wind howling steadily outside. It might become a buran; or it might not. The office stove is blazing, but the commandant is still glad to be wrapped in his oily shuba.

He is just finishing his customary second breakfast of the day—a platter of fried eggs, kolbasa sausage, sliced cheese, dumplings, and blini pancakes, washed down by black tea syrupy with sugar, all essential to keep the cold at bay—when the sealed pouch arrives, marked for his personal attention and carried by rail from Moscow to Vorkuta and from there by truck to the camp.

He opens the pouch and reads through the orders therein. He reads them again. He wipes his plump lips on a napkin and tut-tuts to himself.

The orders instruct him that the services and talents of a number of his prisoners, the holders of certain specified three-digit numbers, are no longer required. Not a problem in itself, as such winnowing was always part of the plan, but these prisoners, like all of them, have just been fed the morning meal. A quantity of food has therefore been wasted. He has his reputation as an efficient administrator to think of. Could Moscow not have allowed him some kind of advance notice of who the individuals were likely to be? He could have canceled rations accordingly.

He tut-tuts again as he rises from the daybed—he prefers to let food settle for a while—and moves to his desk to organize what he needs. He unlocks the floor-mounted safe in the corner and fetches the master list of prisoner names and numbers. He sets the orders beside the list, works out who the lucky winners are and strikes through their names on the master list. Two are already dead anyway: the engineer from Donetsk and the scowling Ukrainian. But he is sorry to see that some of the others are young women, including a couple of his favorites. Still, it cannot be helped.

He makes a fresh list with only the winning numbers on it, laces the shuba tightly about his blubbery body, finds his handkerchief and blows his nose, fortifies himself with a final gulp of the thick sweet tea, and braves the icy wind to issue appropriate instructions to the guard sergeant.

* * *

In the work hut some minutes later there is no fuss, no roll call to stir up unease and thereby distract from the day's productive labor. Pasha is far away in his work. The first he knows of anything out of the ordinary is when Viktor hisses to catch his attention. Pasha looks up to see the sergeant moving slowly between the rows of work tables. He is carrying a sheet of paper, which he consults.

He stops and speaks to a prisoner. Pasha recognizes the woman who was unable to stop weeping on the train. She rises from her table and goes to the front of the room, where a guard unlocks the door and lets her leave the hut.

Pasha concludes that one of the usual visits to Bolotsov is simply being arranged; he goes back to work.

But Viktor hisses again. "Pasha, something's going on."

The sergeant has stopped at another table. This time the prisoner is a man. He, too, rises and is taken outside.

This continues until eight prisoners have been removed from the hut. Among them are the unhinged architect and her lover the botanist, together with the boyfriend of the Bolshoi costume designer. As the doors close after them, the man from the Bolshoi stares at the work table where his lover should be and looks around him in alarm.

* * *

Outside, the eight are loaded onto a truck. They are chaperoned by four of the male guards, including the sergeant. The guards are wrapped snugly in their heavy uniforms, greatcoats, and shapkas but the prisoners have only their indoor camp clothing, useless against the cutting wind.

The truck follows the ice road's winding course farther north. The daylight is thin and ghostly, as if the landscape is lit from below. No horizon is visible through the frosty fog.

"Where are you taking us?" the botanist asks, shivering so hard that he is barely able to pronounce the words. But his effort is for nothing. He receives no reply.

At last the sergeant decides they have gone far enough. The truck halts. The driver keeps the engine running, a precaution to prevent it from freezing and seizing up.

The prisoners are shoved from the truck and made to kneel in the snow. It takes time—they can hardly move their limbs because of the cold or because fear has paralyzed them. They now have no doubt what is about to happen. Some are in tears, some plead for mercy, others know better than to waste their last breaths on such a hopeless course and are praying desperately. Only the architect seems unconcerned, calmly hushing and comforting the botanist.

The weeping woman is the noisiest. The sergeant has had enough of her, so he shoots her first, a single bullet in the back of the head. He lets the other guards see to the rest. The whole affair takes only a few seconds. In the view of the sergeant, who is a decent man with a wife and two children at home in Ivanovo, it is a humane and clinical operation, over in no time at all. A second or two of panic for the prisoners, that was all. A merciful way to go.

The snow is dark with blood. The wind is dropping. No buran on the way after all, by the look of things. When the wind ceases, there will be silence on the tundra until nighttime when the wolves start.

* * *

In the work hut, the ten prisoners hear the gunshots. Sound travels far here, with nothing in the landscape to block it.

Pasha vomits, a sudden, gulping eruption from the pit of his stomach. His work is destroyed, swimming in fluid and sprayed with half-digested shreds of food.

Bolotsov, his eyes dark slits, curses the waste of paper and work effort, and tells him to clean up the mess. A number of prisoners are sobbing—the partners of those who have been executed. Bolotsov orders them to shut up and takes his usual place near the stove.

"There will be no midday meal today," he announces after a few moments' thought. "You will all work straight through until evening." He turns to a guard. "Tell the kitchen. Ten meals saved. Eighteen if I count the others. And eight saved at every mealtime from now on."

This seems to cheer him. He spreads his hands before the stove.

* * *

Out in the snow-covered emptiness of the tundra, the eight corpses wait patiently. They cannot be buried, even if Bolotsov was willing to allow them that dignity. The frozen earth is as hard and solid as concrete, utterly impenetrable. It has never thawed since the Ice Age. Even in summer, only the thin uppermost layer thaws, half a meter at most, so that, once it is scraped away, fires must be set to unfreeze each successive layer beneath. Fire, dig, fire, dig: the only method. And dig with pickaxes. Spades on their own are useless.

But this is not summer. This is winter, when bodies must be put in storage for months or cremated on pyres. Either way a lot of work. For eight worthless artists? Why bother?

There is an easier alternative: let them wait out here, a good safe distance from the camp, where the wolves will deal with them—just as they dealt with the bodies of the engineer and the Ukrainian. There are more wolves than usual this year and they will be all the hungrier in light of the increased competition for food now that the summer pups are fully grown. A polar bear may wander down from the Arctic ice fields to seize its share.

None of them the sort of visitor any gulag camp would welcome. Hence the need to transport the condemned and the dead well away.

Today the patient dead will not be kept waiting long. The gulag is swift to embrace all who enter its republic of bones.

CHAPTER 17

A WEEK LATER, again just as Bolotsov is polishing off his second breakfast, he receives another delivery. It signals the next stage of the camp's work, the stage that he has awaited with the greatest eagerness.

The delivery comprises two boxes, both made of high-grade tempered steel and strong enough to survive a minor war. They are fireproof and waterproof. Both are locked, secured by a sophisticated system of internal bolts. There are only two keys to the lock on each box. One key for each is in Moscow. Bolotsov has the other. He keeps his keys locked away in the corner safe.

The manner in which the boxes arrive is as unusual as the boxes themselves. They are accompanied by four uniformed colonels of the NKVD who have not let them out of their sight throughout the rail journey from Moscow—a journey they passed more comfortably than did Pasha and the other prisoners, with plushly upholstered couches beneath their backsides and waiters to fetch food and liquor.

The colonels catnapped in shifts, so that three of them were always awake. They are armed. They were not known to one another before being assigned to this duty.

Only after they have seen the boxes safely into the commandant's office—which reeks like a chophouse—only after they have stood over him while he signs their forms and have satisfied both him and themselves that his keys fit the locks, only then do the stony-faced colonels snap their blue-trimmed caps back in place, salute the commandant, march back to the truck that brought them here, and depart for Vorkuta and their return train ride to Moscow.

As the sound of the departing truck fades, Bolotsov checks that his office door is locked. Then he wriggles his hands into a pair of white cotton gloves and sets about unpacking the contents of the boxes. For once he keeps well away from his stove. This is not the time to risk a stray spark.

The larger box contains blank sheets of paper—not more supplies of ordinary cartridge paper but sheets of a wholly different kind. There are ten different batches, each wrapped in white cotton. All the sheets in each batch are tinted the same shade: most batches are a particular shade of pinkish-buff, but some are orange, some pale blue. The sheets within each batch have all been made to the same dimensions, which are not large, being smaller than the pages of the document containing Bolotsov's instructions. The sheets, although rectangular, have been finished with various irregularities, their edges frayed and uneven. They are clearly handmade. There are imperfections along edges and corners. Some corners are torn.

All these characteristics, which in handmade paper would be expected to be individual and unique from one sheet to the next, are in fact identical on every single sheet within each of the ten batches. Some sheets have been prepared with grounds of finely crushed bone, ready for silverpoint work and tested to ensure they will achieve a tarnish that matches Leonardo's mellow originals.

All these sheets are precious enough, considering the care and expertise that have gone into them—provided by the chief materials technician in a certain paper mill outside Leningrad—but it is the smaller box that contains the real treasure.

Also swathed in pure white cotton, individually, are ten pages of Leonardo's drawings—no longer photographic prints, for that stage is over and done with, but the original drawings themselves, each sandwiched between two sheets of bulletproof glass.

Despite appearances to the contrary, Igor Borisovich Bolotsov has a heart, he has a soul, he is a man who is moved by beauty, and now he instinctively holds his breath as each magnificent page is revealed. Most have drawings on only one side, but a few are double sided. Most are on pinkish-buff paper but some are on orange, some on pale blue. In terms of their color and irregularities, blemishes, marks of damage, each page has been cloned perfectly by the handmade blank sheets in one of the ten batches from the large steel box.

Even in their protective casings, the pages are small enough for him to range all of them across his desk. And now he sits contemplating the riches before him. He breathes shallowly, in rapid snuffles, the way he does when he leads one of the female prisoners to his daybed.

These drawings are *real*, he tells himself over and over. They are the very drawings Leonardo da Vinci made almost five hundred years ago. These are the actual pages he pored over, alone in his studio or surrounded by pupils, these are pages that he touched and across which his hand moved, changing the world forever—a world that knew no East, no West, no Lenin, no Hitler, no Stalin.

Even Igor Bolotsov's lardy socialist heart beats a little faster in their presence.

And it beats faster still as he contemplates, yet again, the idea that has been taking shape in his mind throughout the numbing misery of his posting here.

CHAPTER 18

THESE ARE THE darkest times for the prisoners. They know they are survivors but they do not know why. Why were the others taken away and shot, and not them?

"Their work wasn't good enough," is Viktor's blunt verdict.

"Who decided that?"

"Your guess is as good as mine."

The prisoners turn in on themselves. The illustrator of children's books and her Byelorussian lover have less to say for themselves than ever. The two academicians are so frightened that they have ceased arguing with one another. The man from the Bolshoi, all alone now, spends every evening weeping softly and hopelessly on his bunk. The little Latvian woman and her Estonian lover watch everyone with suspicion, not just the guards and the commandant but their fellow prisoners as well; they conspire together in whispers, heads touching, and immediately clam up and glower at anyone who comes near.

"It's because they have to speak Russian," says Viktor. "They think the rest of us are eavesdropping."

"Eavesdropping on what?"

"Once again, comrade, your guess is as good as mine."

There are no true believers among the prisoners now, no one who still clings to the belief that the system is always for the best, not with those eight corpses so heavily on their minds, one of them the architect herself, the staunchest believer of all. As for those who never counted themselves among her little band of believers anyway, the executions have confirmed their worst fears. So where there was belief, now there is only the thought of those corpses; and where there was foreboding, now there is the certainty of death.

Josef Vissarionovich can smile all he wants from his portraits, but he is fooling no one. Not any longer.

* * *

It is the morning after the delivery of the two steel boxes. The prisoners are tackling their morning bread and cheese.

"We should refuse to work," suggests Irina. "Even better, escape. Risk the guns. What have we got to lose? We could at least try."

"Madness," says Viktor.

"Why keep working for them? Why must I be Bolotsov's whore? They're going to shoot us anyway, sooner or later. Better to die once than a bit every day, which is what we're doing now. We die and we die and we die. What's the point of prolonging things?"

Viktor shakes his head. "The point for me is my sisters. And one of them has a child. For you it's your parents. For Pasha it's his mother. They're the point." He looks from Irina to Pasha. "If we escape or make trouble, our families will end up in the gulag—if they're even allowed to live. All the prisoners here have family at home. I know because I've asked. This is a contract, a deal between us and the NKVD—if we do what we're here for, they'll leave our families alone. This is about our loved ones, not us. That's the deal and that's how it works." He finishes the last dregs of his black tea. "As for us, the truth is, comrades, we're dead already."

* * *

"Pay attention, prisoners!" calls Bolotsov. His voice is shriller than normal. His hands are clasped behind his back.

Instead of being allowed to go straight to their work tables, the prisoners have been made to wait at the front of the hut. It is the first sign that something has changed, that something will be different today. The second is the tension in the commandant's voice and bearing.

"On each of your work tables there is a sheet of paper, a single page with a drawing on it or a number of smaller drawings. That page is what you will begin copying today. You know what is necessary. You will recognize whatever is on the page you have been given because you have copied it many times already. And you have proven your worth in doing so. That is why you are still here while others less gifted are not."

He pauses and gazes at them one by one, partly to drive this remark home but partly to emphasize his next point.

"You are not permitted, at any time or for any reason, to touch the page assigned to you. If you need it to be moved so that you can study it more closely or if you are ready to copy the content on its reverse, you will inform the guard at your table. I will reposition or turn the page over for you. Only I may touch the pages. No one else."

His hands come into view and Pasha sees the white cotton gloves he is wearing. All at once it is clear what is happening, and he understands the momentous step they are about to take. No wonder Bolotsov is nervous.

"Begin work," concludes the commandant.

Pasha seats himself at his work table. His mouth is dry, his tongue seems to be too thick for his jaw. He can feel the blood pounding in his head. This time the small pinkish-buff page on his drawing board is no photographic print. It is Leonardo's own original drawing.

For a time, he does nothing at all, touches nothing, not a pen or a stick of chalk. He knows that as soon as he begins, everything that constitutes his own self will evaporate; it will burn off as wax burns away on Mama's devotional candles. He knows what his hand will do, but it will not be guided by him. The controlling will singled him out, sent him here. Now another controlling spirit will take over. That of Leonardo himself.

A small stack of blank sheets of paper occupies the place on his table where previously the more generous stack of cartridge paper sat. All the sheets are pinkish-buff in color—exactly the same color as the page of Leonardo drawings he is to copy. There are so few of these sheets because they are more precious than cartridge, rarer by far. They are handmade and match to perfection every aspect of this original page of Leonardo's.

Pasha closes his eyes and searches inside himself, waiting for the moment. From somewhere far distant he hears Sergei Lysenko's rumbling tones.

"Draw as if your life depends on it."

Or Mama's life.

His eyes open. He begins to draw.

* * *

That afternoon, Bolotsov sends for Irina. Viktor's gaze never leaves his work, neither as she is escorted from the hut nor as she returns. That night he and Irina stay together in his bunk.

Pasha moves his belongings to one of the unoccupied bunks. As well as wearing a dead man's clothes, he is now lying in a dead man's bunk. He has worked all day with the dead, been guided by the dead, and now he will sleep with the dead.

CHAPTER 19

IT IS MIDNIGHT. Bolotsov is in the work hut. He is alone. He is excited and exhilarated. He moves from work table to work table, from drawing board to drawing board—spending ten minutes on this one, fifteen on the next, only a dismissive minute or two on another: whatever each merits.

He is examining the progress of the forgeries at the end of this first day of work on them. Sometimes he enlists the assistance of the magnifying glasses and microscopes, sometimes he can see how things are going without such artificial aids.

Unseen by any prisoner, he has scrutinized their work in this way every night since their labors began a year ago. Tonight, however, he studies with particular care what each artist has done. All of it is good, as he expected after the recent cull, but already he can pick out the ones that are just a little less good, by a sufficient margin of failure to leave Moscow dissatisfied. He can tell this. There will be another cull.

He has a heart, he has a soul, he knows perfection when he sees it. So he can also see the work that shines out from the others. He knows whose it is, too. The young silverpoint genius, here is his work; the pretty girl with the green eyes who gratifies and excites her commandant by the way she pretends to abhor his attentions, this is her work; and over here is the work of her gawky boyfriend with the sardonic smile. These three, these are the ones who shine. As he expected.

And he also knows who is supreme among these three. Also as he expected.

He fishes out his handkerchief from the folds of the shuba and blows his nose. Then he moves along the tables again. This time it is Leonardo's originals that he looks at. It cannot be said that he studies them, however. He sees them only hazily. But that will do. When a man's lust is powerful enough, it blinds him. By then he has already made up his mind; he no longer needs to see the object of his desire clearly.

So Igor Borisovich Bolotsov looks with blurred vision upon these objects of his desire as he passes them, back and forth, back and forth.

He is sweating, a rare condition for him and the only time he can recall it happening here.

He knows exactly what he is going to do.

CHAPTER 20

Marya Kalmenova climbs the steps to the militia station and finds a space in the waiting area where she can lean her weary body against the wall.

On the opposite wall is a portrait of Josef Vissarionovich. He looks fine and noble in his uniform with its scarlet flashes. She feels better for seeing him here. It is like being alone in a strange town and happening upon an old friend.

This echoing hallway is not a proper waiting room, just a wide passageway with a couple of chairs, but it is out of the sharp wind. Some of the militia stations she has visited over the last year make people line up outside in all weather.

There is no desk with someone to give information or organize things, which there often is in militia stations. There is just this whole stream of people who are here ahead of her, thirty of them or more. They are standing around or sitting on the tiled floor, squeezed in wherever they can find a space—all types and ages of people, some with children, some carrying wooden cages with chickens or rabbits in them. Marya can smell the rich aroma of the animals.

But it is the people who fascinate her. So many different kinds and colors of faces—who could imagine there could be so many races in this one world? Waiting here will be no hardship, with so much to take in. There are ordinary Slavic and Caucasian types, of course; she would expect them. But she also sees Georgian, Chinese and Asiatic, Mongol, even an Eskimo face. She sees all sorts of garb, from boots made of reindeer hide to flowing robes in rainbow colors.

She is filled with pride. The whole world is represented here, all brought together, all united in common bond of love and fellowship by her Josef Vissarionovich. If Pashenka were here he would be drawing all this wonderful sight.

But if Pashenka were here, there would be no need for her to be here.

Oh, Pashenka, Pashenka. Where are you? Where have they taken you? What has become of you?

There are several closed doors leading off the hallway, none of them with signs to say what they are, so there is no way of knowing which of them Marya wants. But it will be the same door that everyone else wants, so she only has to wait and watch. She will take careful note of everyone who arrives in the hallway after her, to make sure no one cheats her of her place. The trick is to catch the person's eye as they walk in, and stare at them so that they know they have been spotted and will be challenged if they try any nonsense. People are staring at her right now, doing exactly that. She makes a small nod to each one, to let them know that she acknowledges their unspoken message, and they stop staring. This is part of the routine as well.

There is a young woman sitting on the floor beside her.

"How long have you been waiting?" Marya asks. She could have whispered the question so that only the young woman could hear; but instead she says it aloud.

There is a big clock on the wall. The young woman glances up at it. "Two hours."

"Three hours for me," immediately croaks an old man on the other side of the hallway.

This, too, is the usual form: ask one person and others pitch in if they have been waiting longer. This is why Marya asked her question out loud. All part of the routine.

"I'm next," adds the old man, looking about him with a challenging glare. No one contradicts him.

So, thinks Marya, a three-hour wait. This is not too bad.

She does not know for sure how many militia stations she has been to by now. She thinks fifteen or so. She began with the one nearest to Lobachev Row. They had no information for her but suggested some other stations. So each time she goes to a new station, she asks for their suggestions. This is essential, since there is no handy list that a person can look up. People only know the militia stations near their home or place of work, or those near their family and friends. Sometimes when she is doing her sweeping in the streets, she overhears passersby in conversation mention a station. She apologizes for intruding and asks for details. People never mind when she does this: everyone understands; everyone knows how it is when a loved one vanishes.

She has only one day each week when she can go to the militia stations. At first she walked, even to the ones in Dmitrov, but those in Mytishchi and Lobnya were much too far, so she had to go by train. She comes to Moscow by train as well, as she has done today. The awkward part with these distant ones is not knowing how long it will take to find them, then of course how long she will have to wait and whether she will be able to get home before the trains stop running. On two occasions this was not possible; but the militia officers let her stay in the station all night, dozing on a chair until it was time for the first train. It meant she had to go straight to work without having had any real sleep. It was hard, but she managed.

She settles herself as comfortably as she can against the wall, smiles up at Josef Vissarionovich, then turns her mind inwards and begins to pray.

* * *

She is in luck today. She has only been waiting just over two hours and already she is next in line.

The door opens. Someone leaves. The door closes. She waits for a minute. She has learned that this is the right thing to do. Then she knocks on the door, not too loudly or boldly. Another minute passes before a voice tells her to enter.

It is a room like every other she has been to on these missions. Behind a desk sits a tired-looking man like every other man she has encountered in these rooms. But here is Josef Vissarionovich again, behind the tired man, watching. She takes heart.

The tired man goes through the usual preliminaries: her name, address, what her work is, where her depot is.

He frowns.

"So you don't live or work anywhere near here."

"No, comrade officer."

She hands over her passport and propiska. He transcribes various details. She answers the standard question: no, she is not here because she was ordered to attend; she is here to make an inquiry. At this the man looks even more tired and fed up.

"And your inquiry is?"

"Comrade officer, I'm looking for my Pashenka, my son."

"You think we have him here?"

"It's possible, comrade officer. He was taken away by militia a year ago."

"By personnel from this station?" He looks again at her address on the form. "I'd be surprised."

"I don't know where they were from, comrade officer."

This is the moment when the tired men she meets sit back and shake their heads. Which is exactly what this man now does.

"I can't help you, citizen."

"Please, comrade officer—I think he may have been sent to the gulag."

"Why do you think that?"

"Because I can't find him anywhere I go, not in any militia station."

"But if it's a gulag case, then you certainly shouldn't be bothering us here. You shouldn't be bothering any militia station. We don't make those kinds of arrests."

"I realize that, comrade officer. But could you check your records for me, please?"

"It would be a waste of time. If he committed or was suspected of committing an ordinary offense, there's no reason why this militia station would have been involved—we don't have anything to do with your district. And if it was a gulag case, a Red Army unit would have come for him, not militia. Also, a member of the security service would have been present. Was there such a person? They might have been in uniform or plain clothes."

"No, comrade officer. Just some militiamen and their officer."

"Then you're mistaken. He hasn't been sent to the gulag. There now—that's good to know, isn't it?"

"Yes, but in that case the militia must be holding him somewhere. Could you check to see if he passed through this station?"

"No need. I've explained why we wouldn't have been involved—your district is outside our jurisdiction."

"Please, comrade officer."

"We're going in circles."

"Please. I've come a long way." She raises her eyes and looks beseechingly not at him but at Josef Vissarionovich.

Eventually, the tired man does what she asks. Sure enough, no Pavel Pavlovich Kalmenov has ever been brought to his station.

"There. Just as I said. Close the door after you, citizen."

Outside, the wind cuts into Marya's bones. She huddles into her coat and tightens her shawl, the one with the little blue cornflowers.

The same story again. The same story everywhere. No militia station is holding Pashenka. No militia station has ever heard of him. So he must be in the gulag. But he cannot be in the gulag since it was militia who came for him.

Oh, Pashenka! Where are you? When will they let you come home?

She sighs and looks at the piece of paper the tired man gave her. On it is the address of another militia station. Someone in the hallway gave her directions. She can walk there today if she hurries.

She feels the cold of the pavement through the thin soles of her boots. Cold feet make for a cold body. But she will walk the entire world, the world of all the people gathered in the militia station, she will walk from one end of their world to the other in bare feet if she has to, to find her Pashenka. She is a mother; it is what any mother would do.

CHAPTER 21

TWO WEEKS HAVE passed since the first morning when the prisoners began working from the original Leonardo drawings. Two weeks since the task of forgery started in earnest.

The rhythm of the work is different now, slower and more concentrated. Bolotsov seems content with this, but his presence is more evident than before. He remains in the work hut throughout the long working day, which he never did previously. This is partly so that he is at hand when any of the original Leonardo pages need to be moved, but Pasha assumes it is also so that he can keep an eye to their safety.

"He's like a mother hen," says Irina.

Viktor nods agreement. "I guess the stakes are higher for him now."

"Higher for us, too," says Pasha.

One day there comes a strange development. Pasha is the first to experience it—because he is the first to complete a drawing under these new conditions. He has been working for these two weeks on a single drawing—the head of a beautiful girl, every strand of her flowing and intricately plaited hair as lovingly rendered by him as it was by Leonardo, underdrawn in chalk and detailed in pen and ink, with complex line shading and cross-hatching. Now he is putting the finishing touches to the page, carefully inking a tiny oval into the bottom right-hand corner.

Inside the oval is a small symbol of a royal crown and beneath it two very short lines of text. The first line has only two characters, the second has three. He does not know what the significance of the oval is nor the meaning of the writing or the crown symbol. The letters are foreign, Western, that much he knows, because only two of them are recognizable—E and I, with the latter repeated.

This oval device and its contents are not Leonardo's work; Pasha knows that, too. They were applied to the drawing much later. And from the photographic prints he also knows that all the drawings bear this mark.

At last this final small task is done. The oval is complete; the whole page and its drawing are complete.

He carefully slides the page to the top of his drawing board, sets down his pen, and sits back in his seat. He flexes his neck and breathes deeply. Now is the time when he needs to do nothing for a while, remain motionless, until the drawing drains from him.

Bolotsov has been waiting, standing several work tables behind him and watching for this moment. He closes in, leaning over to peer at the finished work and its original. Pasha is unconcerned. He knows that Bolotsov will find no fault.

But the commandant is full of surprises.

"Good," he says. "Very good. Now do another."

"Comrade Commandant?"

"This is good but not good enough. You can do better. Things have moved on. The standard required is now higher."

Pasha looks at the work he has done. The drawing is perfect—the hair, the modeling of the face, every line is there just as in the original. He has worked the black chalk to perfection, including the smudges caused by clumsy hands. Everything is as it should be—indistinguishable from the original, just as Bolotsov has always demanded.

"Comrade Commandant, this drawing is perfect—"

"Are you arguing? Challenging my artistic judgment?"

"No, Comrade Commandant."

"Very wise. So get to work."

A rustle of the shuba and Bolotsov is gone, taking with him his stink and what Pasha knows is an already perfect replica of Leonardo's work.

Do another? Do better? It is like being back with Sergei in the Artists' Union.

He takes another sheet of the handmade paper. He closes his eyes and waits. The drawing is still there, within him. He opens his eyes and begins to draw. All over again.

* * *

That evening he describes the incident to Viktor and Irina, who had seen that something was going on.

"I know your work would have been perfect," Irina says. "What's Bolotsov's problem?"

"I suppose it's as Viktor said—the stakes are higher."

A week later the same thing happens to Viktor when he brings a page to completion. Then to two other prisoners. Then to Irina. It never happens before they finish a forgery; only when the forgery is finally complete.

Eventually all the prisoners have the same experience: "Do another. Do better." All of them tell the same story: they swear their work was already perfect.

Perfection, it seems, is not enough. Bolotsov demands more, he demands something better.

But what can be better than a perfect forgery?

* * *

The answer, Pasha realizes, is two perfect forgeries.

It is evening. He is walking with Viktor and Irina. He takes the usual care to make sure no prisoners or guards are close enough to hear, and waits until the three of them are in the safe zone between watchtowers.

"Viktor, do you remember I once said that whoever is behind this must already have the original drawings?"

"Certainly."

"We couldn't understand why they want copies. Well, now I think I know."

"Enlighten us."

"It's straightforward theft—they're stealing the originals by doing a switch. They replace them with our forgeries so that the theft doesn't come to light—a perfect crime because no one can tell it's happening. Bolotsov returns the original drawings to his masters, whoever they are, when we finish with them, along with our forgeries, and then the switch is made. They keep the originals and put our forgeries in their place—in whatever collection the originals were taken from."

Viktor thinks about this. "I can see how that would work. How do they make sure the absence of the originals isn't noticed while they're here with us for copying?"

"There must be someone who's in a position to take care of that—probably the same person who removes the originals in the first place."

"That would make sense," agrees Irina.

"But listen, that's only part of what's going on here—that was the original plan. I think Bolotsov is going one better. I think he's sending his masters two forgeries of each drawing instead of one forgery plus its original. And his masters are none the wiser."

Viktor stares at him as the implication of this sinks in. "So he passes off one of the forgeries as the original. That's what you're saying. Meaning he gets to keep the original. And that's why one forgery is never enough, no matter how perfect. That's why he wants two. He's stealing from the stealers." Viktor whistles softly. "So that's his game."

"Two perfect forgeries," says Irina. "No one can tell the difference—because they don't have any *way* of telling the difference. He's making a switch within a switch. It's perfect—a perfect crime within a perfect crime."

"Can he get away with this, Pasha?"

"Why not? Irina said it—they can't tell the difference. Besides, who's going to report him or denounce him? One of us? How? Even if we could, why would we? Because we care who gets away with either of these perfect crimes?"

Silence.

CHAPTER 22

Pasha cannot sleep. It is the small hours, and he is in his favored spot beside the dining hut. The night is clear and the sky is rich with stars. Even though the moon is almost full, the wolves are quiet. He is in that state of mind where he may be praying or he may only be allowing his thoughts to wander; sometimes it is difficult for him to know which.

A movement near the inner gate of the compound catches his eye. He sees it is one of the guards on patrol. The figure is small; he recognizes the round-faced Kazakh woman.

He is about to look away when there is another movement, a sudden flurry of action. The Estonian has materialized from nowhere. In the full glare of the floodlights he comes up behind the Kazakh and loops something about her neck. Pasha realizes that he is garrotting her. Despite the camp diet, the Estonian is still a big man; she is no match for him. Within seconds she is on the ground, motionless, and he is bending over her. He rips the bunch of keys from her belt and lopes over to the gate.

Now the Latvian woman has appeared and is hurrying to join him. Still there is no response from the sentries in the watchtowers. The Estonian struggles for a moment to find the right key, strikes lucky, and opens the gate just enough to let them pass through.

They repeat the process at the outer gate and race out into the snow-covered tundra.

Pasha watches, transfixed. This is no sophisticated, carefully planned breakout—not heading out like that, for anyone to see.

He is right. At last the sentries are aware of the prisoners' wild dash. The klaxons wail, the searchlights blaze into life, instantly picking out the two fleeing figures. No targets could be easier. Pasha braces himself for the inevitable roar of the Kalashnikovs.

It does not happen. Instead, the sentry in the nearest watchtower calls for his comrades in the other towers to hold their fire. He shouts for the klaxons to be shut down.

In that instant, Pasha understands his intention. Something else is moving in the tundra other than the two fleeing prisoners. Half a dozen ghostly shadows, indifferent to the searchlight beams, are closing on the two runaways with horrifying speed.

The pack leader brings down the Estonian. The rest of the pack bring down the Latvian woman, whose small body disappears beneath the huge gray beasts. The wolves are not silent now; nor are their prey. Pasha closes his eyes but hears everything.

The sentries allow the sport to continue until the screaming stops and there is only the snarling of the wolves as they compete to feed. Now the Kalashnikovs roar and spit flames. The wolves spin into the air with the force of the bullets. None of them makes any attempt to escape—their greed is too overpowering.

When the grisly dance ends and all the corpses, human and animal, are still, the guard sergeant, who has now appeared, blows his whistle, and the Kalashnikovs cease their roar. Pasha looks around and sees that Bolotsov has emerged from his quarters, bleary-eyed and shivering despite his heavy shuba. The other prisoners have come out into the night as well.

The Kazakh woman has survived the Estonian's attack. She is on her feet, cursing as she rubs her injured neck.

The prisoners are ordered back to their huts as guards set out in a truck to examine what is left and cart everything away.

"I didn't think the Estonian was that dumb," says Viktor. "Now we know what all their whispering was about, he and his little Latvian."

"It was insane," says Pasha. "More like a suicide pact."

"It was exactly that," says Irina. "But they didn't reckon on the wolves. They shouldn't have run so far. They made it hard on themselves. Better a bullet any day."

* * *

Spring arrives. It is as brief as it was last year, giving way to what the prisoners know will be an equally fleeting summer—their second in the camp. Since the death of the Latvian woman, there are only two young women Bolotsov can send for, one of them being Irina, so he now includes the elderly female academician from Leningrad.

Pasha finds he is having difficulty remembering Mama's face clearly. He has to turn to his drawings of her. It is harder still to remember his father.

"There'll be more executions," announces Viktor one evening. He, Irina, and Pasha are playing Preferans with Irina's deck of cards, but from the start it has been obvious to Pasha that Viktor's mind is not on the game.

Pasha sets down his cards and looks at him, then at Irina. The same bleak expression is on both their faces. This seems to be something they have talked over together.

Irina explains. "Remember how we had to put the number of our work table on the copies we made on cartridge paper? A few days after the executions, I saw a list of numbers on Bolotsov's desk, all of them with three digits. I wondered if they were table numbers. I memorized some. In the work hut, I saw they belonged to people who'd been executed. It's possible he made the list afterwards, but I don't think so. I think it was a list of the people he was told to execute. That's how they identify us—not by our names but by our table numbers."

"I don't see—"

"Wait, Pasha. Go on, Irina."

"At the time it didn't seem particularly important. But now I think he's using the same method of table numbers to keep a record of who produces each pair of finished forgeries. The Leningrader says he was doing this with her work when he sent for her one day. He had all three drawings on his desk. She couldn't tell which was the original and which were the copies, but he had mounted one of them between two glass plates. If Pasha's theory is right, that would be one of the forgeries, ready to be passed off as the original. Of course, she doesn't know about that—I haven't told her or anyone else. What took her attention is the fact that he had noted her table number alongside a description of the drawing. She asked why. He said it was so she could be entered for an academy medal. Big joke."

Viktor takes over. "There's only one reason why he'd still keep such records. Nothing to do with academy honors."

Pasha feels infinitely weary. So much death.

"More weeding out," he sighs.

"Exactly. Better make sure you're doing your very best work, comrades."

"What for? You said we're already dead."

"I did, and we are. None of us will leave here alive. But that doesn't mean we should run toward death like the Estonian and the Latvian. Every day when we wake up, even in this cursed place, don't both of you *want* that day, every minute of it? Don't you drink the day as if it's water in the desert? I do. Life is hard, comrades, but death is harder."

* * *

Table numbers instead of names.

Pasha lies awake in his dead man's bunk. He cannot sleep but he cannot stir himself to go outside to watch the stars.

Table numbers because whoever is assessing their work could be influenced if they saw a name they recognized. There can be no other reason.

To assess their work, that person would have to be an expert not only in fine art and drawing but above all in the style and techniques of Leonardo da Vinci.

"Use your eyes, Pavel Pavlovich. See what's right in front of you."

He turns to face the wall. He who has always seen so much behind closed eyelids has been blind. Now, at last, he sees. But sees more than he ever wanted to.

* * *

A few weeks later, the guard sergeant enters the work hut with a sheet of paper and begins to walk along the rows of work tables. There is no disguising what is about to happen.

The prisoners he seeks do not stand up obediently and proceed calmly to the door, as did their unknowing predecessors. Lovers cling to one another in desperation, they scream and beg: the Byelorussian and the storybook illustrator; the two elderly academicians. The man from the Bolshoi, a solitary figure among them, bawls like a child. None of it does any good. The five are dragged away.

Bolotsov enters as the truck departs and warms himself at the stove. Now only Pasha and Viktor and Irina are left. They look at one another across an almost empty room.

"Get on with your work!" snaps Bolotsov. "You're lucky to be alive."

"Are we?" says Irina.

After a time, they hear the gunshots in the distance. This time Pasha is not sick. It seems he has become accustomed to slaughter.

Irina is now the only female prisoner in the camp. She is the only one Bolotsov will be able to send for.

CHAPTER 23

SHY, STAMMERING BERTIE—GOOD King George VI—is dead. His daughter, the pretty little princess, has succeeded to the throne. The king is dead, long live the queen. Everything changes and nothing changes.

Anthony Frederick Blunt soldiers on. Admittedly the hounds, their snouts pressed to the ground in search of any morsel, are still sniffing around, the more so since Guy Burgess and Donald Maclean pulled their little vanishing trick. But the boorish hounds will find nothing. The great pretender is too clever for that. And here is the evidence.

It is one of his Windsor Castle days. A very special one. He has arranged the display cases along one side of St George's Hall, where the light is pure and falls best on them. Each slim case has been placed on its own stand. Mounted within glass in each one is a Leonardo drawing from the hundreds in the Royal Collection, his own carefully handpicked selection. The glass allows the double-sided drawings to be viewed from both sides.

Admittedly, this new young queen is more interested in horses than art. Not her fault: she has been bred among philistines. But he believes he can help to elevate her above this unfortunate pedigree; he believes there is a scintilla of hope. He will certainly try. Of course, she has viewed some of the drawings before; they have been here in Windsor Castle all her life. And for a few centuries before that. At any rate, all the originals have been in the monarchy's mostly indifferent hands throughout that time. Today's informal little exhibition, through which he will guide her, will be her first thorough and proper introduction to them. More accurately, it will be her first introduction to the seventy-odd impeccable forgeries that Her Majesty's Surveyor of Pictures has included, forgeries that are faultless even to the tiny oval stamped in the bottom right-hand corner of each, with the royal crown and the initials *ER VII*—standing for Edward VII, a monarch who did know what art he possessed and cared enough to order his mark to be placed on it, as if he were a child inking his initials in his schoolbooks.

How could the great pretender resist including gems as wondrous as these, the fruit of his own conception, in today's little exhibition?

He sighs contentedly. Still such a glorious game.

* * *

Josef Vissarionovich Dzhugashvili, Stalin, man of steel, Father of the Great Soviet People, is also pleased with himself.

"How many of these drawings have we received so far from our English fool?" he asks.

Lavrenti Beria peers at him through pince-nez eyeglasses. They give him the appearance of a fussy minor functionary, perhaps a factory production planning officer. He settles the eyeglasses more firmly on the bridge of his nose, a tic that betrays the very special effort he is making to remain calm. As Minister of State Security, he has the Soviet Union's vast terror and intelligence apparatus to run. And through the NKVD, he controls the whole gulag, population several million. Yet here he is, frittering time and resources on a gang of bourgeois artists. All because of this whim of Josef Vissarionovich's.

"Upwards of a hundred, Comrade General Secretary. We have completed work on over seventy and sent them to England, where they have been successfully installed in place of the originals—which are now safely stored in one of your personal underground vaults here in the Kremlin, as you ordered. Work is in hand on the others. The Englishman promises more after those. We are satisfied that we have now identified the best artists from the twenty we began with, which will maximize quality while minimizing cost and reducing administrative complexity."

"And security?"

"Always maintained at the most stringent level. Naturally, none of the artists whose services we no longer require poses any risk. We will continue to neutralize any possible future risk by all necessary steps."

Josef Vissarionovich nods approvingly and rises to his feet, indicating the end of the meeting. He stands watching until Beria has left the room, for Josef Vissarionovich is a man who never turns his back on his comrades—not out of courtesy but for the simple reason that there is no knowing what might get plunged into that back. Especially with Lavrenti Beria anywhere near.

The door clicks shut and the security chief's footsteps fade.

Josef Vissarionovich chuckles.

Upwards of a hundred, eh? And more to come. Not bad for a peasant boy.

* * *

Even before Lavrenti Beria reaches the courtyard and is ushered into his limousine, he has made his decision. A decision that has been brewing for a good long while.

Enough is enough. Things cannot go on like this. A change is due. It is time for the Father of the Great Soviet People to hang up his boots—special built-up heels and all. The only question is how Lavrenti Beria can bring this about. But give him time and he will.

Everything changes and nothing changes.

CHAPTER 24

WHEN PASHA, VIKTOR, and Irina work now, just the three of them, they are surrounded by ghosts. Viktor spends each night with Irina in her dormitory hut so that she is not alone there. Pasha returns to his own bunk. Sometimes in the night he thinks he hears the dead Estonian intoning one of his melancholy lullabies.

With only three prisoners in his charge, Bolotsov decides that the detachment of guards is an unnecessary expense. Only the sergeant is to remain in post. The man protests: shift working will no longer be possible, the watchtowers cannot be manned, and he will have to undertake menial kitchen and other duties. The commandant promises him a weighty bonus. The sergeant is persuaded.

The four NKVD colonels return to escort the surplus guards to Moscow. The train will carry no other passengers. The guards are promised a brief furlough with their families before being transferred to other postings. They depart in good spirits. The colonels, whose formerly stony faces have softened, have brought vodka, which cheers the guards even more.

Two hours out of Vorkuta, the train slows down. By now the guards, who have been without alcohol for two years, have consumed much of the vodka. They are drunk. They are enjoying the journey. There is a holiday flavor to the proceedings. The colonels have turned out to be relaxed, jocular men. There has been laughter. There have been coarse jokes. The guards are in fine fettle.

The train comes to a halt. The locomotive wheezes, exhales clouds of steam into the glacial air.

"Let's stretch our legs, comrades," suggests one of the colonels. "I need a piss and a breath of air. Anyone care to join me?"

There are perfectly civilized toilets on the train, private affairs that flush, but the colonel's suggestion is a sociable and manly one. The female guards, not to be outdone, and encouraged by the colonel, decide to venture forth as well.

The guards pile out of the train. They leave their rifles and Kalashnikovs in the compartment and are too inebriated to notice that the four colonels are a little slow to follow—in fact, they stay on board, even the one who issued the invitation.

The Kalashnikovs cough for a long time. The smell of hot steel and gunpowder fills the air. The corpses lie in a muddled heap and the blood-soaked snow is almost black in the spill of light from the compartment. The locomotive builds up steam and pulls away.

As promised by Lavrenti Beria, security continues to be maintained at the most stringent level.

* * *

Another winter passes as Pasha, Viktor, and Irina work on, then a third spring arrives. Viktor adds more columns to his calendar. He no longer mentions Moscow's Alexandrovsky Garden.

Summer returns, then winter falls upon the camp again. It is like an old curse being renewed. Twice every week, Irina must submit to Bolotsov. Pasha wonders at what point a human being ceases to be human.

He fears for his sanity. He fears for the sanity of all three of them. Especially Irina.

CHAPTER 25

ON A BITTERLY cold February morning, Sergei Lysenko presents himself in the usual way at the Lubyanka. The usual uniformed guards take him to the usual staircase, the usual guardians in dark suits escort him to the usual reserved room.

"Hot lunch today," says one of the guardians. It is the first time in Sergei's three years of coming here that either man has ever spoken to him. Taken by surprise, Sergei stares at him for a moment, then enters the room.

It has been made ready for him in the usual way—one of the tables for the original drawings, another for the copies; magnifiers and microscopes to hand; ashtray safely distant; chandeliers bright on this overcast morning. No workmen in white boiler suits, however; they have not been needed for two years.

During these two years, Sergei's monthly duty has been much as it was during the first year: to assess and compare—except that the work he assesses now is the finished article: proper forgeries on proper paper alongside their originals.

Supposedly.

Only supposedly, because he knows that things are not what they seem. The act of deception to which he has been enlisted, however unwillingly, has multiplied itself. What he would find today—if he cared to look; which he does not—is what he has found on every previous occasion for two years.

Will there be perfect forgeries on perfect replica paper suitably aged and flawed? Yes, those will be here for his inspection. Works of genius in their own right. But the authentic original drawings against which they are to be assessed for their accuracy? No, they are not here. Leonardo's originals will not be here. Because throughout these two years Sergei has been comparing perfect forgery with equally perfect forgery, not forgery with original.

He remembers well enough his immediate response on discovering this, right from the first set of finished forgeries. He recalls his terror when he saw the choice he had to make. Did those who had put him to this task know the truth? Was he himself being tested? Should he speak out to protect himself? But if they did not already know, that would be assisting them. Why should he do that? If they were being duped, why should he warn them?

Fear struck him dumb, paralyzed him. He said nothing and waited for the worst to happen. Perhaps in his heart he might even have welcomed that, to put an end to this long betrayal. After all, what was his life worth these days?

But nothing happened. No one called him to account for his acceptance of what were being passed off as original drawings. No one arrested him. The reasonable men who had come to him in the beginning seeking a name, the men to whom he gave the very best name he knew, they never reappeared, nor anyone like them.

So he has continued coming here to the Lubyanka. The uniformed guards have continued to receive him, their faces as blank as ever. Month after month his guardians in their dark suits have escorted him to this long room blazing with light, never to a bloodstained cell in the basement.

No one but him knows the truth. Which is to say, no one but him and whoever has put this further deceit in hand. He does not know who that might be. Nor does it matter. Nor what has become of the true original drawings. He is finished with all this, finished with the betrayal and his cowardice, and the sickness that gnaws at his soul.

No one but him sees the truth. He will take it to the grave.

As the door closes behind him, he knows that there is now a moment during which his guardians' attention is not on him. Just for a few seconds. It is long enough for him to do what he has planned. Which, he has decided, must be done here—the sickness must be expunged here.

The tall windows do not lock. He has checked previously. No need for locks at this height to keep out intruders; besides, who ever heard of anyone wanting to break *into* the Lubyanka?

He opens a window and climbs up to its sill, his tired old legs shaking. He hopes they will not give way; he hopes he can be fast enough. He steps out onto the narrow ledge. His cape billows like a sail in the brisk air currents, his long hair rises in a white halo. Overhead, hidden from his view by the overhang, is the large clock on the front face of the building. He looks down. He is directly above the central main doorway. A woman is hurrying past. Something prompts her to glance up. She sees him. Her hand flies to her mouth.

Behind Sergei the doors of the room burst open. There are shouts. Down on the pavement the woman screams.

Sergei is thinking about Pasha Kalmenov.

"Forgive me, Pasha," he calls into the wind. "Do you hear me? Are you listening?"

He leans slowly forward, as if following the curve of his stoop. Gracefully. Calmly.

Movement is a river. It never comes back.

* * *

February becomes March.

Josef Vissarionovich wakes to a mystery. He is flat on his back on this rug on this floor. Somewhere. Wherever this floor is.

How did he get here?

He is a rational man. He thinks matters over. There are curtains on that window over there—closed curtains—but he sees daylight along their edges. So, daylight but the curtains are still closed and that lamp over there is on. Does this mean he has been on this floor all night?

He is a rational man. He turns his head to examine the rug more closely. He recognizes it now. It is a rug he often walks across. Of course—it is the rug that covers the floor of his study in his private chambers in his Kuntsevo dacha. A beautiful Georgian rug, of venerable age, part of Nadya's mother's dowry and passed on to Nadya. See—he still has a soft spot for his wife, Nadya, despite her selfishness, despite what she did, despite how she disgraced him with her suicide. Appendicitis, that was the story that had to be put about to cover things up. All a long time ago now, but it still rankles, the bother of the whole affair.

The lamp is his reading lamp. The telephone on that table is his.

So he is in Kuntsevo. But how did he get to be down here on the floor? Did he trip? Did he drop something and bend to pick it up and lose his balance? But if a man trips or stumbles like that, he falls on his front or side, not on his back.

He remembers certain things. Dinner, here at the dacha. That must have been last night. He remembers who was with him. Or remembers some of them. Lavrenti Beria, certainly. That beast, that monster. As to the others, their faces are vague. He will find them in a moment, put names to them. He remembers telling them all how useless they were. They knew damned well what that meant. It meant they were on borrowed time and any day now he might call in the debt.

He remembers being alone in this room afterwards. Yes, he remembers walking across the room, even stepping on this very rug.

And then?

Then nothing. He remembers nothing.

Ah. Wait. Is it possible . . . ?

The dizzy spells. The weak turns. He has been having them for weeks. But nothing to do with his heart. His heart is fine, the new doctors have said. Always supposing he can trust them any more than the old ones. Say this has nothing to do with his heart. Say it has nothing to do with stumbling or tripping either. What does that leave that could have put him here?

The answer comes to him like a hammer blow.

Poison.

Lavrenti Beria. That bastard. This is his doing.

Josef Vissarionovich knows he must act quickly. There will be an antidote. There must be. Someone will identify it and bring it to him. It is not too late—it cannot be. That is why he regained consciousness—he is as strong as an ox. He must alert someone.

But he discovers that he cannot stand up. He discovers that he cannot move. Not even an arm, a hand. He can no longer move his head. He can only swivel his eyes from side to side. The telephone might as well be on another planet. He cannot even bang on the floorboards.

He tries to call out.

He discovers that he cannot speak. He cannot move his mouth. He can only make little grunting noises.

But surely someone will come in of their own accord to check on him, a member of his domestic staff, a bodyguard.

No.

No one will do that. They have their orders. He has forbidden them ever to disturb him here in his private chambers, no matter what the circumstances. And they never disobey him. Never. Who would dare disobey Josef Vissarionovich?

Now there is a warm sensation in the region of his groin. It is spreading over his legs and belly.

His bladder has let go. He groans, the only sound he can manage. The mighty Josef Vissarionovich, man of steel, is pissing in his pants.

* * *

The doorman at the Artists' Union watches the old woman as she wanders back and forth in the street outside, first this way, then that, then crosses the wide road only to cross back again. Throughout her wanderings, her gaze never leaves the door—his door, the door he guards as though it is the Kremlin's Spassky Gate.

He is used to seeing all sorts here. Artists are a peculiar species. There are the ones who get themselves up to look like ruffians, with wild hair and mad eyes, paint splattered everywhere, and there are those who are always fastidiously turned out, looking more like sleek government bigwigs than painters or sculptors. Every variety in between.

But this little old babushka is no artist, dressed all in black with her ratty old coat and dowdy shawl. He has never seen this one before. So when she plucks up courage and opens the door and steps into the lobby, he plants himself squarely in her path.

"What's your business here, citizen?"

She gazes up at him, blinking. He sees now that she is not the ancient crone he took her for. She is younger than that, but shrunken and bent and wizened by whatever life has thrown at her. Moscow is full of souls like her. Come to think of it, the whole country is full of them.

His heart softens.

“Are you lost?” he says, more gently. “Looking for directions?” After all, she can hardly have any other reason for being here.

“I’m looking for someone,” she whispers.

He bends down to hear her better and notices the blue cornflowers embroidered in the shawl. In its time it cost a pretty ruble or two, that shawl. And in her time, her better days, someone loved this worn and weary woman.

“He’s a professor. Very important professor. I don’t remember his name. The schoolteacher isn’t around any longer, you see, she’s been reassigned, so I can’t ask her. I don’t know the professor’s name but he might know where my Pashenka is. He might know where they took him. He can help me find him. The militia stations are no use. And there are so many of them. I don’t know what else to do. I said to myself if I came here—”

The doorman raises a hand to hush her. “You’re looking for a professor but you don’t remember his name. Yes?”

“I might know it if I heard it.”

“You think he’s here, at the Artists’ Union?”

“Oh yes. He’s definitely here. He’s very important here. Pashenka used to come all the way here to study with him. Every Saturday. He’s a great artist, you see, my Pashenka.”

“Can you tell me anything about this professor—maybe what he looks like?”

She produces a folded sheet of paper and smooths it out with loving strokes. “This is him. Years ago now. My Pashenka was very little when he did this drawing.”

For the doorman, one glance is enough. Although the man in the sketch is younger than the man he knows—the man he *knew*—and his hair and beard are dark, the likeness is still plain. He sighs.

"This is Professor Lysenko. There was an unfortunate accident involving a motor vehicle as he crossed a road. Seems he wasn't looking. I'll tell you what little we know. He's sadly missed by everyone here . . ."

Afterwards she cries a little, very softly, though the doorman realizes it is not because of the tragic loss of the comrade professor; it is from despair at her own predicament.

She wipes her tears and looks up at the portrait on the lobby wall. A thought seems to strike her. Her face clears.

"Comrade Stalin would help me," she says. "I know he would. I'll try writing to him."

"Good idea," agrees the doorman.

* * *

They have gathered at the dacha out in the woods at Kuntsevo. Everybody who is anybody in the inner circle is here—Beria, of course, plump Malenkov, Molotov the old Bolshevik, potbellied Khrushchev, and others—a good dozen of them altogether. Malenkov has new shoes. They creak. He takes them off and shoves them under his arm as if he fears they might be stolen.

It is clear that Josef Vissarionovich is fast approaching the end of his time on earth. The men tell each other that they are here out of anxiety and to pay their last respects.

Nonsense. They are here in case he names a successor in his dying breath. And to prevent false claims.

Fear is in the air, as sour and strong as the stench of urine. The doctors tending Josef Vissarionovich are afraid because they know full well that they will come under suspicion. The domestic staff and bodyguards are afraid, for it was only after hours of agonizing over Josef Vissarionovich's failure to emerge or even make a sound that they eventually dared to enter his chambers. Their fear is that they will be accused of failing to save him, of neglecting him until it was too late.

And Khrushchev and the others of the inner circle are afraid because none of them knows where power will gravitate to and what will become of them.

Ah, but they are also afraid of the one man among them who is not afraid. The man who has files on each of them. The man whose agents creep about in the shadows after them and report their every move. The man who knows their mistresses and lovers—who may even have sent those lovers their way—and who sees what goes on in every bedroom and hears what is whispered behind every closed door.

Lavrenti Beria is the man who is not afraid.

Why would a man be afraid when his time has come?

CHAPTER 26

IRINA IS ILL. It begins with a fierce headache and a hacking cough. Her body shakes from head to foot with each outburst of coughing.

"I've had headaches before," she says, dismissing Viktor's concern. "Which of us hasn't? In this hellhole? We all cough and splutter like babulki."

Pasha sees the dark rings beneath her green eyes. Eyes from which the life seems already to be fleeing. He says nothing of this to Viktor, but a chill of fear runs through him.

Before the day is out, work becomes agony for her. She brings up her evening meal. Pasha learns later that Viktor is kept awake all night by her thrashing and wild outcries. She burns with fever. Viktor does what he can to cool her and reduce her temperature, wrapping handfuls of snow in bits of clothing with which to sponge her down.

In the morning the guard sergeant refuses to let him wake Bolotsov so that a doctor can be sent for.

"There are no doctors," the sergeant says. "Not for zeks."

"She should be in hospital. There's one in Vorkuta."

"That won't happen."

Viktor tells Pasha the situation, twining and untwining his long fingers anxiously.

"It's typhus," he says. "I'm sure of it."

"Don't say that. Don't even think it."

"My father described it. He could have been describing Irina. This thing is moving fast, Pasha, far faster than it should. It's because she's so weak. It's devouring her."

"No doctor, no hospital," rules Bolotsov later. "No point. It's typhus."

"You want to keep us alive to work, don't you?"

"There's nothing doctors or hospitals can do." He orders Viktor and Pasha to get to work. He forbids Viktor to enter Irina's dormitory. "Either she'll come through it or she won't. Nothing you can do will make a difference."

"Let me be with her."

"The lice that infected her are carriers. If they infect you, you'll die, too."

"I don't care."

"I do—and it's my view that counts. As you helpfully pointed out, there's work to be done. I don't plan to lose another artist. Unless I'm forced to have you shot."

Viktor curses Bolotsov to his face and tries to push past the sergeant. The man fells him with a blow to his stomach from the butt of his rifle.

"Don't damage those valuable hands," Bolotsov warns the sergeant. "Get these two to work, then take water to her hut. Don't approach her—she can help herself if she's up to it. See if she lasts the day."

That day is unbearable for Viktor. He works but only to make the sergeant think he is doing something. Instead of bothering with the evening meal, he goes to Irina's hut while the sergeant is visiting the latrines.

"Where is he?" demands the sergeant when he returns.

He does not wait for whatever lie Pasha might concoct but goes directly to the hut. A few minutes later, Pasha follows and finds Viktor standing outside, his head bowed. The sergeant is fixing a padlock in place on the door of the hut. No dormitory hut has ever been locked before. Pasha only has to look at Viktor's face to know what has happened.

As for himself, he had thought there was nothing more of his heart left to break, but now he finds he was wrong.

Irina's body is left in the locked hut to allow time for as many as possible of the typhus-carrying lice to die from lack of sustenance. That night the sergeant dusts her with delousing powder as an extra precaution, wraps her in a tarpaulin for his own protection, and takes her away on the back of a truck.

Once again, a hut is locked—this time the men's, with Viktor and Pasha inside, to ensure no further difficulties or interference from either of them as the sergeant goes about his task.

Viktor does not speak. He shuffles Irina's playing cards. He picks out the four queens. Pasha created a different portrait of Irina for each suit, a detail that pleased her. Even the mirror images on the individual cards are subtly different. Viktor's gaze remains fixed on the eight Irinas as he slides them from place to place on the table. Pasha watches. Just as he can see several Irinas, so he has come to know several Viktors: Viktor the knowledgeable; Viktor the lover; and now Viktor the broken.

After a while Viktor goes back to shuffling the deck, like an old man that the world has forgotten. Shuffle, shuffle, never dealing, no one to deal for. It is the madness of pointless repetition. Eventually Pasha reaches out and gently takes the cards from him.

Viktor looks up, as if noticing him for the first time.

"You know, Pasha, people make plans when they're in love. But Irina and I knew we couldn't do that. You might expect that would weaken our love. It didn't. It made it stronger. It was as if we were condensing love, boiling it down, and discarding anything unnecessary. But I'm nothing now, Pasha. Without Irina, I'm nothing. My life is nothing. Nothing, nothing."

He reaches out and reclaims the deck of cards.

CHAPTER 27

THE NIGHT IS uneasy for Bolotsov as well, but for reasons other than the death of an artist—even one as pretty as the little green-eyed girl.

His suspicions begin as he listens to his wireless in the privacy of his quarters. He is tuned to All-Union First, the Moscow home service. Under normal circumstances, no man in his right mind could listen to All-Union First for any length of time, allowing his brain to be pummeled by its droning political announcements and reports on successful economic plans. But tonight, for some reason, normal programs are not being broadcast. Instead, there is only solemn music and a news bulletin with nothing of note in it. The bulletin is repeated through the evening.

Something is wrong. But what?

By one in the morning he can take it no longer. He turns the tuning dial slowly and carefully. The music is replaced by the crackle and hiss of static. But here and there this becomes the squeaks and buzzes of Soviet jamming transmissions—meaning that he has found a Western station. He turns the dial with extra care, past the spot and then back again, because he knows that there are occasional windows of clarity and he might just find one.

At last he hears what he is seeking—a voice whose tone and delivery suggest a news bulletin. A foreign voice. He does not know what language it is speaking, nor does he have any idea what it is saying, but he stays there, listening for clues, for several minutes. Then he gives up and turns the dial some more.

It is a frustrating process. He can never lose the jamming noise completely. He spends over an hour searching and switching between wavebands. Finally, just as he is about to give up, he picks out a word that he recognizes. Yes, there it is again, behind the buzz and crackle. Not merely a word, but a name. An unmistakable one.

Stalin. Not once, but repeated several times.

But *what* about Stalin? Obviously he has announced something or done something—but what? Changes in the Praesidium? Another atomic bomb test? It is clear that the foreign broadcasters know something that the Soviet people are not being told—and not for the first time.

Some minutes before three he retunes to All-Union First and lets the doleful orchestral music play while he fortifies himself with a snack of cold meats. Without warning, the music stops. For a moment there is nothing, then bells ring out, as if the station is broadcasting from within a cathedral. The bells cease and the strains of the national anthem emerge. It, too, fades and a somber male voice comes on air.

"The Central Committee of the Communist Party, the Council of Ministers, and the Praesidium of the Supreme Soviet of the USSR announce with deep grief to the Party and all workers that on the fifth of March at nine fifty in the evening, Josef Vissarionovich Stalin, Secretary of the Central Committee of the Communist Party and Chairman of the Council of Ministers, died after a serious illness."

Bolotsov stares at the wireless. Stalin dead?

"The heart of the collaborator and follower of the genius of Lenin's work, the wise leader and teacher of the Communist Party and of the Soviet people, has stopped beating."

Bolotsov's own heart is thundering so hard that he presses his hand to his chest. What does this mean for the nation? No, never mind that—what does it mean for Igor Borisovich Bolotsov? What does it mean for his careful plans?

"The immortal name of Stalin will live forever in the hearts of the Soviet people and all progressive mankind," promises the solemn voice. "Long live the great and all-conquering teachings of Marx, Engels, Lenin, and Stalin! Long live our mighty socialist motherland! Long live our heroic Soviet people! Long live the great Communist Party of the Soviet Union!"

Bolotsov switches the broadcast off. His gaze shifts from the wireless to the telephone. He reaches out and lifts the receiver.

But immediately checks himself. It is the middle of the night. Beria will not be in his office at this hour.

Wrong. Stalin has died. Beria will be there regardless of the hour.

Wrong yet again. At this dangerous moment, the Minister of State Security will be wherever he has to be and will be doing whatever he has to do to secure his position.

Besides, the telephone connection to Moscow is via a radio link with Vorkuta—who knows who might be listening?

Reluctantly, the commandant replaces the receiver. He will have to wait. As will many others, no doubt, including those far mightier than Igor Bolotsov.

Then a further possibility presents itself to him, as he considers those mightier than himself. Another reason why Beria might not be available is if he is sprawled in a basement cell of the Lubyanka with a bullet in his brain.

CHAPTER 28

Lavrenti Beria is not sprawled in a basement cell of the Lubyanka. He does not have a bullet in his brain. He is safe and comfortable at home, working in the study of his handsome mansion on Little Nikitsky Street just north of the Arbat district. He is signing government orders and official pronouncements—of which there are many, for he has moved swiftly to strengthen his grip on power.

He passes the final document to his aide, who notes the serial number for his records, checks it off his list, and slips it into a folder. He also notes the name of the individual who is to action it: one Igor Borisovich Bolotsov.

* * *

Three days later, just after second breakfast, Bolotsov welcomes into his office an NKVD colonel who has made the long journey from Moscow on his own. He is not one of those who came to the camp before.

"Comrade Bolotsov, perhaps you have heard the tragic news about Comrade Stalin."

"A terrible loss."

The commandant's face registers no emotion. The colonel is the same. The reason is simple. Who can say what will happen now? Who knows whose side anyone is on? Who will climb, who will fall, who will simply disappear?

The reassurance to which Bolotsov clings is the fact that this colonel has come alone. If Beria has fallen and the colonel's purpose is to take Bolotsov back to Moscow or simply execute him on the spot, he would not be here all by himself. Executioners do not work alone.

But, just in case, the commandant keeps his hand in the deep pocket of the shuba, where he feels the weight of the pistol he slipped in there on the colonel's arrival. He notes that the colonel's own weapon is safely holstered. He keeps an eye on it and on the colonel's hands as the man removes his gloves and places them on his attaché case.

"The Soviet people are now in mourning," says the visitor. "Moscow and the Kremlin are draped in black. Comrade Stalin's body has been embalmed and made available for public viewing. It will be laid to rest in the mausoleum in Red Square, alongside the body of Vladimir Ilyich himself."

"Embalmed, you say?"

"As soon as was possible after death, comrade."

So that settles it. However Josef Vissarionovich met his end, whether by natural causes or with a little help, even the man of steel cannot come back if his innards have been forked out and replaced by the contents of some mad mortician's chemistry kit.

There is a nasty moment as the colonel's hand reaches inside the attaché case. The commandant's grip tightens on the pistol. But the colonel merely produces one of Moscow's sealed communication pouches.

"I am here by command of First Deputy Premier and Marshal of the Soviet Union, Comrade Lavrenti Beria," he says. "Here is his formal letter confirming new instructions for you."

Bolotsov's face is without expression as he takes the pouch, though his thoughts are racing. So Beria is now First Deputy Premier, no less. He has done better than simply hold on to his position; he has actually improved it. Beria is safe. For the present.

Which means that Igor Borisovich Bolotsov is also safe.

For the present.

As the door closes behind the departing colonel, Bolotsov sinks onto the daybed, his nerves in tatters. He places the pistol on the couch but keeps it cocked until he sees the colonel board the truck and then sees the truck depart. Only then does he make the weapon safe.

He opens the pouch, scans the document within, and at last relaxes. Beria requires just two things of him. Neither poses a problem.

One: terminate the project immediately. Two: liquidate all evidence. Terminate the project because Beria has never seen the point of it. Liquidate evidence because, depending on how the political wind blows now, evidence of the project's existence could be used to compromise Beria, to show how he allowed the NKVD and the gulag to become Josef Vissarionovich's personal playthings rather than serving the Party and the people.

Bolotsov calls the guard sergeant into his office.

"I must inform you that Comrade Stalin has died."

The sergeant knows the ropes. He is as deadpan as were his commandant and the NKVD colonel.

"Death is a bitter blow," he says evenly. "Thank you for informing me, Comrade Commandant."

"No need for our two prisoners to be told."

"Very well, Comrade Commandant."

"One other matter. It concerns our duties here. All good things must come to an end. It is time to begin planning our return to Moscow. In the next few days I will have a task for you. Listen well . . ."

CHAPTER 29

"WHERE'S KALMENOVA?" GRUMBLES the foreman. "She's over an hour late. She's never late."

The depot yard is deserted. All the other sweepers from his work gang are out on their streets. Marya Kalmenova's streets are being left unswept.

"Nothing's been right since we lost Comrade Stalin. The country's going to the dogs."

He likes Marya Kalmenova. She is one of his best workers. So the foreman calls in on the chief foreman, explains his problem, and goes to Lobachev Row.

But no one comes to the door of Marya's apartment when he knocks.

"She's in there—she hasn't gone out," says a voice behind him.

The foreman wheels around, startled. Two wary little eyes are peering at him from the adjacent doorway. The door opens a crack further, revealing a small, unshaven old man.

"I'm Griboyev," he says. "My wife was talking to her in the kitchen last night. We haven't seen her this morning, but she can't have gone out. I would have seen her if she had."

"You spy on all your neighbors, do you?"

"Nothing of the sort. I want her to do an errand for me, so I'm waiting to catch her. She helps me out. I hope she's all right. The caretaker has a key if you think something might be wrong—you know, if you want to go in."

"Why would I do that? I don't spy on people."

But the foreman fetches the caretaker anyway. They practically have to shove Griboyev back into his apartment to stop him sliding in behind them.

The foreman enters the room and immediately stops. He and the caretaker stand there, astonished. It is like stepping into an art exhibition. The walls are covered with pictures—not proper framed pictures but sheets of paper with drawings on them. They are everywhere the foreman looks, and there are tidy stacks of paper on every surface, evidently with yet more drawings.

In the midst of this gallery is Kalmenova. She is lying on the sofa, sound asleep. On the wall above her, hemmed in by drawings, is a picture that is, in fact, properly framed. It is a portrait of Comrade Stalin. A somber black mourning ribbon has been tied across one corner.

"Kalmenova!" says the foreman. "Hey there, Marya!"

He touches her arm to give her a gentle shake. The arm is cold. Too cold. He searches for a pulse. There is none.

"I'll fetch a doctor," offers the caretaker.

"I think it's too late for that, but I suppose you should. An ambulance, at any rate, to take her away. Close the door—don't let that old busybody in."

"Oh, Marya," says the foreman when they are alone.

She seems so peaceful. Younger, too. The lines of worry and tiredness have disappeared from her face. He thinks he remembers her mentioning that her son had some artistic talent. That was many years ago. The boy must be grown up by now. The drawings must be his. What was his name? Ah yes—Pasha. The foreman has heard no mention of Pasha for . . . oh, for quite a while. Well, Marya always did keep to herself. Never one for chatter or gossip—one of the reasons for his high regard of her.

As he examines the room, he discovers a holy icon almost hidden among the wall-mounted drawings, on the wall directly opposite Comrade Stalin. At sight of the icon, the foreman automatically crosses himself. He notices, too, that the candle beneath it has been allowed to burn out—dangerous among all this paper, but it pleases him to think that Marya may have been praying when Jesus came to fetch her.

He comes upon a cardboard shoebox on the little table, a box that Marya—no buyer of new shoes—has obviously salvaged on her sweeping rounds. It is neatly filled with sheets of paper—the same good-quality paper as the drawings.

The sheet on top is not a drawing, however. It is a letter. He would never read Marya's private correspondence, but he cannot help but see how this letter begins.

My darling Pashenka . . .

If Marya has been writing to Pasha, he cannot be living at home. But there is no recipient address. So it occurs to the foreman that if he can find out where Pasha is, he might be able to arrange for him to be told the tragic news about his mother.

He lifts the letter from the box, feeling a little uneasy at this act of trespass but reminding himself that it is being done for the best of reasons—Marya may have mentioned her son's whereabouts in the text of the letter.

He does not get that far. Beneath the letter is another one. It is also to Pasha. But again, there is no recipient address.

The foreman flips quickly through all the sheets in the shoebox, lifting only their corners. They are all letters to Pasha. Judging from their dates, Marya has been writing a letter almost every day, since goodness knows when. There is never any recipient address.

Why would she feel the need to write to her son so often? Why are the letters unposted? Why is there never an address for Pasha? It is as if Marya does not know where her own son is living. Have mother and son become estranged? Such things do happen, sadly.

An untidy pile of crumpled paper in a corner behind the sofa catches the foreman's eye. He frowns. The crumpled balls are out of keeping with the care that Marya has taken with her son's drawings and her mysterious letters to him. What has caused her to cast these particular sheets away so dismissively?

He picks up one of the balls and opens it out. He cannot help gasping in surprise. It turns out to be another letter, but this time an unfinished one, containing only a few lines of Marya's careful handwriting—no doubt her very best effort, considering the person to whom she was writing.

This time there certainly is a recipient address. And this time the foreman does read what Marya has written.

He opens another of the crumpled sheets. And another. A good six or seven. They all begin the same way:

Dear Comrade Stalin . . .

The various attempts that follow this salutation differ in minor ways from each other, as if Marya was trying to find the best way of expressing herself, but in essence they all say the same thing:

Please help me find my son, Pavel Pavlovich Kalmenov, who was arrested and taken away from me. I don't know why he was arrested or where he is.

Unlike the letters to Pasha, all these unfinished and abandoned letters bear the same date—the day before the announcement of Comrade Stalin's death.

"Oh, Marya," says the foreman again.

He flops onto the room's only chair. He must wait for the ambulance. But as for what he will do about these letters of Marya's and her missing son, he has no idea.

Overhead, Christ and Josef Vissarionovich—the late Josef Vissarionovich—continue to stare each other down.

CHAPTER 30

PASHA WAKES COUGHING. When he breathes in, his throat seems to be filled with some dense mass that blocks air from reaching his lungs. At first, still half asleep, he thinks it is the same kind of cough that racked Irina, a typhus cough. Dread of that jerks him fully awake.

But no, it is not a typhus cough. The blockage in his throat feels and tastes and smells like smoke. His mouth is full of it, his nostrils are clogged. He cannot see because the hut is in complete darkness, which it has never been previously. Are the compound's floodlights off?

He is certain now that it is smoke. His eyes are stinging—tears stream from them. The temperature in the hut is higher than he has known it before, even though the stove is always kept burning through the night.

The stove must be the culprit. It must be spewing out smoke. He peers in its direction but in the darkness all he can see is its normal dull glow.

"Viktor!"

No reply. Either the smoke has yet to reach Viktor and he is still asleep or it has knocked him unconscious. Pasha stands up and shakes him. No response. He shakes him again, hard. To his relief Viktor begins to stir.

"Get up, Viktor! The hut's on fire!"

He goes to the doorway and switches on the light. He is shocked at the sight of the thick clouds of black smoke. It is coming up through the floorboards and is starting to creep between the boards of the walls in long dark tendrils. He returns to his bunk and shoves his boots on. In the far corner, the farthest corner from the stove, he sees the first tongues of flame. They are coming from the floor and beginning to lick their way hungrily up the wall.

Viktor has jumped down. He coughs and curses as he struggles into his boots.

Pasha tries the door. The latch lifts but the door refuses to budge.

The heat is greater here. He places his hand against the wall but has to whip it away immediately—the boards are scorching. The smoke continues to seep through them. The walls are burning—but from outside.

Neither the stove nor anything else inside the hut is to blame for this. Then who or what *is* to blame?

Viktor has gone to a window. Outside there is only solid darkness, not a glimmer of light visible. The window frame is fixed, not designed to open, so Viktor grabs a chair and smashes through the triple panes of glass. The glass falls away but the chair can go no further. The darkness beyond the window is now explained. He calls to Pasha.

"Some bastard's closed the shutters—barred them."

He attacks the heavy wooden shutters with the chair, but it is no use. The shutters are too solid.

Pasha goes to another window. Pointless to try it—he can see that it, too, is firmly shuttered outside. Same thing with the next window.

There is no way out of the hut.

* * *

Outside in the compound the floodlights are as bright as ever. The guard sergeant stands at a safe distance from the dormitory hut as it burns.

He has done a thorough job. He built a few stacks of thin dry timbers beneath the hut in the gaps made by the piles. He soaked the stacks in truck fuel and set them alight. The flames are starting to penetrate the hut at one corner and soon the other stacks will achieve similar results. He poured fuel over the walls of the hut and they, too, are now ablaze.

He reflects on what will happen with the two prisoners. If they are lucky, they will die of smoke inhalation before the fire reaches them and begins to engulf their bodies. At the very least, they might fall unconscious. Either fate will be better than being fully aware of what is happening as they burn to death. He would spare them that. The truth is that he would not have disposed of them in this way. Nothing beats a bullet in the back of the head. He would choose that for himself. A merciful way to go. But the decision was Bolotsov's, who announced that the whole camp is to be torched, and that might as well include the final two prisoners.

Thinking of which, the sergeant decides it is time to move on and begin setting the other buildings alight.

Odd how quiet the two prisoners are being. He would have expected screams by now. Could be that the smoke has put an end to their woes already.

He bends down to grasp the can of fuel.

* * *

Considering his girth, Igor Bolotsov is light on his feet. He can move surprisingly swiftly and stealthily. The crackle of the flames helps. The sergeant hears nothing as the commandant approaches from behind.

The weighty bonus that Bolotsov promised him a while ago weighs in at exactly nine grams: a rifle bullet in the back of his head—a merciful way to go, as Bolotsov has often heard the sergeant describe it. Impelled by the force of the bullet, the man falls flat on his face in the snow. On his way down, a small sigh escapes his lips, not of protest or even of appreciation for the consideration shown to him, but simply as his last breath departs. The snow around him turns dark.

Bolotsov grunts with satisfaction. An easy job, without the other guards to get in the way. He returns to his quarters, leaving the sergeant where he has fallen.

* * *

In the burning hut, Pasha and Viktor hear the gunshot. For a moment they are motionless, listening. But there are no more shots.

"Whatever that's about, we still have to get out of here," says Viktor. A spasm of coughing catches him.

"The stove," says Pasha. "The flue. You're tall enough."

Instead of venting through a chimney, the flue exits through the wall of the hut, close to the roof. A metal plate is set into the wall to accommodate it.

They carry one of the tables over to the stove. Viktor climbs onto it and Pasha passes him a blanket. Viktor wraps it about the hot flue and tugs and shakes the metal tube from side to side. No good. Pasha passes him a chair. Viktor uses it to strike the flue again and again. Pasha knows he himself is growing weaker and that Viktor must be doing so as well—more so, given the energy he is expending.

The entire wall where the flames entered is ablaze now. More tongues of fire are appearing all over the floor, even close by Pasha's feet. He can only look in snatches of a couple of seconds before the smoke forces his eyes closed.

At long last, over the crackle and hiss of the fire, there is the sound of tearing metal as the flue detaches from the plate. Viktor continues swinging the chair until with a loud creak the flue falls out of his way. He wraps the blanket over part of the rim of the hole in the metal plate. He wrenches the plate, pushes it outward, pulls it back, does this again and again. It begins to loosen.

Pasha's chest feels as if it is being crushed. He breathes in short gasps. He is aware that most of what he is taking in is smoke. Now he can barely open his eyes at all. But, in fact, he does not want to open them anyway. He wants to sleep. Nothing matters now but that. It is an alluring and peaceful prospect, to lie down and just drift away.

Something smacks his head. It is Viktor's open hand.

"Pasha, stay awake!"

Pasha looks up to see a square of light near the top of the wall. The metal plate has gone and the light is from the floodlights in the compound, which apparently are still on.

Viktor bends down toward him. "You're going out first, comrade. I'll give you a leg up."

Pasha feels himself being lifted bodily off his feet by Viktor and scrabbles to find a footing on the table. Another powerful shove by Viktor, then the cool air hits him and he is outside.

Seconds later they are both lying in the snow, close by the fence. It is as far as they can crawl from the inferno that the hut has become. They are out of sight from anyone in the compound. In this regard the flames offer protection.

Pasha feels the chill of the snow beneath him. Nothing on earth could feel better. Nothing could taste purer than the chill Arctic air he is sucking into his lungs, however much it stings. He grabs a handful of snow and scrubs his face. Viktor does the same. They have no gloves, which would normally make this an act of folly. But not this time, with such fierce heat pouring over them.

Viktor rinses his mouth, spits the snow out. When he speaks, his voice is hoarse. "This was no accident, Pasha. Someone tried to roast us like boar on a spit—Bolotsov or the sergeant."

"Or whoever fired that shot."

"No, there's no one else. It's one of those two bastards. Something's changed. Something's happened that means we're no longer needed."

Pasha is watching the blazing hut. Eventually there will be only ash left—cold ash, all heat gone from it. Not only are they without gloves, but all they are wearing is their uniforms in which they were sleeping.

"When the fire burns out, we'll freeze to death."

He peers along the snowy ground into the gap beneath the raised hut. He can see how the fire was made, the blazing stacks of wood that got it underway. But beyond the hut he sees something else in the snow.

"Look over there," he tells Viktor.

Viktor looks where he indicates. The dark form clearly visible in the glare of the floodlights is the body of the guard sergeant. Close by lies an overturned fuel can.

"One down," says Viktor. "That leaves Bolotsov. So where is he?"

"I don't know, but I can tell you we won't survive without better clothes. You got us out, Viktor, so this next job's mine."

Pasha's scramble to the women's dormitory hut is frightening. He will be a perfect target if Bolotsov is lying in wait. But he stays close to the fence and makes it safely. The hut has remained unlocked since the sergeant took Irina's body away. The clothing left behind by the executed female prisoners is hanging near the door. Pasha chooses the four largest greatcoats he can find, adds gloves and shapkas, and hurries back to Viktor. They each put on two greatcoats and find the best fit among the gloves and fur hats.

"At least no one tried to shoot me," mutters Pasha.

Which leaves them wondering again where Bolotsov is and what he is up to.

CHAPTER 31

The commandant is hurrying into the barn where the trucks are kept. He is lugging one of Moscow's steel boxes in his left hand and the rifle in his right.

In the box are all the original Leonardo drawings, more than a hundred now in total, including three that were still being copied. The drawings are no longer in their casings of bulletproof glass—too bulky. Instead he has interleaved them with sheets of the hand-made blank paper. In theory this could expose them to the risk of being rubbed and smudged, but there are so many and he has packed them so tightly that this is unlikely.

He hefts the box into one of the trucks. The rifle follows. He removes his gloves, digs out his handkerchief, and deals with his nose. When he climbs into the driving seat, his size and the bulky shuba mean that he ends up with the steering wheel pressing into the folds of his stomach. Throughout, he can hear the roar of the flames that are consuming the dormitory hut. The blaze is a fine sight against the night sky.

His destination is Vorkuta, to make tomorrow evening's rail departure to Moscow. He will pass the time until then in the whorehouse, quieting the restlessness in him since the loss of the green-eyed girl.

In Moscow he will report to Beria that the security chief's orders have been carried out to the letter. Beria will simply shrug. He has bigger things to worry about by now, weightier matters of state more pressing than whatever may have transpired out here in the backside of nowhere. Moscow will be in turmoil, he and the others snarling and snapping at one another like rabid dogs. The security chief—correction: First Deputy Premier—will have only one concern: Can any of this come back to bite him?

"You liquidated all evidence?" is all he will say. "Then the matter is closed."

He will not ask about the original drawings. Why would he? As far as anyone knows, all but three are already in Moscow anyway; and those three, Bolotsov can claim in the unlikely event of being asked, were lost in the fire that he set to destroy the camp—in order to liquidate all evidence, as Beria required.

And that will be that. Who gives a damn about a few drawings when control of the entire Soviet empire is up for grabs? Time will pass, the dust will settle; and when all is quiet, Igor Borisovich Bolotsov will make his move. Leningrad first—he has family there; no eyebrows will be raised when he applies for a travel permit. Then to Finland, only three or four hours by road from Leningrad. There are crossing points if a man has contacts. As Igor Borisovich Bolotsov does.

With which reflections he glances across the seats at the steel box—fireproof and waterproof, strong enough to survive a minor war—and turns on the ignition.

* * *

Seconds later, Pasha and Viktor hear the whine of the truck's engine as the vehicle emerges from the barn and crosses the compound.

Pasha breaks from the cover of the burning hut in time to see it swing through the open gates and toward the ice road. There is no mistaking the singular figure in the driving seat.

"That's him, Viktor!"

Viktor does not hear. No need—he has seen for himself. He has already grabbed the dead sergeant's rifle and is sprinting across the compound. Pasha races after him. But once Viktor passes through the gates, instead of continuing after the truck, he turns in the direction that will allow him to intersect the ice road's meandering course.

* * *

Bolotsov has a moment of doubt as the truck enters the slope to the ice road. He brakes at the right moment, but the suddenness with which the vehicle's nose dips, together with the steepness of its angle, pitches him forward so that his head almost collides with the windscreen. Only the fact that his belly is pinning him firmly in place behind the steering wheel saves him from a bad knock.

Soon he is safely on the level surface of the ice, slicing through the churned-up tracks as he follows the ice road's twists and turns toward Vorkuta. The weather is calm, the truck's headlights show the route ahead. He begins to relax and enjoy the ride, snug in this island of light from the instrument panel and the steady, comforting drone of the engine. He keeps his speed slow and careful and congratulates himself on a plan well conceived and well executed.

He has negotiated two of the ice road's long loops when he feels the truck lurch sharply to the right. He presses the accelerator and wrenches the steering wheel to the left as quickly as his belly will allow.

But immediately the truck lurches again. He accelerates again. Another lurch to the right. He hears a clunk and sees that the rifle has slid along the seat and come to rest against the door on the other side. The steel box, heavier and more inert, is also starting to slide slowly in the same direction. Even his own body is tilting; it, too, wants to slide across the seat.

The truck is tilting to the right; he realizes that the ice on that side is giving way.

He puts his foot to the floor, gunning the engine. It is an instinctive response, to accelerate away from the problem. It is also a wrong response. The road wheels spin uselessly in terms of producing any forward motion. Their tires pass through the layer of snow; the snow chains begin to saw into the ice.

He curses and eases off the accelerator, takes the truck out of gear. The vehicle is well and truly stuck; he will never free it. He will have to return to the camp on foot and take the other truck. This means a long and tiring walk in temperatures that, even in March, are still hovering around twenty below zero. But it can be done. There will still be time to make the train, time enough for the whorehouse, too.

He retrieves the rifle, flings the door open, and drops the weapon on the snow. Getting hold of the steel box is more difficult because it is so heavy. But again he manages. He has the pistol with him and will take the rifle as well in case he encounters wolves, but the box can await his return.

Now he must squeeze himself out from behind the steering wheel. He grabs the back of the seat and begins to turn his body. Not easy. As he does so, he glances through the open door.

His heart falters.

A man is standing no more than four or five meters away on the ice road, hands by his sides, calmly watching him. He is at the edge of the headlight beams, not caught directly by them but perfectly visible.

He is a man who is supposed to be dead. In fact, he might yet be dead, so streaked with filth is his face as if he has just hauled himself from his grave, so pallid is the face beneath that filth and so devoid of any human expression. He is the tall, gawky prisoner with the sardonic smile. Lover of the pretty green-eyed girl.

Now, as if he has waited to be sure of having Bolotsov's attention, he moves. He is in no hurry. He is holding something. A crisp one-handed action is accompanied by a loud metallic clatter. His arms rise, he spreads his feet, turns slightly so that one shoulder trails.

Bolotsov groans.

The man is pointing a rifle at him. He has him in his sights. He has just loaded a round into the chamber.

And he is not smiling, sardonically or otherwise.

CHAPTER 32

PASHA REACHES THE place on the riverbank from which Viktor descended to intercept the truck. As he arrives, a flurry of hail starts, not a buran but bad enough and driven by a cruelly chill wind. Behind him in the distance, through the sheets of hail, he can see the flames of the dormitory hut shooting high into the night sky like a beacon.

The chase across the deep snow of the tundra has left him exhausted. The weight of the greatcoats did not help. Smoke still clogs his lungs and throat. He halts at the top of the slope, gasping for breath, and tries to focus on what is happening down on the ice road. Bolotsov's truck appears to be ensnared and Viktor is holding the commandant at gunpoint.

"Don't be a fool!" Bolotsov shouts at Viktor, over the noise of the hail and rising wind. "Do you know what's in that box?"

"Of course I do—the drawings you've been stealing."

"Half of them are yours if you help me. Imagine what they're worth! Take them to the West and sell them—you'll have more wealth than you can count."

"Like you were planning to do?"

"We'll share them."

Viktor raises the rifle. "I don't want them. I never want to set eyes on the cursed things again."

Bolotsov has managed to get his left leg out of the truck. He pushes back against the seat and tries to stretch down. The hail batters him.

Viktor seems not to notice the storm. He is trying to take aim. His gloves make him clumsy.

Pasha hurriedly begins to descend the slope. He cannot let this happen. He has had enough of death. He cannot let Viktor be a cold-blooded killer.

But he has delayed too long. The rifle flashes, a shot rings out. Pasha ducks instinctively. There is a metallic clang as a bullet buries itself somewhere in Bolotsov's truck.

The commandant yelps. He stops trying to free himself.

"Viktor!" calls Pasha. "Stop!"

Bolotsov and Viktor both turn to search for him in the darkness and curtain of hail. He descends closer, bringing himself into the pool of light where the steep banks reflect and intensify the truck's headlights.

"He's not worth it, Viktor."

"Stay out of this, Pasha. He's a murderer."

"But you're not. And you don't want to be."

Bolotsov senses an opportunity.

"Take your friend's advice," he tells Viktor. A bluster of hail slashes across the ice. He turns to Pasha. "Tell him we can all benefit here, we can all do well for ourselves."

Viktor's face streams with hail and streaks of smoke. "Don't interfere, Pasha. Keep in mind what he did to Irina. It's time for justice."

Pasha comes all the way down, skidding through the loose snow of the slope.

"Justice without legal process, Viktor? You'll be judge and executioner? That makes you no better than him and what he stands for—all the lies. Would your father approve if you pull that trigger?"

"You think we can get someone to put our good commandant on trial? Who would that be, Pasha? My father would tell us to get on with it, right here. This is the only courtroom we'll ever have. Zeks' justice."

"Listen, both of you," persists Bolotsov. He is calmer now. "We can work something out. My connections in Moscow are the best—I'll fix you up with top positions, anything you like. Now that Stalin's out of the way—"

"He's what?" snaps Viktor. "How is he out of the way?"

Bolotsov is all innocence. "Stalin's dead—didn't you know? I ordered the sergeant to inform you. This was Stalin's project. He's dead, so it's dead, too."

"Is that who this was for? Is that why everyone died? Is that why we ended up in the gulag? My Irina's gone because Stalin wanted some nice pictures? That's what gave you license to rape and kill—and then try to incinerate us like trash?"

"That was the sergeant, not me. I told him to release you."

Bolotsov has been fumbling with the folds of the heavy shuba. Pasha's mind races. Something here is not right, something other than Bolotsov's lies. The commandant is too calm.

Suddenly Bolotsov is brandishing a pistol. Viktor has not seen it. Pasha yells a warning.

But before Bolotsov can use the weapon, a massive cracking sound fills the air, far louder and deeper than any gunshot. It lasts for several seconds. It has no single source but envelops everything, like thunder directly overhead.

But the sound is not overhead. It is below them. It sounds like the earth itself is breaking open.

It is not the earth. It is the ice. Long fissures open around the truck and begin to spread in every direction.

Bolotsov is no longer calm. He shrieks as the vehicle suddenly plunges down and tilts through ninety degrees. The pistol has vanished, lost in the chaos. The truck's right-hand side disappears from view. The ice creaks and protests. The commandant is still pinned behind the steering wheel but now he is perched at the highest point of the tilted truck. Pasha suspects that inside the cab the water must be reaching him; he must be feeling its first icy caress.

Bolotsov writhes and twists. His fur shapka has gone. His upper body swings from side to side, hail bouncing off his shaven head, his Asiatic eyes now round orbs of terror.

The collapse of the ice has not weakened Viktor's resolve, even if his aim is no better. Another shot rings out. The bullet shatters the truck's windscreen. He loads the rifle for another shot.

The truck plunges again. The ice screeches and groans as the breaking slabs are pushed aside to let the vehicle pass through. This time the whole of the truck slides into the water, which rises black and thick around it.

Bolotsov's squeals are unremitting, louder than the roar of the wind and the rattle of the hail. The commandant knows there is no escape. Only his head and arms remain visible, his head still weaving from side to side, his eyes bulging as if they will spring from their sockets, his arms flapping uselessly and beating the water into black foam.

The shifting slabs of ice are rocking the section on which Pasha is standing. He loses his balance, regains it for a moment, but then the ice tilts again. He tries to step back. He trips, his arms windmill as he tries to steady himself, but he knows that he is overbalancing and heading straight for the dark scar of water that has opened up before him. There is nothing he can do.

Something slams into him. He falls backwards onto ice that is solid and stable. Viktor has flung himself across the disintegrating slabs to propel him to safety—but in doing so he has lost his own balance and is now slipping into the black water that awaited Pasha.

His hands claw at the ice, but they cannot gain a purchase. He slides into the water.

Pasha throws himself forward on his belly. Snow and hail blind him for a moment. When he reaches the edge of the ice, Viktor has vanished.

Seconds pass. Bubbles of air break the surface, then there is an explosion of water as Viktor comes back up. He sees Pasha and stretches toward him. Pasha plunges his arms into the water to catch him. He pushes even closer to the edge, until he is in danger of going over.

Their fingers almost touch. Almost. Their eyes meet.

"Pasha," says Viktor, though the name is not audible, only mouthed.

That is all. Nothing more. Viktor's eyes are wide, the arcs of his eyebrows high as if in wonder. He is still holding Pasha's gaze as he slips beneath the black water.

Pasha beats the surface in the same useless way that Bolotsov did. Eventually he stops. The water settles. It is as black as death. Hailstones pock the surface. Gradually they cease, as the storm blows itself out.

Now Pasha becomes aware of the stillness around him. He tears his gaze from the black water. The truck and Bolotsov have gone. The commandant's rifle has gone, the steel box as well. Viktor's rifle has gone. The only sound is of air bubbling up through the water from the drowned truck.

After a while the bubbles stop. All that is left is the glow of headlights in the black water. The glow wavers, grows dim, and is finally extinguished.

Pasha pushes himself to his knees. He is motionless for a moment, like a man in prayer, then he throws back his head and cries out Viktor's name. Afterwards there is silence again. Then, across the empty tundra, the wolves reply.

CHAPTER 33

IN THE TRANQUILITY of his little flat in central London, Anthony Frederick Blunt is cooking dinner, a simple omelette. He will dine alone this evening, as so often nowadays.

It is not wolves that he hears in the lonely stretches of his imagination. It is the baying of the hounds. They are coming closer than ever these days. His life has become a not-so-merry-go-round of investigations, interviews, interrogations. The hounds are persistent, he gives them that. Their dealings with the great pretender are unfailingly courteous and restrained, notable for their English decency and civility, but the fangs are there nonetheless. And a little more bared than they used to be.

He tells himself that these tête-à-têtes are more an annoyance than a threat, for they get nowhere; but they do take time and disturb his work. His official work, that is, as opposed to the unofficial kind. As well as his duties at Windsor, he has his writing to get on with, a demanding program of lecture tours, many of them involving overseas travel, and of course his role at the Courtauld.

But now the press has weighed in—publishing lurid piffle about Guy Burgess and that clown Maclean, lumping them together as the "missing" diplomats, plus much innuendo about the Cambridge set and the Apostles, and endless grubbing about in search of any smutty titbit with which to thrill their readers. They ambush him in Portman Square, so that not even his refuge, this beloved flat, is safe for him to come and go.

To hell with all of them. The hounds will never get anything out of him. And the press can go hang. Because—goodness, despite all the vulgar clamor—he continues to receive knowing winks from the right quarters regarding the knighthood that is on the cards for him.

Sir Anthony Blunt: it has a pleasing ring to it.

The thought of it bucks a fellow up. His dear old mother will be pleased. How glorious the game still is.

Or so he tries to tell himself.

A shame about today's news, though. No getting away from that, even for the great pretender.

It was the familiar jaunt from Windsor up to London. There he was, in first class as required, settled contentedly with the briefcase beside him, and in it another consignment of original drawings. A delightful spring evening, sun slipping down over the water meadows at Windsor, daffodils everywhere, the fields rolling past and then the rows of little houses as the train approached London.

In due course, his usual contact appeared. But with no briefcase—meaning no forgeries for Blunt to take back to Windsor, as has been the procedure for the last couple of years.

No preamble either, no beating about the bush. And no interest in having anything to do with Blunt's briefcase and its contents.

"Terminated." That was the word the man used: "The project has been terminated. With immediate effect."

Then he stood up and went to another compartment.

Blunt shakes his head angrily as he remembers the frigidity of the encounter. The anger is unwise: at once he feels the muscles in his face contract. He leaves the omelette and goes through to the bathroom to look at himself in the mirror.

This thing with his face. Bell's palsy, his physician calls it. The entire right side spasms and becomes completely immobile. It makes him look like a half-wit. The side of his mouth is paralyzed, as if he has been to the dentist. His right eye can only blink in slow motion. Utterly hideous.

He attempts a smile, in order to see what a smile looks like, and regrets it immediately. It is Quasimodo who leers back at him.

"It'll pass," the physician has reassured him. "It may take a while, but it'll pass."

"How long is a while?"

"Weeks. Probably only a few weeks."

"Probably?"

"It could take a year."

"But I have to give lectures. I have to be seen in public. Good God, will I start dribbling?"

"The usual cause is stress. Anxiety, pressure. Anything of that sort going on with you?"

"Nothing comes to mind. Calm as a duckpond."

CHAPTER 34

PASHA HEADS BACK to the camp. He is shaking with cold. The water in his gloves has begun to freeze. He abandons them and shoves his hands under his greatcoats in search of warmth. But the sleeves are soaked through and by the time he reaches the camp he is conscious of a tingling sensation in his hands—he is no stranger to cold but he does not recall a feeling like this before.

The men's dormitory hut has been reduced to charred timbers and heaps of smoking ash; even the hailstorm was not enough to quench the blaze. But there is little warmth in the ashes now. He remembers there was still some clothing in the women's hut, so he collects what he needs from there, including gloves and another two greatcoats, adds scarves and an armful of blankets.

In Bolotsov's quarters he finds that the stove is still lit. Stripping off his wet uniform and other clothing is hard work—his hands are stiff and the waterlogged garments are heavy. This is when he notices that the tips of his fingers have become white and bloodless. When he tries to flex the fingers, they move more slowly than they should, and erratically, as if the communication link between brain and fingers has been stretched to the extent that breakages in transmission are occurring. He thinks of Leonardo's anatomical studies and of his own drawings, and pictures the nerves and tendons and muscles involved in the complex ballet of even the simplest finger movement. It would be all too easy for that ballet to be disrupted.

Finally he manages to change into the dry clothing. He sits on the daybed, letting his body soak up the heat, and tries to bring his thinking into order. The one thing of which he is certain is that he has to get away from here. But not to Vorkuta, where he would be immediately identifiable as a fleeing zek. To where, then? And how?

He forsakes the stove and goes to the barn, where he investigates the other truck. He has never driven a motor vehicle but he can try. He knows he needs a key to make the engine start but he finds none anywhere in the truck or the maintenance area of the barn.

So, transport but no way of using it; and in any case no destination that would offer safety.

He returns outside, searches the sergeant's body, and finds an assortment of keys on a large ring. Back to the barn and the truck. None of the keys fits the ignition.

The female guards' hut is completely empty. No keys anywhere. In the other hut he finds only a few clothes, clearly the sergeant's, in a military backpack along with a shaving kit. There are photographs of a woman and two children, presumably the man's family.

Again, no keys. If Bolotsov had the key for the truck with him, it is now at the bottom of the river.

He goes to the work hut. No sign of any key. But he lingers, even though standing here is not a good feeling. There are more ghosts than ever. When his gaze falls on any work table he knows who sat at it. He sees them there now. He can make the room as full and busy as it ever was in its quiet industriousness. Here is Viktor. Here is Irina. Here is himself, lost in the work, deep inside the day's drawing. Here are the guards. Here is Bolotsov—he even smells the stink of the long shuba.

He goes to his own table. His sketch pads are where he left them, in the sliding tray beneath the table. They contain his old work that he brought with him, going right back to his time with Sergei, along with many of the drawings he made here. He turns some pages, hears Viktor laughing, feels Irina's lips on his cheek.

He closes the pads and slips them into the inside pockets of the greatcoats.

At Viktor's table, he finds Irina's playing cards. For once, Viktor was not carrying them with him. He takes them.

By the time he explores the dining hut he has given up on finding any key, but what he does discover in an annex is the store of food, much of it packed in ice, from which the prisoners' meals were prepared. There is far more than ever came their way, and in greater variety—beef, pork, chicken, fish, some smoked or salted, as well as eggs, cheese, vegetables, and apples. For the first time he realizes how well Bolotsov and the guards must have eaten.

All this is still getting him nowhere. All he is doing is wandering about aimlessly, and the only thing he has come up with is transport that he cannot use and that would take him only to a destination he dare not go to. In the meantime, his whole body, not just his hands, has begun to grow stiff from the cold. It was folly to leave the warm stove.

He is still in the dining hut when he becomes aware of a faint sound in the distance. He hurries from the hut and crosses to the gates of the compound where he can see across the dark tundra.

It is still a couple of hours before daybreak. Far away to the south there is a flash of light. It comes and goes as he watches. It is somewhere on the ice road, at present farther away than the spot where the truck went down. He understands at once what it is. It is caused by headlight beams spilling intermittently over the high banks of the ice road. It is getting nearer. The sound he hears is the drone of a vehicle engine. A truck is on its way to the camp.

He is angry with himself for failing to anticipate this. The flames of the blazing dormitory hut must have been visible for many kilometers around—certainly as far as the mining camp and probably in Vorkuta itself. Unsurprisingly, someone wants to know what is going on.

He returns to Bolotsov's office, pushes his discarded clothing out of sight beneath the daybed, and moves a rug to cover the wet patch on the floor. He goes to a watchtower and climbs the ladder to the sentry post. He has only just clambered into the enclosure when the truck arrives. Up here he is behind and above the floodlights, and cannot be seen from below, just as sentries could sometimes not be seen during darkness by the prisoners.

He peers out. The truck has brought soldiers. They are regular Red Army. With any luck, they are here only as a matter of form; they will have no real interest.

He watches and listens. There is some excitement when they find the dead sergeant, which turns to speculation over what might have happened and who might have killed him. Someone suggests that his death, the result of a single bullet in the back of his head, looks more like an execution than a dispute or the result of a breakout. His pistol has not been fired and is still holstered, a further indication that he was ambushed from behind. One of the soldiers takes possession of the pistol.

The visit is as half-hearted as Pasha hoped. The soldiers walk around the remains of the dormitory hut but make no attempt to look for evidence of what caused the fire. Nor are they interested in establishing whether there are any bodies among the ashes. They wander into the barn and the other huts, and report on the stoves still lit, on the healthy stocks of food—some of which they help themselves to—and on the impression of a hasty and unplanned, maybe even forced, evacuation. Perhaps some vehicle driven with less skill than theirs went through that hole in the ice road, but so what? Nothing can be done about that. Not their problem, one of them points out.

Finally, they regroup at the truck, where there is talk of sending a report to the NKVD.

"What about him?" someone asks, meaning the dead sergeant. "If we leave him here the wolves will have him."

"He's NKVD," is the reply. "Wolf meat is all they're good for."

When he is sure they have gone, Pasha climbs warily down. He returns to Bolotsov's quarters and adds more coal to the stove until it is hot enough for Bolotsov himself, then retreats beneath the blankets on the daybed.

What happened on the ice road repeats endlessly in his head. Each time there is a different revision—if only he had kept his balance, if only he had stretched a little further to reach Viktor, if only Viktor had fought harder.

Eventually exhaustion consigns him to merciful sleep. It is a sleep so deep that he does not hear in the distance the shriek of the great locomotive as the train from Moscow approaches Vorkuta—the train that Igor Borisovich Bolotsov will not be boarding for its return to the capital.

CHAPTER 35

LATER THAT DAY, Pasha goes to the work hut, takes a sheet of cartridge paper, and seats himself at his work table. He removes his gloves and arranges the guides on the drawing board. His fingers are still stiff but the diagram he intends is simple. It is based on Irina's estimates of the distance from the camp to the rail line. He marks a point on the paper, representing the camp, then draws two vertical lines eight and nine centimeters distant from it—one centimeter for every ten kilometers—these lines representing the rail line. He joins the point to the lines with a horizontal line that intersects the vertical ones at ninety degrees. He uses the guides on the drawing board to mark deviations from the horizontal line in steps of five degrees, then makes a series of measurements and calculations based on the resulting right-angle triangles. The result is as he hoped.

He goes to the male guards' hut and empties the sergeant's backpack of its contents. In the dining hut he fills the backpack with meats, bread, and a few apples. He takes some boxes of matches. He chooses a large, broad-bladed chef's knife and puts it into the backpack. The knife is not only to cut the food but also for protection against the wolves. He will be traveling south, so the likelihood of encountering polar bears is reduced, although there are also brown bears to consider. He is not convinced that a kitchen knife will save him from either.

The dead sergeant's boots are better than his and are knee high. It is a struggle to remove them, again partly because of his own awkward hands but also because the corpse has frozen during the night and the ankles refuse to bend. When he gets the boots off, he sees that the socks are long and thick, so he pulls these off, too, both pairs, and takes everything to the barn. The socks go on over his own, and with the extra thickness the sergeant's boots fit well enough. He returns for the man's greatcoat—an even more difficult struggle but worth it for the heavy quality of the garment—and puts it on in place of one of the women's coats. The dead keep on clothing the living.

There is a coil of rope in the useless truck. It is thin, but length is more important than strength for what he has in mind. He lays it out along the barn floor. It measures about thirty meters, which is less than he had hoped, but since it is the only rope he can see, it will have to be enough. Instead of coiling it again, he winds it about his chest inside the greatcoats. So rather than carrying it as dead weight until the time when he needs it, he has an extra layer of insulation.

In the workshop area of the barn he saws a deep, wide notch into the end of the shaft of a snow shovel.

He chooses one of the kerosene lanterns hooked to the truck's cab for emergency use, its glass clear on one side and red on the other. He ensures that its reservoir is full and lights the lantern to test it. If the kerosene is poor quality, wax will form and clog the burner. He adjusts the lantern to its highest setting and lets it burn for a minute or two until he is reassured. When it has cooled, he secures it to one of the cords on the backpack.

In Bolotsov's office he rolls up two blankets and tethers them to the backpack. He slides the shaft of the shovel through loops on the side.

Finally, he searches every hut and the barn for a gun of any kind. He has no success. He should have taken the dead sergeant's pistol while he still had the chance, before the Red Army soldiers came.

He goes to the dining hut, eats there so as not to deplete the supplies in the backpack, and returns to Bolotsov's office and the warm stove to wait for nightfall.

He examines his hands. Everything he has done today was more difficult than it should have been—the simple geometric diagram, his work in the barn, the struggles with the sergeant's boots and greatcoat. Sometimes his hands function as he tells them to. Sometimes they ignore him, as if they belong to someone else.

His fingers are the most worrying. When he commands them, he feels the tension all the way up his arms, as if the message is being blocked there before it can travel as far as his fingers. The harder he tries, the more the blockage builds up, like water behind a dam. There is no getting away from it: last night and this morning his fingers were bad; this evening they are worse.

Only one thing distracts him from his anxiety—the distant shriek of the locomotive as it leaves Vorkuta for Moscow.

CHAPTER 36

AFTER A LONG twilight, the daylight finally ends. He stands for a while outside the gates of the compound, watching the sky and the empty tundra. The night is cloudless and starry. The moon is in its first quarter; he will have its light each night as it waxes.

He recalls the free workers in the mining camp and how he wondered how desperate a person must be to take such a gamble with their life. Well, this is his gamble. He has no compass nor any way of making one, so he will rely on the stars and moon for navigation—he has watched them often enough. He will travel only during darkness, and each dawn he will check the sun to make sure he has not strayed too far off course. Each evening when he sets off, he will verify his direction with the setting sun. There is room for error—his diagram showed that even ten or fifteen degrees of deviation add only a few kilometers to the total distance.

He will not travel in daylight because if he is found in the gulag zone without papers he will be known at once to be an escaped prisoner. Wiser to rest and stay out of sight during the day. Temperatures will also be higher then, reducing the risk of sleep becoming a hypothermic coma.

He will also avoid bears by traveling at night, but they may be a danger in daytime when they are active. There is the risk they will smell him. He can do nothing about that.

He has a week for the journey.

* * *

He does not use the ice road, instead clambering over its banks and crossing its twists and turns. He walks directly across the snow plain, holding as straight a line as he can over the hillocks of the permafrost, where water forced upwards in the brief summer thaw is refrozen into domes of ice in winter, and over the flat expanses between them. He trudges forward to the sound of the wolves far away—God preserve him from them—and the crunch of snow beneath the dead sergeant's stout boots. He does not light the lantern, for its light would be of limited use; and it might be seen. His body is weak, the snow is knee deep, the backpack, lantern, and shovel are heavy and cumbersome, and his progress feels pitifully slow.

But it is progress. With every step he feels increasingly confident that it is progress.

After what he thinks is a couple of hours, he sees over to his left an arc of yellow light on the horizon. It is either the mining camp or Vorkuta, or it might be the lights of both. It is reassurance that he is traveling in the right direction, passing west of the town and the camp, and continuing to head south.

The rope about his chest is doing its job, providing extra protection against the cold. He has tied the scarves over his nose and mouth. The air he breathes is therefore warmed, however slightly. He hopes this will protect his lungs, though he can still feel the prickle of ice as it forms in his nostrils. His eyebrows and eyelashes become caked with ice from his exhaled breath, and the cold eats at his eyes so that he has to close them for a while every few paces; but he cannot keep them closed for long in case his eyelids freeze together. He is being covered by a layer of frost and ice crystals that grows steadily thicker and whiter. He gives up trying to sweep it off.

Four or five hours into the journey, the stars and moon are swallowed by cloud, and snow begins to fall, soundless and persistent. It is not a storm, above all not a buran, for which he is grateful, but it comes in a dense, steady fall of large flakes that make it impossible to see more than a few meters ahead.

Now that he has to manage without the moon, he discovers how much light it was providing. He might stumble into one of the frozen pools that lace the tundra. The depressions they create bring the risk of a sprained ankle or broken leg, which would put an end to everything. But he is not prepared to stop and wait for the snow to pass. After all, how long might that be, each time? And how many times?

He presses on, watching where he places every step, doing the best he can to hold as straight a course as the horizontal line he drew in his geometric diagram.

CHAPTER 37

It is a simple funeral. Marya reposes in a plain wooden coffin. It is unvarnished, made of cheap wood, with no fancy metalwork. It has been provided at no charge by the welfare administration section of the local soviet. Someone has added blankets and a pillow to take the bare look off it and, as is the tradition, to give Marya some ease in her rest.

The watery sunshine of this early spring day is cold. A thin dressing of snow still lingers on the ground. As the procession makes its way from the church to the cemetery, a sharp wind snaps at the priest's cassock, wafts the sweet tang of incense far and wide when he swings the censer, and nips the cheeks of the mourners, most of whom wish he would walk a little faster. The memorial meal, to be taken at the graveside in the old way, will be a chilly affair. But in any case, there will not be much on the menu to detain the mourners for long.

Old man Griboyev is here, with his wife and all four of their daughters. It was his wife who, in the absence of any known family, washed and clothed poor Marya's body.

A few other neighbors from the dom on Lobachev Row have come along, as has the caretaker. Marya's foreman and her fellow workers have also shown up. The foreman persuaded the work gang to cough up a few rubles with which to pay the priest, he himself making the heftiest contribution when he saw that the total was looking a bit light.

But the priest has done right by Marya; he has given full measure. It was a good solid service, with plenty of Scripture readings and hymns, and, of course, that long funeral psalm, the Bible's longest. The little congregation held candles and stood throughout the service, though Griboyev was worried that his knees might not last the course. "I am laid low in the dust," lamented the psalmist—a fate that Griboyev feared for himself. But he got through.

Then everyone came forward in turn to whisper a final goodbye before the priest sprinkled a little soil and holy oil in the coffin and closed the lid.

At the foreman's urging, Griboyev has agreed to hold Pasha's drawings and Marya's letters in safekeeping, along with the shawl she loved so much, the black one with the tiny blue cornflowers, as well as the portrait of Comrade Stalin and her precious icon of Christ. There was nothing else in the apartment worth keeping.

"Her son will want those things," the foreman assures Griboyev as they shuffle behind the coffin. "You never know, he might come back one of these days."

"He might," agrees Griboyev, who does not believe it for a moment. In any case, he is wondering how long he will be able to hang on to the items. There is little enough space for the six Griboyevs in their apartment; and his wife, while she has a good heart, does have a habit of disposing of things without warning or consultation. There is, though, one gem she has her eye on: that shawl of Marya's.

"She'd want me to have it," she has already remarked to her husband, more than once. "Who was it who washed her as if she was family? We were like sisters. You know that."

As for himself, he would happily keep young Pasha's drawings forever. He misses the boy. He misses the sheer joy of watching him do his magic.

He sighs and scratches his stubbled chin. More pressing than these matters, of course, is the question of who might be allocated Marya's apartment. Will his family ever have as good a neighbor again?

Another sigh. All in all, death can be such a nuisance.

* * *

Here is another funeral. But this one looks more like the eve of war, for every branch of the military is represented, in unimaginable numbers, with column after column of perfectly drilled men and women assembling since well before dawn. Endless fleets of military vehicles course through the Moscow streets. Fighter aircraft will pass overhead in a last salute.

There is snow on all the roofs, but Red Square and the streets along which the cortège will pass have been swept clear of every last flake. Marya would be moved to see such love and respect shown to her Josef Vissarionovich.

Above all, here are his beloved people. The capital has never known such crowds. They are a river in full spate, all in black and darkest gray, their faces gaunt and sorrowful, their collective breath a white cloud in the cold air above them, like souls ascending. They flood the wide boulevards from wall to wall of the buildings on either side, pressed so close together that individuals can lift their feet from the ground and be carried forward when the crowd surges.

And, alas, the crowd does surge. People scream as they are swept against walls and lampposts. They see the danger rushing toward them, they know what is coming—but who can do anything, who can stop this torrent? No one intends harm but no one can stop it either. Faces smash against metal and stone, bones are crushed, bodies slide to the ground and become a soft carpet from which the life is trampled. Short people have it hardest—some simply suffocate.

So it is that, even in death, Josef Vissarionovich contrives to keep his beloved people close.

CHAPTER 38

By the time dawn arrives, Pasha is ready to collapse. His legs are like lead.

The snow has stopped at last. He is covered in snow and frost from head to foot, a living snowman. He watches as the red sun breaks the horizon, turning the white landscape pink and coral as if a brush is sweeping washes of color across it. The sky is clear and the distant mountains over which the sun is rising can only be the Urals—meaning that he has kept to the correct bearing. The relief is like a dawn blossoming in his own heart.

He does not know how far he has walked or how much farther it still is to his destination. Neither matters. What else is there for him to do? Where else would he go?

He looks back the way he has come and sees the tracks in the snow that he is making. They are clear evidence of his whereabouts. He has to hope they will soon be buried by fresh falls of snow.

But who out here will see them? Wherever he turns to look, from horizon to horizon, there is only the snow plain. Nothing moves. There is not even a shadow to break the monotony of the snow, only swirls and curves that form and reform across the landscape with the gusting wind. He heard the wolves through the night, but looking around now at this endless wasteland, he could be the only living creature on the planet.

He knows it is a deceptive notion. Worse, it is dangerous. It would tempt him to break his rule about not traveling during daylight. It is the kind of conceit that the emptiness of this place conjures up. Some remote Red Army detachment might embark on maneuvers that would result in their coming upon him; or the soldiers who investigated the camp might already have been ordered to search for escapees and even now be only minutes from him. Those empty horizons that seem so far away—are they really that far, are they really devoid of other human life? To assume he is alone and therefore safe could be lethal. He hardens himself against doing so. Danger is never far away. To believe anything else is a mirage.

Weary as he is, he knows he cannot rest yet—he has work to do first, to keep himself safe during the hours of daylight. He chooses one of the frozen pools where a large snowdrift, as tall as himself, has formed in its dip. He uses the shovel to dig his way into the drift and beats the floor of the tunnel until it is flat and solid, making a shelter, a sort of cave. He works steadily but slowly, careful to avoid sweating, since perspiration would reduce his body temperature dangerously as it cools.

He crawls inside, taking the shovel with him in case the construction collapses; at the very least he can use the shaft to make a ventilation hole. He leaves the entrance open to allow some light, and removes his gloves so that he can examine his fingers.

They are soft to the touch, as if the flesh is melting. There is no pain in them. There is still no feeling of any kind, neither in any finger he touches nor in the tip of the finger of the other hand with which he probes it.

He unpacks the knife and tries to slice slivers of fat from some cuts of cooked beefsteak. His hands are clumsy at this. He cannot grip the knife firmly. He cannot push or pull it accurately in the direction he wants. Such a small thing, but he cannot do it.

When he finally manages to hack some slivers off, he wraps them about his fingers and tries to put the gloves on again. Both of these tasks prove as impossible as manipulating the knife. In desperation he inserts the slivers of fat into the fingers of the gloves however he can and pulls the gloves on, hoping that he will still achieve some extra measure of insulation.

He tries to eat some of the meat and bread but he has no appetite despite the energy he has used. He knows it is because of anxiety. All he can manage is to swallow some snow, first letting it melt in his mouth in tiny quantities so that it does not sear his throat or stomach.

After this he closes the entrance to the shelter with his backpack, leaving a small gap for air. The shelter will retain his body heat.

It is dark now inside the shelter. It is like a womb. It is also like a grave. He lies down with his head by the entrance, wraps himself in his blankets, and curls up to concentrate his body heat in as small a space as possible. He winds a scarf about his head to prevent his eyes from freezing while they are closed. He wonders if he will be able to sleep. He wonders if he will wake.

* * *

He does sleep. And he does wake, because the shrieking of the wind makes sure of that, a shriek that he recognizes immediately as the sound of a buran. He is helpless. There is nowhere to go. He can do nothing but stay where he is as the storm rages over him.

But something is changing inside the shelter. At first, he cannot identify what it is. He twists his head to look up. A patch of light has appeared above him. A hole. He is seeing daylight, the white fog of the buran. The change he senses is the change in air pressure caused by the storm. Now the darkness in the shelter is changing, too, dispersed by light as the hole enlarges. The wind is peeling the top of the snowdrift away. The shelter is beginning to disintegrate.

The suction of the storm is such that he can hardly breathe. He stretches out full length, making himself as flat as possible, trying to press his body down into the snow. But he has packed the snow solid and it yields hardly at all. As the snowdrift is ripped apart, hail hammers along his body, large frozen chunks as hard as rocks. The wind tears at him, trying to pluck him up and carry him away. He realizes that the blanket that covered him has gone, though he was unaware of its departure. The shovel is still by his side. He must not lose it, so he shifts his body to pin it in place. In doing so, he takes some of his weight off the blanket beneath him. Instantly it is gone. He has lost both blankets.

He is clinging with two hands to the backpack but he can feel his fur shapka beginning to lift from his head. The fastening has been torn. He cannot let the shapka be taken—the hailstones will crack his head open; or if he survives that, he will freeze to death if his shaven head is bare.

He takes his left hand away from the backpack and clamps it on top of his head, securing the shapka. The wind immediately detaches the lantern from the backpack. He tries to pull the backpack closer so that he can hook his right arm into one of the shoulder straps and grab hold of the untethered lantern. But he is too clumsy, too slow, and the wind has other ideas.

With sickening clarity, he realizes that he must choose between the backpack and the lantern; he cannot have both. In fact, it will be a feat against the odds if he can hang on to either.

He must decide quickly. The backpack has all his food. Without it he may starve to death. And he will have no knife, no protection against the wolves.

But without the lantern—

He dare not lose the lantern. He frees his right hand from the backpack and stretches out in time to slam it down on the lantern. At once, just as he feared, the backpack shoots away from him. In desperation, he lunges with his left hand, jeopardizing the shapka. But he is too late. The backpack is gone. He clamps his hand back on the fur hat. He shouts into the storm—no words, just a howl of anguish. There is a malevolence in the wind that seems conscious, intentional. After everything he has been through, it is unjust.

He wants to chase the backpack, find it, retrieve it. But if he climbs to his feet, the storm may carry him away, too.

But if he does not chase the backpack, he may starve.

It is one decision too many for him. He cannot handle it. So he does nothing—which is a decision in itself. He stays where he is. Let the storm do what it will.

* * *

The buran ends as suddenly as it began. The wind dies. The hail stops. The sky clears. Astonishingly, the sun appears. He even feels its warmth.

He pushes himself slowly to his feet and takes stock. Nothing is broken, though his limbs are still stiff and awkward. He aches all over, but the greatcoats and the rope around his trunk have protected him from the worst of the hail's battering. He feels something move on his face. When he touches his cheek there is a stream of blood on his glove, its bright scarlet vivid on the crusted snow. He finds many places on his face where the razor-sharp shards of ice carried by the buran have cut him.

He checks the lantern. Its glass and burner are intact and the reservoir is undamaged; he hears the kerosene sloshing inside.

He looks around. The buran has done him one favor—it has obliterated his tracks not only in this immediate area but also far beyond. But there is no sign of the backpack or its contents, neither the food nor the knife. They could be anywhere, several kilometers away, scattered who knows where—or they might be only meters from him. They could be buried deep in snow or concealed by no more than a thin covering.

He wanders about for a while, searching and poking with the shovel and kicking through drifts, ridges, any uneven rises of snow, widening the scope of his search as he goes. But he is wasting his time. He is wasting energy, too—with the food gone, a more important consideration than ever.

So he stops his wandering about, abandons his search. He can still survive, he tells himself, food or no food.

Perhaps it is a foolish thing to believe. Perhaps a blue sky and a bright sun have made him delusional. Hope is a perilous companion, inclined to treachery. He of all people knows that. But he does not care. He adds the buran to the list of adversaries and circumstances he has overcome. He will overcome the lack of food as well. It is water that is the essential, and he will not be short of that. His plan can still work—it *must* work. He will not give up. He can still survive.

In his heart he knows he has to tell himself this, because he has no choice but to believe it.

He finds another deep snowdrift, digs another shelter, and waits for night.

CHAPTER 39

By that second night of travel, he knows his body is failing him. Hunger is to blame. Even while he slept, its pangs gnawed ceaselessly at him. The meals in the camp now present themselves to his imagination as rich repasts. All he has eaten are small portions of the slivers of beef fat he slipped into his gloves the first morning. His method is to make them last as long as possible by sucking them for short periods as he walks and only allowing himself to bite off a corner and chew it when the hunger becomes unbearable. He has no idea how much food value there may be in the fat, if any. It hardly matters, since he has nothing else. What he does know is that the times when the hunger becomes too much are coming closer together and are more intense. These are times when the pain ratchets so high that he moans aloud.

He wonders if the fat will become rancid. Or if it already has. He wonders if that would stop him from sucking and eating it. But he knows the answer to that question.

His fingers above their top joints have taken on a grayish-blue tinge. Yesterday when he examined them, they were soft, but now they look as if they are made of wax; and they have become hard, like wax. He nips the flesh between fingernail and thumbnail and as usual feels nothing.

Suddenly, his head spins and the black sky seems to ripple like water, like the black river that took Viktor. The dizziness is so bad that he does not trust his ability to remain upright and instead falls to his knees. He drops the shovel and lantern, lurches forward, his hands outstretched to support his weight, and retches. He brings nothing up, but the dry heaving is painful. He stays there, head down, eyes unfocused, saliva dripping from his open mouth.

There is no goodness left in his body. He is empty, a husk, a shell. He wonders if there is blood left in his veins. He wonders if there is blood left in his fingers.

Throughout the rest of that night and the night following, there is more snow, thick and heavy. There is wind, but nothing with the malice of a buran. The snow falls for most of the hours of darkness.

His mind becomes as numb as his body. He has been reduced to a mechanical structure of muscle and bone that stumbles through this unending emptiness. It seems to be all he has done since the beginning of time and all he will do until time ends.

There must be pain in his body, he reasons, but he no longer feels it, neither in his hands nor in any other part of him. He does not notice his swollen and broken lips, scorched by cold. He is indifferent to the frost in his eyes and the icicles in his eyelashes and the cracked skin in his frozen nostrils.

Nor does he grow tired. This is not a benefit; on the contrary, it is worrying. It is as if the numbness is blocking any sense of tiredness—as if his body's warning systems are shutting down: no pain, no tiredness, and even the hunger pangs have stopped. He just keeps going forward, one boot following the other, his mind as blank as the wilderness around it. The risk is that he will keep on until his bodily functions simply stop.

But would that be such a bad thing? If death comes softly and peacefully, if it steals upon him, if it is nothing worse than a quiet cessation, with neither pain nor fear, would that not be a blessed relief, a release?

No. He will not allow death to come, he will not let it in so easily. He will not open the door to death as if it is an invited guest. He has fought and fought; death is a thief, not a guest. It, too, will have to fight if it wants to take him. And it must fight like the very devil that sends it.

He toils on.

* * *

He becomes aware that he is being plagued by thoughts that he cannot dislodge. One is a growing conviction that he was wrong to abandon the search for the backpack and his food. He should go back and look more thoroughly for them.

Another is a belief that he is being followed, that someone is hunting him, tracking him and watching him, keeping behind him and beyond his vision.

His mind keeps turning to the small animals he knows there are in the tundra, that serve as regular prey for the wolves, bears, and Arctic foxes—tiny creatures such as shrews and mice. He, too, could eat them. They are here somewhere, all around him, burrowing beneath the snow in tunnels and tiny caves. They are right beneath his feet as he walks. Surely he could gather them in handfuls, cram his mouth full of them. All he has to do is pause, bend down, and catch them. It would be child's play—as simple as plucking fruit from a tree.

But the most distressing notion is that Viktor did not die in the black river. He climbed out only to find that Pasha had gone, had forsaken him. He would have survived if Pasha had stayed a little longer. He called for help but Pasha was too far away to hear.

These fancies are like constant background noise in Pasha's mind. He remembers fearing for his sanity in the camp. Now he thinks that if these imaginings are not proof that he is already insane, they will soon drive him that way.

* * *

Something else is tugging for his attention, always in the background, a feeling that he cannot at first put a name to.

It cannot be fear, because he already knows he is afraid and has long since come to accept that. There is nothing new in fear.

It is not hunger, for he has come to accept that, too.

It is not sorrow—though it is in some way akin to sorrow and gathers itself into a black, sluggish heaviness inside him in the way that sorrow does.

Finally, he understands what it is. He stops walking, as if a physical obstacle has been placed in his path.

The feeling is loneliness.

He is infuriated by this. Loneliness is self-pity by another name. Just as he will not open his soul to death, neither will he open his heart to loneliness.

He raises his foot, places it, hears the crunch of snow as he steps forward, and tramps on.

* * *

It is daybreak. He hears a faint buzzing as he is making his shelter. He stops digging and listens. It is far too early in the year for mosquitoes and there is no liquid water. Besides, the buzz is steadier than that of mosquitoes.

It is growing louder. It is an aircraft.

In panic he flings himself into the half-dug shelter. There has been no snow for some hours. His tracks are visible, both his route here and the area where he has been working, circling the shelter and dumping the excavated snow.

He lies there, his heart pounding, as the buzz reaches its maximum volume, then diminishes as quickly as it came.

But he does not leave the shelter. Fear still grips him. It is no longer fear of the aircraft itself; it is fear of what he discovered was happening to him while he cowered in the dimness beneath the snow. As the aircraft passed overhead, there arose within him a fierce urge to rush outside and do everything he could to attract the pilot's attention. A blind instinct in him was ready to sacrifice everything for the sake of one simple thing: contact with another human being.

So it is not only hope that is a perilous companion; this loneliness that has crept up on him can betray him, too.

He does not sleep that day. Thereafter he never stops listening for the aircraft's return—not in order to give himself up, but to make sure the loneliness can never win.

* * *

He no longer itches. He cannot strip off his clothing to look for lice, but in the parts of the garments he can see, there are only a few small gray corpses as hard as ice.

The cold is too much for them. Either that or his blood no longer has enough nutrients to sustain them.

* * *

He is not always alone now. Sometimes he is aware of a presence close by as he tramps through the darkness, someone who matches him pace by pace, from time to time pressing ahead and gazing back to urge him on.

It is Viktor.

* * *

By that night he knows how sick he has become. He knows he is coming close to death—or rather that death, the uninvited thief, is coming close to him. It is death that has been stalking him, tracking and watching him.

The shivers that grip his body are constant now, but he knows that if they stop at this stage, it is the beginning of the end. There will then follow a time when he no longer feels cold but feels hot and wants to discard all his clothing. People have been found naked, frozen to death, yet with all their clothing neatly folded beside their bodies.

Mental confusion of any kind is a danger sign, so he sets himself tasks to make sure that he does not descend into such a state. He counts backwards from one hundred in units of seven, then six, then three, then awkward combinations of these. He tries calling up from memory a Leonardo drawing—the one that surfaces is a series of designs for war chariots—and begins to trace each line. But he abandons this when he realizes that he has entered the drawing as if he is at his work table or in the Tretyakov Gallery with Sergei in that other life he once had—the chariots race past with their slingshots and saw-toothed wheels, he feels the breeze of the arrow the archer has just released, hears the snap of the bowstring.

The same thing will happen with any other drawing he tries—the power of Leonardo's images is too strong and he falls too readily into them. Losing himself in the drawings will not sharpen his mental functions; it will bypass them and make him more vulnerable. He needs something else.

Suddenly the prayer is in his mind, one that Mama taught him. He is standing by her side before the holy icon.

"Pray with me, Pashenka. We'll pray together."

His fractured lips form the words. "I will lift up my eyes to the hills. From where comes my help? My help comes from the Lord, who made heaven and earth."

He hears Mama respond. "He will not allow your foot to slip; he who keeps you will not slumber. The Lord will protect you; the Lord is your shelter at your right hand. The sun will not burn you by day, nor the moon by night. The Lord will preserve you from all evil; the Lord will preserve your soul."

The prayer ascends into the darkness. The globe of the world consists only of this frozen desert iced over with loneliness and grief, but Pasha prays and believes with all his heart that he will not be lost, that death will not prevail.

CHAPTER 40

IT IS NIGHT now. But which night? His sixth? He has lost count. Walk, rest, walk, and sometimes sleep. He just goes on, always on, head down, boot following boot, always watching every step, always as straight a course as he can, with always the crunch of snow at every step.

The thoughts that have been tormenting him are joined by another, the most unsettling of all. He is now bedeviled by the fear that his navigation has gone wrong, not merely by a few degrees but to the extent that he is walking in circles or doubling back. He should surely be there by now. He was a fool to think he could get this right.

The hunger pangs have returned. They are worse than ever. Hunger obsesses him completely now. He is nothing but an empty stomach riven by craving, a stomach with no brain, no humanity, no emotions or feelings except hunger. The slivers of fat are gone, all of them consumed. He is tortured by endless images of food: everything from lavish dishes he has never in his life set eyes on, with bizarre combinations of foodstuffs, to the simplest things—a crust of bread, an apple. He can taste them, he even salivates. The saliva runs down his chin and freezes.

In this state he is only vaguely conscious that the moon has emerged from behind its cover of cloud. He raises his head and glimpses something.

He is not sure if the shape is really there or not. It is still some way ahead. He comes to a halt. The snow is still falling, still thick. He peers through its lacework, moving his head from side to side in an attempt to see better.

A gust of wind sweeps the snow aside for a second. It is long enough. He sees clearly. The shape is there.

It is a long, low contour on the ground, a low ridge, so low that it is only just discernible. It intersects his path and stretches across as much of the landscape as he can make out. It runs as straight as an arrow. Here and there it is interrupted by drifts of snow but it resumes its straight course after each one.

There can be no question what it is. There is nothing else in this empty landscape that it could be.

He moves forward again, his stride lengthening with each step. There is urgency now, as if he fears that the vision might be snatched from him. But if it is only a heartless illusion, the sooner he knows the better.

He pushes himself to a pace that is as close to running as he can achieve. It is the fastest pace he has set since he chased after Viktor. The falling snow is joined by cascades flung up by his boots. The scarves slip from his mouth and nose, exposing his throat and lungs to the air, but he is unaware. He misses his footing several times but manages to right himself and carries on, never losing his grip on the lantern or the shovel.

He arrives, panting so hard that every breath sounds like a death rattle, the freezing air burning his throat, his chest in agony. He doubles over and clutches his knees for support, and has to wait for his body to recover and his eyes to clear.

And at last, here it is. It was no illusion. Here are the two low ridges, parallel, running straight and true through the drifts of snow to disappear into the darkness. He thrusts the shovel into the crust of snow. It strikes metal. He has reached the rail line. Just as Irina's crude sketch promised.

* * *

He retraces his steps until he is fifty or sixty meters from the rail line, and digs a shelter.

The sky is still dark when he feels the tremor in the ground. Then he hears the distant rumble. He leaves the shelter but stays hidden behind the snowdrift. The tremor grows stronger. The rumble resolves into the unmistakable clackety-clack of the train. The hairs rise on the back of his neck, not only from hearing that sound again but because he knows he would have to wait another full week for this moment if he had failed to arrive here in time. He would have to stay here, with no food, not knowing if he would still be alive when the train finally passes again.

He bows his head. "The Lord will protect you . . ."

Almost before he knows what is happening, the beams of light are carving through the darkness and the mighty locomotive is roaring past, shaking the earth and casting huge waves of snow to either side. Its thunder pounds through his body as it did before; he sees the lit windows of passenger carriages and the dark voids that indicate cattle wagons. A mixed consignment: perhaps military or mining personnel or whatever other passengers are privileged to travel as human beings rather than animals, and with them new batches of prisoners for the mining camp.

It will be daybreak when the train reaches Vorkuta. And night when it passes here again on its return.

He will be ready. He has come this far, he has achieved this much and survived. He will be ready.

CHAPTER 41

He tries to sleep but he is too full of what must be done and what is to come, the risks involved and how—indeed, whether—he can overcome them.

He will not die now, he reassures himself. God will not allow him to die. He only needs to hold on for a few more hours.

He watches the snow throughout the day. It never stops for long, which is good—the tracks he made in reaching the rail line are soon buried. The sun never breaks through the clouds, but he catches enough faint glimmers to follow its course across the sky as the day passes.

When he judges it is time, he picks out the tallest snowdrift that has piled up on the rail line since the train passed. He plants the shovel upright beside the track and hooks the lantern into the notch he made at the end of the shaft, the red side of the glass facing outwards. He unwinds the rope from his body and ties it to the shovel. He leaves enough slack so that he can lash the lantern securely to the shovel as well. Lantern and shovel must stay together.

No part of this task is easy. He is still trembling throughout his whole body—powerful shivers that shake his legs, his trunk, his arms and hands. The work with the rope is the hardest. Even with his gloves off, his fingers fumble and are unresponsive. He notices that they are now red and blotchy, as if they have been scalded.

He is mindful of the engineer who fell against the steel fence, and is careful never to touch the metal lantern with his bare hands. Because of his shivers it takes him several attempts to light it. Then he moves the shovel to the snowdrift, planting it right in the middle of the rail line, positioning it as high up on the drift as he can.

He assesses his work. Everything is done. He is almost fainting from the lack of food and whatever sickness is ravaging his body. He knows death is still waiting for its chance—but he is not dead and he has accomplished everything as he planned it. Death has not won.

Nor will it. Not now.

He walks away from the rail line, paying out the rope as he goes. When he reaches its end, this is where he must wait. He wishes the rope were longer so that he could be farther from the rail line. Here there is no snowdrift within reach that he can tunnel into or hide behind; and now that the light is beginning its slow fade into night, he cannot simply drop the rope in the snow, for fear of never finding it again. What he wants is the snow to continue falling, to cover as much as possible of the latest set of tracks he has made. Bad enough that he will leave fresh ones in due course.

In the absence of any snowdrift, he crouches down and lets the snow cover him, as it has done throughout his journey. His hope now is that the living snowman will merge into the landscape.

He watches the red glow of the lantern. It is his comfort, like the candle beneath Mama's holy icon. The flame flickers in the darkness but it holds.

* * *

The locomotive driver, one of the two men who share this marathon journey between them, is a seasoned and attentive man. He never takes his eyes off the rail line stretching ahead. This is not because of the dangers of meeting another train, for there is no other train to meet in this godforsaken expanse of nothing. As he comes closer to Moscow, yes, conceivably, or even once he passes Pechora; but not way out here.

Reindeer and brown bears, these are what are on his mind. No animal is large enough to pose a danger of derailment to the locomotive, but the pelts and meat of reindeer and bear are worth a fortune. The difficulty is that the very size of the locomotive means that even a bear would be flicked aside like a fly by the snow scoop without the impact ever being felt at all. What a loss that would be. So the driver watches the rail line carefully.

This is why he sees the red light up ahead the instant it emerges from the screen of snow. He knows there are no signals anywhere near here. The light has to signify someone working on the line.

But at night? That can only mean serious trouble, an emergency.

Even as he thinks these things, he is already braking the huge locomotive and sounding the whistle's warning.

* * *

The instant Pasha hears the unearthly shriek and the screech of the wheels grinding against the rails, he rises to his feet and yanks the rope as hard as he can, a sudden sharp tug. Lantern and shovel are whipped from the snowdrift together. The lantern extinguishes. He reels the rope in as fast as he can, looping it over his arm. When he has retrieved about half of it, he begins running at a crouch toward the train, which has not yet stopped. He continues to reel the rope in as he goes. He has to turn sideways every few steps to do this, but his hands keep losing their grip on the rope, so that he is in danger of tripping on the loops.

He is beyond the beam of the locomotive's front lamps now, and glad of it even though he knows that the driver's attention is probably wholly on the rail line and the place where the red light was. There are passengers here and there in the carriages, but Pasha knows they will not see him. He is well below their line of sight, and in any case, all they will perceive, if they even bother looking, is their own reflections in the windows.

The train finally comes to a halt just as he reaches one of the cattle wagons. He has all the rope in his arms now, along with the shovel and the lantern. But he has left evidence behind, as he knew he would: tracks in the snow, including the drag marks as he reeled in the rope.

He can see the locomotive, but he sees no movement there. He cannot see the driver or what the man is doing. He does not know if he is safe. He may have only seconds before the driver raises the alarm. Or before the train simply moves off again.

But he cannot do anything more just yet. He has no strength left. He slumps against the wagon, clings to it, and tries to find reserves from somewhere.

He looks up at the side of the wagon, but in the darkness he cannot see whether its door is padlocked. If it is, he will have to try another wagon—if there is time. How many might he have to try? What if all of them are locked?

Then all will be lost, all will have been in vain. He will perish beside this railroad of the dead. Death will have won after all.

Death and, from beyond the grave, Josef Vissarionovich.

* * *

The driver has jumped down from the locomotive. He cannot understand what is going on—one moment the light was there, the next it had vanished. Either someone extinguished it or they carried it off. In either case, why?

He calls out. No one answers. He sets off along the track, toward where the light was—if it really was there at all. He is beginning to have his doubts. He feels foolish. A certain quantity of vodka flowed earlier today. Out here a man needs a drink to keep him going.

Behind him he hears the fireman calling.

"What's going on?"

"There was a red light."

"Where?"

"Up ahead."

"No light now."

The driver shakes his head. A real intellectual, the fireman.

There is nothing to be seen. Only snow. Only snowdrifts. So, what else was he expecting?

It is bitterly cold. Not a night for standing about. His warm cab is waiting for him. Besides, what if a bear is watching him from the darkness?

That last reflection is enough for him. He does not look beyond the rail line; he does not see the tracks or drag marks in the snow. He turns around and slogs back to the locomotive as fast as he can.

Easy on the vodka next time, he vows.

* * *

The door is not padlocked. Pasha summons what he knows is the last of his physical power, grabs the edge of the door, and drags it sideways. It slides open. He tosses the rope, the lantern, and the shovel through the doorway and pushes himself up after them.

The interior of the wagon is pitch black, darker than the night outside. He pulls himself all the way in and collapses on the floor.

He is just in time. The locomotive's whistle blares. The train begins to move off. The door is slammed shut behind Pasha.

"Who the hell are you?" demands a voice from the darkness of the wagon.

CHAPTER 42

As far as Pasha can reckon, there are about a dozen men in the wagon. Someone has grabbed the lantern and lit it so that they can have a look at the intruder.

"You're a zek," someone says.

He manages to sit up. No one offers to help him. He sees their striped clothing in the lamplight, just as they have seen his beneath his greatcoats.

"So are you," he replies. "You're zeks, too."

"Not anymore we're not."

"You escaped?"

"No need. They released us. We were in the mining camp."

The men fire question after question at him—they demand his name, want to know where he has come from, which camp, how he escaped, how he got to the rail line. Eventually, exhausted, he stops answering.

There is one man who takes no part in the interrogation, though he listens to everything. He is wearing spectacles carved from wood, with thick lenses held in place by rims of glue. The glue makes Pasha picture Irina mending her boot on the evening she drew the map for him.

It is a relief when the man tells the questioners to stop. They do not argue. They seem to be used to deferring to him. He introduces himself to Pasha as Gennady. He says he is a doctor.

"Pasha, when did you last eat?"

Pasha has to think about this. His brain seems to have slowed down.

"I had some pieces of beef fat. Before that, about a week ago."

Gennady swipes the worst of the snow and ice from Pasha's clothes and face, then wraps him in blankets.

"We need to raise your body temperature."

He prepares a thin broth by immersing a small square of beef in water and heating it in a tin cup over the flame of Pasha's lantern. He makes sure that the broth is not too strong and waits until it has cooled, then passes the cup to Pasha.

"Slowly," he warns. "Small sips only."

He removes the crust from a hunk of bread and soaks the softer flesh in the broth so that it is easy to swallow and poses less risk of choking, and for the same reason makes him chew the beef until it breaks down to small shreds. Pasha has to fight hard against the urge to devour the food in one desperate gulp.

Gradually his shivers subside, though they never stop entirely. Gennady, his eyes made large by the lenses, watches him closely as he squats beside him. It is like being observed by an owl. The other men stand or sit, whispering or talking quietly. They still glance suspiciously at Pasha.

"So you were in the camp out beyond ours in the tundra," prompts Gennady. "The one along the ice road."

Pasha nods.

"No one seemed to know much about that place, not even our Red Army guards. What was going on there, what sort of work?"

"Art forgery. I'm an artist. All of us were artists. We were forging foreign art."

Gennady does not conceal his surprise. "Why did they have you doing that?"

"We never knew. By the time it was brought to an end, most of us had been executed or had died in other ways. There were only two of us left. They tried to kill us by torching the place."

"That explains the flames we saw."

"I'm the only one who got away. I want to get to Moscow and then home. In the meantime, just forget about me. Thank you for what you've done."

"Well, you see, Pasha, we can't just forget about you. As an escapee, you're a wanted man. That puts us at risk."

"No one saw me board the train. If they had, it wouldn't have got underway."

"That's not what I'm referring to. As of yesterday, the rest of us here are free men. You're not, which means we're harboring a fugitive. If you're found, that puts us right back in the gulag."

"What do you want to do—put me off the train?"

Gennady sighs and shakes his head. "We won't do that. You're still one of us. We'll figure out something."

"Why have you been released?"

"There's been some kind of amnesty following Stalin's death—well, for some of us, namely non-politicals with sentences of less than five years. Also pregnant women, mothers with young children." He frowns. "You do know Stalin's dead, don't you?"

Pasha nods. "The controlling mind and will."

"What?"

"Just something I couldn't figure out until a while ago."

"Apparently, releases like ours are happening in many of the camps. From the way our guards were talking, it sounds like everything's upside down in Moscow. No one knows what will happen now or who's calling the shots. Plenty of rumors but no way to tell what's true and what isn't."

Pasha tries to concentrate on what Gennady is saying, but it is becoming difficult. The restorative effect of the broth and bread is wearing off and his energy is fading.

He is also worried about his hands. He removes his gloves and begins to rub his hands together in the hope of restoring some kind of feeling. There is still no sensation in the fingers. He investigates them in the light from the lantern. They are still red and blotched and the nails are discolored with unnatural splotches of dark green and blue, almost black; but his eyesight seems to be going wrong as well and there are strange colors and shadows everywhere.

Now that his nostrils are clear of ice, he is also aware of a foul odor, as of something rotting. He does not know if it is coming from the wagon, which is filthy, or from himself—from his hands.

Gennady continues watching him for a few moments.

"No more talk now, Pasha. You need to rest. But first I think I should examine those hands. Have you been physically sick?"

Pasha does not reply. Slumped in the slime and filth of the cattle wagon, he has slipped into unconsciousness.

* * *

He awakens to pain. Excruciating pain. He has never known such pain. Out on the frozen tundra he was numb, a vacuum, a husk that felt nothing. That is no longer the case. Now he is a mass of raw nerves, all of them in agony. Pain that he never imagined possible racks his body, deep physical pain rooted within him. He is on fire. There is no stopping it. It hurts when he inhales, hurts when he exhales. His eyes are burning in their sockets. He is no longer sitting but is lying on his back, the blankets tight around him. When he tries to move his head to look around, the pain is terrible, his head throbs, his chest is exploding.

Everything is confused. It is daylight, bright daylight—impossible daylight, for it was dark just a minute ago except for the glimmering lantern. The door is wide open. This accounts for the daylight. But what became of the night? The rocking motion of the wagon has ended, there is no clatter of train wheels. So the train must have stopped. People are moving about, figures silhouetted against the daylight.

Now the pain is contracting, somehow drawing its force together. It is not reducing in magnitude, it is simply focusing its location, as if being concentrated through a lens. The pain no longer courses through his body. It is in his hands, only in his hands. And it is fearsome, terrible. It is all the worse for being concentrated in this way. It feels as if all the pain in the world has flown into his hands.

Then Gennady is beside him, gripping his shoulder.

"Easy, Pasha."

Easy? Why does he say that? Did Pasha cry out? Was he thrashing as Viktor said Irina did in her fever? Has he been unconscious? Was he delirious?

"We're in Moscow," continues Gennady. He speaks calmly, soothingly. "Yaroslavsky station. I've convinced the security unit who'll check us off the train that there's been an error, that our release docket should include you. Frankly, I think there's such disarray in Moscow that no one cares much. You'll come home with me. It's not far. There's only my wife, we have room for you. You must rest. That's what you need now—plenty of rest and proper food."

Yaroslavsky station. Pasha is sure he knows that name. Images come to him, though they are confused and for the moment he has difficulty locating their origin: an ocean of light; lofty curved ceilings gleaming like marble; a cacophony of inexplicable noises.

"You've been out cold for the entire journey—morphine, the last I had and there wasn't much. It'll be wearing off now, but you'll still be groggy for a while; it's still in your system."

Gennady pauses and seems to be weighing his next words. His gaze never leaves Pasha's face.

"Listen to me, Pasha, there's something you need to understand. You're physically weak—well, all of us here are, but you especially, after what you've been through and the lack of food. And you were hypothermic. You were as close to death as I've ever seen, and I've seen many such cases these last years. I think you're through the worst now and out of danger, but your hands . . . Pasha, listen, you contracted severe frostbite. There was the risk of gangrene. Gangrene—do you understand? Gangrene kills. Are you taking in what I'm saying? I couldn't let you run that risk. I'm sorry, I know you're an artist, but there was no other way. Are you listening?"

Pasha is in the Artists' Union. Sergei is lecturing him and grumbling.

"Yes, Comrade Professor. I'm listening. I'm always listening."

Gennady blinks but says nothing.

The Artists' Union is gone.

Gangrene.

Pasha discovers that his hands are pinned across his chest within the tightly wound blankets. With Gennady's help, he withdraws the left hand. He raises it before his face. He needs a moment for his eyes to adjust to the glare of the daylight. The hand slowly comes into focus.

There is an immediate sick feeling in his stomach. No, no, this is wrong, it cannot be right. What is this, what is he looking at? It must be a trick of the light, still blinding him.

He squints harder. There is no improvement in what he sees. There is no mistake. The thumb and all the fingers are individually bandaged. But they are too short. How can they be so short? They are no longer fingers. They are only stumps. The hand is no longer a hand. It is a paw.

Desperate now, he asks himself if this is part of the delirium. But he knows it is not.

He works his right hand free and raises it. It is the same.

* * *

"Pasha—are you awake?"

He manages a weak nod. Has he been asleep? No, he realizes; this time he knows he was unconscious, in a dead faint. He remembers Irina's description of waking from her sleeping dream and how bad it felt when memory came back.

There is activity in the wagon. Gennady rises from time to time and exchanges a few words with his companions. The men have obtained ordinary clothing from somewhere and are changing into it, becoming regular citizens again rather than zeks. They and Gennady share handshakes and embraces, and the men depart in ones and twos.

After the last of them has gone, Gennady returns to Pasha and squats down beside him.

"You won't be up to walking, Pasha. A couple of my comrades are fetching a stretcher. They won't be long."

There is a flutter of movement beside them. A city sparrow has flown into the wagon. Gennady shoos the bird out. It withdraws to the platform but returns as soon as he looks away. It pecks at the crust of bread that he tore up for Pasha, then seizes the whole crust and takes flight. It alights on the platform, triumphant with its prize.

Pasha watches the little bird until the morphine takes hold again and he escapes back into sleep.

PART TWO

CHAPTER 43

Days and weeks—the remainder of March and half of April—are lost to Pasha as his body uses sleep to heal itself. Long afterwards, fragments of memory will drift into his mind, small unbidden cameos from this closed portion of his life: Gennady's face floating over him, anxious eyes behind murky spectacle lenses; his wife, Valentina, changing Pasha's bandages; the taste of the broth she spoons for him; the soft murmur of the couple's voices in conversation, as soothing as parents' voices to an almost-sleeping child.

Gradually, he sleeps less, and his periods of consciousness become sharper. Sleep was protecting him from the worst of the physical pain, but now as his mind begins to clear he has the psychological and emotional challenge of coming to terms with his ruined hands. The most basic physical tasks must be relearned: how to handle clothes—buttons are the worst thing—how to grasp cutlery, everyday functions of personal hygiene.

It is late April before he can pick up and grip a pencil and hold it for long enough to scratch a word or two on a sheet of paper. The strain of this undertaking and the pathetic result produced by his labors force tears to his eyes.

But this is only writing. In these weeks he confronts the most cruel truth of all: he cannot draw. The gift that defined him is gone forever. Then who is he—*what* is he—if he can no longer be the person he once was?

Through the fog he reminds himself that he is fortunate to be alive. Every day he tells himself this, tries to drum it into his stubborn head, until slowly the message begins to get through—tempered by the reminder that there are still many dangers: he has escaped the gulag but he is far from being safe. He is not a free man.

This does not bear only on him—there are Gennady and Valentina to consider, given the risk they are running in sheltering him. He is alarmed to learn that their neighbors already know of his presence in their apartment.

"What have you told them, Gennady?"

Gennady shrugs. "The truth. Or as much of it as anyone needs—or wants to hear. That you and I came back from the gulag together. Such returns are an increasingly familiar story these days, with releases of prisoners from the camps continuing. I said you're recuperating from severe injuries and staying with us for a while because I can give you the medical attention you need without troubling a hospital. It's all true."

"Except I haven't been released. I'm a fugitive. You said so yourself. I'm illegal, I have no papers, and I'm putting you in danger. I must leave. I need to see my mother and show her that I'm alive."

"Of course—but only when you're up to it. You're not strong enough to travel any distance. I'm saying this as your physician. You're as weak as a baby. Your body took a lot of punishment and it needs time to recuperate. I'm not just talking about the surgery—three years in the gulag have taken their toll, plus almost dying of hunger and wandering through half the Arctic. Give your body a chance to recover."

He closes the copy of *Pravda* he has been reading and passes it to Pasha.

"I've been catching up with what's going on. The political situation is still confused. Nobody knows what to make of this new man at the top, this Nikita Khrushchev. See for yourself what *Pravda*'s reporting—whole ministries are being merged; their numbers halved. Anything's possible right now. I reckon Beria's days are numbered. Don't be surprised if they construct a case against him—already it's said he tried to mount a coup and seize power when Stalin died. There are even those who claim he had a hand in Stalin's death. It doesn't matter whether or not any of this is true; what matters is that the rumors are being spread—they're getting people ready for whatever's in store. The word is, Khrushchev's behind it."

"Khrushchev? I don't know that name."

"You see? You make my point for me. You've been away too long, you're out of touch. So you stay here a while longer. No arguments."

* * *

Pasha knows Gennady is right—he must build up his strength. He cannot even write to Mama or ask Gennady to do that for him—as the close relative of a fugitive, she may be having her mail intercepted. Concealing his whereabouts if he were to write would be no help; she would be taken into custody to force him to turn himself in. Nor does he have any way of getting a private message to her. There are no telephones in Lobachev Row and it would be wrong to call her at her work depot—it would compromise her foreman, who is a good man.

Going to her in person is the only way—and that means making himself strong enough for the journey. So from the middle of April he begins to take short walks in the surrounding streets, initially at night, then also in daytime. He wears an old leather cap of Gennady's—all his clothing is Gennady's—and keeps his head down as he crosses the open yard of the dom to leave and return. At the beginning he is shocked to find that an outing of only a few hundred meters leaves him drained of all strength. This will be a long process; he will have to be patient.

Gennady and Valentina live in the old Basmanny district. It is an area that the city planners are trying to modernize, with old buildings being torn down and new ones rising, but there are many places where the past survives in hidden lanes dotted with small grassy parks. It has its grander corners but nothing like the Arbat—and its privileged areas must still rub shoulders with run-down sections scarred by neglect, on which the builders have not yet started work. Pasha picks his way through the streets with caution, day by day increasing his range and always watching for militia units. He steers clear of the wide boulevards and squares that bound the district and sticks to the lanes and narrower streets, resting from time to time in the parks when fatigue overcomes him.

Sometimes his mind plays a trick so overpowering that it brings him to a standstill. The city vanishes, and once again the vast white emptiness of the gulag stretches all around him—a blinding nothingness wherever he turns, devoid of color or form, without even a horizon to break the infinity. Figures rise from the mist: the republic of bones is giving up its dead. He knows these wraiths, every one of them—Viktor, Irina, all the others as well, even Bolotsov.

Then, as suddenly as it descended on him, the horror is gone. He is dizzy with relief. He is not in that place of death. He is not closed in by steel fences and guns. These are apartment blocks around him, not watchtowers. He may not be a free man in the way he desires but there is something here on these pavements and in these quiet spaces that tastes and feels close to freedom. To be able to walk where he chooses, to eat and drink like a human being, to hear birdsong, to look upon a tree and see its buds open day by day as he passes, to watch the wind stirring the blades of soft green grass at his feet—these are at least the seeds of freedom.

In these moments he thanks God for what has been given to him. He may have lost a precious gift but he has been allowed the gift of life. He has survived. Like the sparrow in the cattle wagon, he must snatch what he can from the world.

A survivor. That is the person he is now.

* * *

Valentina is a nurse. Her wage is low but it is the only wage in the household—and now, with three mouths to feed, it is being stretched to the breaking point. Gennady goes out every day to look for employment.

"There's a shortage of doctors," he explains to Pasha. "Every hospital and clinic in the city is short-staffed. But that doesn't mean they'll take on someone who did time in the gulag. The dom's housing committee will terminate our tenancy of this apartment if I don't have work—I'll be classed as economically unproductive, a hanger-on, someone who isn't repaying the investment that society made in his training. What am I supposed to do—give up medical practice and become a caretaker somewhere and get a room that way? How does that repay anything? It's stupid beyond words."

But at least he can look for work, however dispiritedly. Pasha cannot even do that. So one morning he makes his way to the nearby Yauza River, one of the Moskva's tributaries. It is his most ambitious expedition so far. But as he follows its course, he sees immediately that, as a place to fish, the river is useless, its water scummy with waste washed down from industrial areas outside Moscow. Tellingly, there are no fishermen.

Having come this far, rather than abandon the venture, he follows the riverbank south and crosses to the Lefortovo estate on the opposite side. It is a bold move, because not far away is the notorious prison; but here by the river is a broad swath of rolling parkland, once glorious but now neglected and overgrown with copses and scrub. The old palace, built for Catherine the Great, now houses a military academy, and although the estate is supposedly a closed zone, the fences and boundaries, like the land, are poorly maintained. He sees no security patrols and no one bothers him as he pokes around among the undergrowth and ponds.

He returns the following morning and sets snares. The wire is difficult to bend and twist, and it cuts into his fingers, drawing blood, but that evening and as often as he can manage the trip to Lefortovo, he brings rabbit or hare to Valentina's table.

There are nights when he dreams that he glances down at his hands and they are just as they once were—uninjured, every finger and each thumb intact and perfect.

Then he wakes up.

CHAPTER 44

MAY BRINGS GOOD weather that feels to him like the sweetest warmth he has ever known. His walks are longer now, though he still needs frequent rests. One day he sets no snares in Lefortovo, and instead makes for the center of the city. This means using the great boulevards he has avoided so far. He joins knots of people heading in the direction he needs, working himself into their midst and making himself as inconspicuous as possible.

His destination is Red Square. He is nervous at the sight of the Kremlin guard and so many Red Army soldiers posted everywhere, but here finally is the goal he set himself: Viktor's beloved Alexandrovsky Garden.

The place is a blaze of color, rich with spring blooms. The scents are intoxicating. One corner of the garden is devoted to the tulips that Viktor loved. Children are playing by the fountains, their laughter ringing out bright and clear. Lovers steal kisses when they think no one is looking.

But for Pasha it is suddenly all too much, too glorious, too happy. It was a mistake to come here. He is here for Viktor, but there is no Viktor to see any of it, no Irina. He, Pasha, has survived, but there are those who did not, so many of them, too many—not only Viktor and Irina, not only the other artists, but all the millions who have been swallowed by the republic of bones.

He turns away and hastens back to the apartment.

* * *

"You're out of touch" was what Gennady said.

The judgment stings, but he knows that once again Gennady is right. So one morning he goes beyond Red Square to the massive pillared building that houses the Lenin State Library. He settles himself in one of the reading rooms and scours *Pravda* and *Izvestia*, not only current issues but back issues as well, as many as he can persuade the Leninka's librarians to dig out from the archives. The action of leafing through the pages of newsprint is wearying, and he knows that what he is reading is propaganda, but he learns to read between the lines. Soon he has caught up on world events—or the Kremlin's version of them—and gains a better sense of what is going on in his country and of the men that Gennady rails against, these latter-day tsars: Khrushchev, Malenkov, Molotov, Bulganin. He also sees who was running the NKVD at the time of his arrest and during his years in the gulag. It was Lavrenti Beria.

This is when he recalls Viktor's question: "Who can take over a chunk of the gulag and set up militia arrests, transportation, a complete prison camp? Not to mention enlisting the services of the NKVD."

None of it, Pasha now sees, could have happened without Beria. He was the one who made it possible. The controlling will and mind may have been Josef Vissarionovich's, but the NKVD was, and still is, Lavrenti Beria's fiefdom. His is the gulag, his the republic of bones that still haunts Pasha and will haunt his nation forever.

* * *

He puts the great library to another use. It holds scores of books on Leonardo da Vinci, many of them authored or edited by Sergei Lysenko. Pasha remembers them well—but he has a different area of study now.

His search takes a while. The first indications come quickly enough, but he wants to be sure, so he is thorough. The evidence accumulates. It is consistent.

In the end the Leninka tells him everything he needs to know. He has followed a trail and can see where it is leading. He is not yet at the end of this trail. But that day will come. He does not know how he will manage it. But he will.

"Thank you, Vladimir Ilyich," he tells bronze Lenin as he leaves the library for the last time.

That night he remembers the shiver he felt on seeing Sergei's name on the books about Leonardo. Once again he hears Viktor: "You must be a good artist, Pasha. Someone somewhere knows that."

Yes, someone somewhere.

CHAPTER 45

THE DOORMAN AT the Artists' Union shakes his head. He looks unhappy at Pasha's question.

"The comrade professor is no longer here, citizen. No longer with us, so to speak. You're not the first to come looking for him. And you're going to be just as disappointed."

Behind Pasha the door opens and two middle-aged men enter the lobby, both of them well dressed and prosperous looking.

"But right now you're in the way," adds the doorman in a whisper. He guides Pasha to one side of the narrow lobby. The men hurry past in the direction of the dining room.

"Lunch is a busy time," explains the doorman. "They flock here like gulls that haven't seen scraps for a month."

Pasha knows this; it is why he came at this hour. He recognizes neither of the men who passed him.

"So who else has been looking for Professor Lysenko?"

The doorman tilts his head, remembering. "A woman. Small and elderly."

It is as if a jolt of electricity shoots through Pasha's body.

"She was here just once, a month or two ago." The man breaks off to greet another arrival. "Yes, that's right—it was March, just before we lost Comrade Stalin, because she said something about writing to him. It angers me, you know, the things some people are saying about him these days. If you ask me—"

"Did she tell you her name?"

"She wasn't much of a one for names. She didn't even know Professor Lysenko's. She had a drawing of him—that's how I knew it was him she was after."

"Why will I be disappointed about the comrade professor?"

The doorman sighs. Pasha listens to what he has to say.

Afterwards the man frowns at him and leans in close. "Do I know you? Have I seen you before? A good while ago, maybe?"

Pasha puts his cap on and leaves quickly. He no longer bothers to look at the men who pass him in the lobby.

When he gets back to the apartment, Gennady is already there, having returned from another of his searches for work. He is drinking tea; Pasha smells it as he lets himself in. Unasked, Gennady fills a glass for him. Pasha uses both hands to raise it to his lips. As he drinks, he is aware of Gennady studying him in his peculiar way. The owlish eyes are large and unblinking.

"You had a good walk?"

Pasha nods without meeting his inquisitive gaze.

Sergei is dead. Sergei who seemed indestructible. Whether he was guilty of Pasha's suspicions is something Pasha will now never know.

And Mama has been here in Moscow. There is that old tightness of anxiety in his chest when he thinks of her making her way all alone to the city—that tiny figure buffeted by the capital's bustle, trying to find her way through this alien place. As for seeking out Sergei, her only conceivable reason would have been to ask if he knew anything about her Pashenka. It is time for him to go home to her.

With a start he realizes that Gennady has just said something. He looks up.

Gennady smiles sympathetically. "I was asking where you went today."

"The Artists' Union."

"The place where you used to train with the professor?"

"I wanted to ask him something."

"And did you?"

"He's dead."

"I'm sorry to hear that."

"Gennady, you and Valentina have been good to me. But it's time for me to leave. I'm fit enough now."

Gennady has taken a slip of paper from his pocket. He places it on the table.

"I, too, looked up an old friend today," he says. "Actually, I saw him a couple of weeks ago. That was when I asked him if he could help me locate someone. I figured it might be a long shot but I caught up with him this morning. He's a pediatrician. Very distinguished. You won't find him scrubbing up for the proletarian masses. His clientele is politicians' wives, daughters of ministry directors, mistresses of the high and mighty. He lives near Tishinskaya Square, which alone speaks volumes. Do you know it? It's in Presnya."

Pasha is listening closely now.

"Presnenski district," he says.

Gennady nods. "He has access to medical records. And if we Russians are good at anything, it's medical records. I asked him to look for any information on a family by the name of Cherviakov, currently or previously resident in his district. I told him that both father and mother are deceased but the father had been a judge in the Supreme Court—and had spent time in the gulag. I said there was an adult son called Viktor, also sent to the gulag—but that this might not appear in any official records, medical or otherwise. I said I believed the only remaining adult members of the family might be two daughters, but I didn't know if their name is still Cherviakova or whether they might have married and taken their husbands' names. I said there's at least one child."

Now he pushes the slip of paper to the middle of the table.

"You told me you wondered what might have become of them. Well, here they are—your friend Viktor's sisters, both of them." He glances at the paper. "Nina and Sofya. Nina was married briefly. It didn't work out and she came back to the family home. She has a son, Alexei, born after the divorce, so he took her family name rather than his father's. Alexei's records were the easiest to find, being the most recent. Then the other details fell into place." He pauses and looks at Pasha. "There's something else in the medical records—concerning the father, the judge. How he died. Do you know about it?"

Pasha nods.

"This is their address—and an impressive one it is, too—still the same privilege apartment originally allocated to the parents for the whole family." Gennady makes a wry smile. "I wonder how they pulled that off. That's the elite for you. Still, you wouldn't think they'd want to stay there after what the father did, would you?"

Pasha shrugs. "Some people don't mind ghosts. They get used to them."

He puts the paper into his pocket. So now there is one more thing he must do before he can go home to Mama.

CHAPTER 46

THE BUILDING, A five-storey dom in pale green stucco, is in a narrow cul-de-sac called Khlynovsky, running north off Great Nikitsky Street, a busy avenue that leads directly to the very center of the city. Gennady did not exaggerate—the location is one of the most prestigious in Moscow. It is also only a few minutes' walk from Restaurant Praga in the Arbat; little wonder that Viktor was familiar with the eating house.

Pasha takes care not to approach too close, keeping to the junction with Nikitsky, where he is less conspicuous among the busy flow of pedestrians. There is no question of someone like him going right up to the dom and entering it: such a fine residence will have a doorman, unlikely to be as amenable as the one at the Artists' Union where all sorts roll up, to whom he would have to explain himself—and how would he do that? What legitimate purpose could a man with no papers claim? All he can do is wait to see if a woman who might be one of the sisters appears, possibly with a young boy.

In the half hour he spends watching the dom, most of the people he sees entering or leaving are elderly. Most likely it is a place where tenants, once they have been awarded such a favored residence, make sure they stay for the long term, just as Viktor's sisters seem to have done. Certainly all the residents he sees are well dressed; some even come and go by motor car, confirming their status.

As he is crossing the junction with Nikitsky and thinking it is time to depart before someone reports him, the wide door of the dom swings open and a woman steps out to the covered portico. A chilly drizzle has set in. She glances at the gloomy sky, then arranges a brightly colored headscarf over her head and ties it in place.

There is something familiar about her brisk movements, the way in which she raises her chin to fasten the scarf, the set of her shoulders as she lowers her arms, something in her bearing that Pasha recognizes at once. He watches from the corner of his eye as she descends the steps to the pavement. She is tall, like Viktor, and slim. But Viktor was lanky and all elbows; this woman is graceful.

He looks the other way but he knows that step by step she is coming closer. In a few seconds she will be gone.

He does not know which sister she is.

"Cherviakova?"

Surprised, she pauses and turns to look at him. She is unsure, ready to continue onward again if she has made a mistake and only imagined that this poorly dressed stranger spoke to her or if he has no good reason to detain her. She takes half a step back.

He raises his head and meets her gaze. Her eyes are dark, sharp, watchful. They are Viktor's eyes, beneath a feminine version of Viktor's finely arched eyebrows. Pasha is so disconcerted that for a moment he can do nothing, say nothing. He was not prepared for this; it is as if Viktor is gazing at him.

"Nina? Sofya?"

Now there is puzzlement in the dark eyes. But anxiety, too. Her body stiffens.

"I'm Nina," she tells him. "Who are you? What do you want with me or Sofya?"

He removes his cap. The drizzle is cool on his forehead. He is grateful for it.

"I was with Viktor."

Her right hand tightens on the empty shopping bag she is carrying. Her left hand presses into her side, as if she has been struck.

"Where is Viktor? Has he sent you?" She steps forward and looks more closely at Pasha. "Why are you here? Why not Viktor?"

In reply he makes the slightest shake of his head.

"I'm sorry," he tells her. "I have bad news. The worst possible. Viktor died."

He is doing this all wrong. Has the gulag turned his heart to ice? To tell her like this, in a public street?

But she is stronger than he thinks. Her voice is steady. "Tell me what happened. How can my brother be dead when he wasn't guilty of anything?"

"Nobody among us was guilty. That didn't matter. What was done to us had nothing to do with being guilty."

"We tried to find out where they sent him. It was like talking to stones. The gulag, I suppose."

"Yes."

"And now prisoners are being allowed home. We couldn't help thinking there might be a chance. So you've been released."

"No, it was different with us. No amnesty."

"Yet here you are. Are you telling me you escaped?"

"Yes."

"With Viktor?"

He shakes his head. "I'll explain but not now—not here. I have to go. Anyone can see I don't belong here, and we've talked long enough; we might have been noticed. That could put us both in danger."

In another movement that is achingly familiar to him, she squares her shoulders and stands a little more upright. She casts a glance back down Khlynovsky.

"I live in—"

"I know where you live."

This admission does not seem to surprise her. "Our apartment is safe. But don't come to the front door. There's a door at the rear of the building. Come tonight, at nine. Not before. I have a child."

"Alexei. Yes, I know."

Again she shows no surprise. "He'll be asleep by then. There'll be Sofya and me, no one else. Wait by the door, but not too close. Don't knock. Make sure you're not seen. Wait for me to open the door." She frowns. "I don't know your name."

"Pasha."

"Pasha. Well, you're getting wet, Pasha."

She walks away. Her back is straight, her pace purposeful. She is in control of whatever anguish is raging within her.

* * *

That night he tells the sisters Viktor's story. When he comes to the manner of their brother's death, he spares them as much as he can.

"In such extreme temperatures the body feels no pain." He wonders if they will believe the lie or will persuade themselves into it.

He tells them about Irina.

"So Viktor found love," says Sofya, the younger of the two. Her eyes, as dark as her sister's, are soft with emotion. "I'm glad he did. And I'm glad he had you as a friend, Pasha. I think you loved him, too."

"I failed him. I owe him my life but I was unable to repay him."

"You tried to save him. You didn't abandon him. You were the last person he saw on this earth." Her gaze falls on Pasha's hands. "You've paid a high price."

"What will you do now?" asks Nina.

"Leave Moscow. Go home to my mother." He thinks for a moment. "And then I must get to Ukraine, to Lvov."

It is the first time he has admitted the decision to himself, though he knows it was made the moment he encountered Nina today. It is the right thing to do, the only thing. It is the duty he owes to Irina, just as he owed a duty to Viktor and is now fulfilling it.

Nina raises an eyebrow. "All the way to Ukraine? You'll go to Irina's family?"

"If I can find them."

"That means considerable travel. Do I assume your papers are in order?"

"Everything will be fine."

"You don't have papers, do you?"

"They took them away when they arrested me."

"You're undocumented, unregistered. And an escaped prisoner can't apply for new papers."

Sofya exchanges a swift glance with her sister. "Pasha, without papers, you're taking a big risk."

He shrugs. This is not their concern.

"How much money do you have?" asks Nina.

"I'll manage."

The three of them are quiet for a time. Pasha surveys the elegant room. It is one of many rooms that make up the apartment: he saw several doorways in the entrance hall. As he passed them, he thought about Viktor's father and what he did behind one of those doors, and about Viktor finding him and rushing to shield his sisters.

A luxury apartment like this is a world away from Gennady and Valentina's simple home—not to mention Lobachev Row. Everything in this residence is private, available only to its occupants. It is not a place where kitchen or toilet must be shared—Pasha glimpsed the private kitchen through an open door. There may even be separate bedrooms for each person, some of which will now be empty and unused in the absence of Viktor and his parents. What would Gennady make of such extravagance?

Yet Pasha also sees something else. He sees clues that indicate a different truth. Yes, everything is of a quality he has never experienced before: the floor rugs, the furniture, the chandeliers, the delicate porcelain tea set in which Sofya served tea—poured from a teapot, not drawn from a samovar—though he declined to accept any, so terrified was he of dropping the tiny cup.

But the elegance has a shabbiness. The rugs are marked by wear, the furniture is scuffed and becoming threadbare in places, there are outlines on the walls where pictures have been removed, and he suspects that the displays of expensive-looking ornaments are more sparsely spread than was once the case. In the sisters' clothing he sees small repairs as skillful as anything Mama could do.

So it seems that Nina and Sofya have their financial difficulties just like everyone else. They, too, must scrimp and save, make do and mend. And piece by piece they are converting their possessions into cash to support themselves and Nina's growing son—perhaps also to bribe someone to let them stay here.

As if to compensate for these sacrifices, there are Viktor's paintings and drawings on the walls of the entrance hall and in this room—rural landscapes, still lifes, studies of Nina and Sofya, watercolors of Moscow, including, of course, the Alexandrovsky Garden.

Then there are the photographs—so many of them, their very quantity another indication of past affluence, carefully arranged about the room, all in frames of silver or polished walnut. Perhaps one day the valuable frames will also have to go, but for now they grace portraits of individuals and family groups. There are photographs of a boy that Pasha assumes is Alexei, and of a tall, distinguished-looking man in court robes, a dark-haired woman by his side.

But most numerous are the photographs of Viktor, on his own or beside his sisters or his parents, sometimes holding Alexei, but always with his crooked smile. These are the photographs that clutch Pasha's heart.

Nina has been observing him.

"Some of the photographs are my own work," she says. "I took up photography some years ago. Viktor encouraged me. I have my own little studio here where I develop and print, though it's not always easy to get the materials and chemicals. I took all the later photographs of Viktor." She pauses. "Allow me to photograph you, Pasha."

She leaves the room before he can protest.

Sofya is smiling. "Please let her."

In Nina's absence she quizzes Pasha about himself, about his life before his arrest; she asks about his home, his childhood, his mother and father. He is embarrassed to speak about himself—it is not what he came here to do, but she gives him no choice. He is flustered to be the object of such attention, so that when Nina returns with a folding camera, he allows her to position him beneath one of the bright chandeliers. The shutter clicks. She winds the film forward in a smooth, practiced movement.

"Another, please. Stay there."

She takes four or five photographs, all very quickly, with no fuss. For one of the shots she coaxes a smile from him; in the others he is serious, gazing directly into the lens.

At last she folds the camera shut. It is late now, very late, more morning than night. The sisters look tired.

Pasha stands up. "I must go."

Nina sets the camera aside. "Come back in a week's time if you can. I hope you will."

"We both do," adds Sofya.

"Wait at the same door, at nine. If I'm not there within ten minutes, come back every second night. Not every night, because then you'd be taking twice as many risks."

"You know it could be dangerous for you."

"Even so. We'd like to see you again."

He nods absently, preoccupied by one more matter he must deal with.

"I want you to have these."

He fans the sketches out on the table. Viktor is in all of them. Irina is there, too, in several. He knows that the shaven-headed zek in the ill-fitting gulag uniform is not the brother they remember, and he debated long and hard with himself whether to bring the drawings. This is not the Viktor of Nina's photographs.

But the drawings are all he has to give them. All that is left.

The three of them gaze without comment at the creased and damp-stained sheets of paper. The images within them say everything that needs to be said. Sofya begins to sob softly, but Pasha knows his decision was right.

Nina leads him down the back stairs.

"I don't think Viktor's death was as easy as you'd wish us to believe," she says as she unlocks the door. "But thank you for trying to protect Sofya. The drawings are hard to look at—I can't pretend otherwise—but when we love someone we must bear the hard things as well as rejoice in the joyous ones. I hope you'll come back to see us again next week."

Something rustles. She is holding out some ruble notes.

"It's not much, Pasha. Don't be offended. This isn't charity. It's love."

"I welcome your love. But I won't take this."

He walks quickly away.

* * *

Dawn is breaking. In Great Nikitsky Street the road sweepers are just starting their morning shift. He wonders what shift Mama is working today.

He heads north where he can pick up Tverskoy Boulevard and eventually Dolgorukovsky Street, the beginning of the road that runs due north out of the city. Militia patrols will be thin on the ground at this hour.

It is a fine morning. Unlike yesterday, the sky is clear. The day will be warm and dry. His heart lifts as he contemplates the journey ahead, one he has yearned for so much, not only during these months in Moscow but above all during the long years in the gulag. Today his body feels strong and there will be no meter-high drifts of snow for him to struggle through, no blizzards or Arctic burani to sweep him away. The distance before him is half what he covered in those conditions. It will be a pleasure to walk through the city and the villages of his homeland on a day like this. Even allowing for a few hours' rest in a barn or an abandoned shack along the way, he will be home with Mama by tomorrow.

CHAPTER 47

THOUGH THEY ARE weary after the long night, and their hearts are heavy with sorrow for what Pasha has told them, Nina and Sofya do not retire to bed. There is too much to do and none of it will keep. Sofya quickly washes up and tidies away the cups and saucers and teapot. Nina locks the drawings in her dressing table. There is nothing to suggest the presence of any late-night visitor.

Now both sisters go to Nina's so-called photographic studio. This is a converted walk-in larder off the kitchen. It has just enough space for the two of them to stand side by side, closed in by shelves laden with developing trays, mixing jugs, and bottles of chemicals. But the sisters are well practiced in their complementary roles and they work smoothly together, with scarcely a word needing to be spoken: Nina doing the technical tasks involving the chemicals and judging when each step is complete, and Sofya fetching water, rinsing the film, and clipping the negatives and then the final prints on hanging lines to drain.

By the time they hear Alexei beginning to stir, everything is done. They breathe a sigh of relief as they examine the outcome of their work. Nina's camera, a Moskva, always gives good results and these are no exception—the photographs of Pasha are perfect.

Sofya moves the prints to her bedroom, which is warmer than the larder and where they will dry more quickly. She hides them in her wardrobe, rumples her bed and changes into a nightdress and dressing gown, as Nina has already done, as if she has just risen. Then she joins her sister and Alexei for breakfast.

It is a normal morning like any other. Alexei has plans for his day and recounts them excitedly. If his mother and aunt yawn a little more than usual, he does not notice.

CHAPTER 48

Lobachev Row is the same as always. Pasha might have left only last week. The roads and lanes are dusty and sleepy; insects buzz and hum. He hears the rumble of a goods train passing behind the dom. The water of the canal sparkles in the sunshine. Children still clamber through the branches of the lime and chestnut trees exactly as the youngsters of Lobachev Row have always done; the one difference is that he recognizes none of them—a new generation has arrived.

It is a workday. The place is quiet. The only adult he sees is the clothes seller, the old woman whose evil eye he feared as a child. Not right in the head but harmless and still trying to earn a few kopecks. The good weather has prompted her to nail a makeshift awning to her shed for her to sit beneath, but it would be no surprise if the garments she is displaying are exactly the same as throughout his childhood. When she grins at him with her empty gums, he smiles in reply, though he knows she has no idea who he is.

The concrete stairs in the dom are still crumbling and treacherous. How many times did he climb these stairs, day and night, all his life, that simple little life he once had? How often has he sat on these stairs with friends? How many Saturdays did he haul his portfolio case up and down? Until that night when the militiamen hustled him down the stairs at gunpoint, with fear like a lump of granite in his belly.

He reaches the apartment door only to find he has no key. The thought of it had never occurred to him, all this distance he has come. He feels foolish, but that is not all: there is something wounding in the absence of the key. A final insult. They took so much from him, and now here he is without even a key for his own home.

He is hungry. He has eaten only what country stallholders were willing to give him for free along the way—overripe tomatoes and damaged courgettes that no one would buy, broken pieces of wild mushroom.

But his hunger is only a vague sensation. It is not like the savage hunger that gnawed at him on the trek from the gulag. It is not the hunger of desperation; it is the hunger of anticipation, a reminder that Mama will have shchi warming; she always has shchi on the stove.

He knocks. Waits. He imagines how joy will light up her face when she opens the door and sees him.

He knocks again.

"Mama?"

She must be on the afternoon shift. He could wait here for her or go to the depot. But she will be out with her work gang, not in the depot. So perhaps he should try to surprise her in the streets.

A rasping voice makes him jump.

"Who are you? What's your business here?"

Pasha chuckles. He recognizes this voice. How could he not? Here is another feature of Lobachev Row that is just the same as ever—old man Griboyev.

And yes, here are two cagey eyes squinting up at him from the next doorway. They blink, then withdraw slightly, back into the shadows of the apartment.

"They're all at work," adds the old man. "What do you want?"

Pasha feels a first cold shiver of doubt. *All* at work? *They?*

A woman's voice calls from within the Griboyev apartment. "Come away. None of our business. Leave it."

Griboyev ignores her. He opens the door fully and emerges, squinting in the light. His head stretches forward as he peers at Pasha.

"Pasha? Young Pasha? Is it really you, my boy?"

"Of course it's me. Who else would it be?" He grins at the old man. "Where's Mama—at work?"

Griboyev does not smile back at him. His wife appears. She sees Pasha. She stops short. Her mouth falls open.

Griboyev is scratching the stubble on his chin. "You'd better come in, Pasha."

That lump of granite from long ago is in Pasha's stomach again.

"Where's Mama?"

"You'd better come in."

* * *

He stays four nights. All the Griboyeva girls are at their Komsomol and Young Pioneer spring camps, so he is given their sleeping corner. He tells the old couple he was in a gulag work camp, confirming what they always believed anyway. But that is as far as his explanations go. He reveals nothing of the nature of his work in the camp. They think he was accused and convicted of some offense, but they do not bother asking what it was; they know any accusation would have been a lie. They think he has been officially freed and he does not disabuse them. They assume that the damage to his hands happened during his incarceration.

He uses the communal toilet in the courtyard only when the dom is quiet during work hours or late at night. He never sees the family who have been allocated Mama's apartment, nor they him. They work long hours, leaving early each morning and not returning until late evening. When he hears them depart each day, he escapes from the dom to walk the lanes and fields. It is only in this solitude that he can grieve for Mama.

Yet again, he is being fed and housed by those who have little enough to meet their own needs, so, as in Moscow, he tries to provide whatever he can—here it is perch that he catches in the farther reaches of the canal where he is safely out of sight of Lobachev Row.

When he comes and goes, he is as circumspect as he was in the streets of Moscow, but here it is not only militia he watches out for; it is also anyone from his old life. He does not want the endless questions that would inevitably come from former friends, Komsomol comrades, and neighbors who have more inquiring minds than the Griboyevs. And he does not want to be the object of their ghoulish sympathy, watching their gaze constantly returning to his hands and knowing they are pitying poor Pasha Kalmenov who once had such a bright future before him.

It takes him until the fourth day to bring himself to go to Mama's grave. There is no headstone with a glass-encased photograph, no marble cross; only a clumsy wooden cross. He looks at the piece of paper he has brought with him. Once again he is mindful of his journey from the gulag through the icy wastes to the rail line, but this time it is because of the prayer that sustained him when he feared he was lost. He knows from the Griboyevs that Mama had her trying journeys, too—week after week to far-flung militia stations where she begged for news of her Pashenka.

He pins the piece of paper to the cross. His handwriting is a barely legible scrawl: "The sun will not burn you by day, nor the moon by night. The Lord will preserve you from all evil; the Lord will preserve your soul."

Before the day is out, the paper will be taken by the wind; or overnight dew will wash away the words. But Mama will hear the prayer.

* * *

He returns to Moscow and fulfills his promise to Nina and Sofya. And now, in their apartment, he is staring in amazement at the small green-backed booklet in his hands. The sisters are seated on either side of him, not speaking, giving him time to absorb what he is seeing.

The internal passport is battered and dog-eared, the threads of its cover fraying, as any passport would be from always being carried by its bearer, as the law demands. Indeed, it is in much the same condition as was his own genuine passport on that fateful night when he last saw it.

He opens it to the first pages. Here is his name, complete with patronymic, here are his date and place of birth—these details being the result of Sofya's determined quizzing of him. Here is his photograph, unsmiling as required—one of the rapid shots Nina took, with a section of blank white wall as background.

Here is his propiska. And on the pages reserved for military service, again all is in order—here is the military commissariat's official confirmation of his exemption. It looks identical to the one in his original passport.

He returns to the first pages and examines the official stamps, particularly those that endorse his photograph. Nina fetches her own passport and places it on the table for comparison. The stamps on Pasha's are flawless, more than good enough to convince any militiaman or Red Army trooper. He says so.

"But how did you arrange this?"

Nina explains. "A judge of the Supreme Court builds a network of many contacts during his career. Not all of them are on the right side of the law—the more so if he serves a sentence in the gulag. Friends made in such adversity are the truest friends of all. You know this. Some of those friends of our father's are our friends now. They're there for us when we need them. They can be trusted—and some of them, as you see, have very special skills."

"This must have been expensive."

"It cost us nothing. They're friends, Pasha. But even with this, you must be careful—you'll have to come up with a good reason for your journey if a security detail gets officious with you."

"Medical treatment. I've heard there's a surgeon in Lvov who may be able to restore the nerve endings in my hands."

"Is there such a surgeon?"

He shrugs. "I may have been misinformed."

Nina looks unimpressed. "When will you leave?"

"Tonight if possible. By train. I'll find an unlocked freight wagon. If not tonight, then as soon as I find one." He smiles. "I'm used to wagons. And they don't have security checks."

As she leads him to the door at the rear of the residence, she produces a paper package.

"Food for the journey, Pasha. Bread, smoked sausage."

He has an old fishing bag that Griboyev gave him so that he could take some of Mama's possessions away with him—though not the portrait of Stalin. The bag also holds a selection of his early drawings and the things he brought from the gulag. He thanks Nina and slips the package into the bag.

As he is crossing the Borodinsky Bridge toward Kievsky railway station, he stops beneath a streetlight and unwraps Nina's package. He sees bread and a thick chunk of dark sausage. But there is something else. In a separate small envelope is the little bundle of ruble notes—as she said a week ago, not much, only a few threes and fives. No, not much. But, he suspects, dearly bartered.

CHAPTER 49

THE OLD CLOTHES seller of Lobachev Row is not as soft in the head as she seems. She knows all the children in and around the dom, both the present generation and the ones before them, their mothers and fathers, and all their histories. She knows what the children say about her evil eye. She loathes the wretches, generation after generation of them.

Evil eye or not, she is not blind. She is certain it was Pasha Kalmenov she saw. There was something odd about his hands, but it was him nonetheless. The same Pasha Kalmenov who was taken away over three years ago—no one ever found out why, or where he ended up. Poor Marya Kalmenova put herself into an early grave over him, surely as useless a son as a woman ever bore.

In her slow, shambling way the old woman thinks things over. It begins to dawn on her that there may be gains to be made here. Clearly Pasha Kalmenov had to be guilty of something. People do not get arrested and disappear without good reason. That makes him a criminal. The Griboyevs took him in. Unless he was set free as part of the amnesty she has heard about, that makes them criminals, too.

Eventually, she packs away her merchandise and goes to the militia station—the very first station that Marya Kalmenova herself went to when she began the grueling search for her Pashenka.

"But you're telling me he's gone now," says the duty officer. "What took you so long? Why didn't you tell us while he was still there?"

"I'm a busy woman. I have my shop to see to."

"Your shop?"

Behind the duty officer, his sergeant coughs to smother a snigger. Both men are familiar with her lines of scraggy, worn-out rags.

"And how was I to know he'd be off again?" she adds. "What do I get for this information?"

"The satisfaction of knowing you've fulfilled your responsibilities as a good citizen."

"I remember this case," the duty officer tells the sergeant when she finally leaves. "Kalmenov's mother came here looking for him. We had no record of his arrest. I heard we weren't the only station she pestered—with the same result. Without a record of arrest, there can be no determination of whether he's an escaped prisoner."

"Which means no determination of whether the Griboyevs have committed a crime."

"Exactly."

The duty officer tears off the report sheet in which he has filled in only the date, the time and the old woman's name, and drops it in the bin.

No one troubles the Griboyevs.

CHAPTER 50

THE RAIL JOURNEY to Lvov takes twenty-four hours. But Pasha is lucky enough to find an empty wagon, the journey is without incident or security checks, and no other free riders try to board at any of the stops along the way. On his arrival he is able to spend the night in the wagon before setting out in search of his objective.

And now, after a morning's walking, he has found it: Irina's Korniakt Tower.

His gaze travels up the length of the square-sectioned structure. It must stand a good sixty or seventy meters high. He looks again at the pencil drawing on the back of the playing card. It is slightly smudged but it portrays the church tower faithfully, with its four stepped levels topped by an elaborate bell tower. In the small monochrome drawing, the bell tower is delicately shaded; in reality it is the vivid green of oxidized copper, glinting in the sun. It is a handsome edifice; he can understand Irina's affection and pride.

As he searched the streets, he found many churches—so many in this one city—and here at the foot of the tower is yet another, a complex affair of interlinked buildings, their green domes clustering together like mushrooms.

It is only now that he notices the bearded black-clad priest watching from the shadows of one of the doorways. He is leaning comfortably against the stone jamb, his arms folded. How long has he been standing there?

Pasha shoulders the fishing bag and goes over to him.

"I'm looking for a man called Petrov."

The priest's expression does not change. Perhaps he does not like the look of his questioner. Or perhaps he does not understand Russian. For one thing, this is Ukraine, with a language of its own, similar but not identical to Russian; for another, this particular region of Ukraine was once part of Poland, complicating linguistic matters further. Lvov has submitted to many masters in its blood-soaked history, of which the Soviet empire is only the latest; and that just a few years ago. Perhaps standard Russian has not yet taken root properly.

"Petrov. Do you know him? He comes to this church. At any rate, he used to."

Still no reaction. Pasha shrugs and turns away. Evidently he must find himself a more cooperative guide. Or a Russian-speaking one.

"I don't know any Petrov," the priest declares in faultless Russian.

Pasha turns back to him. He is certain the man is lying, priest though he is.

The priest's gaze is on the playing card. "What were you looking at just now?"

Pasha holds up the card so that the man can see the drawing of the tower.

The priest grunts. "Playing cards are Satan's picture book. But the drawing's not bad."

"It was done from memory."

"Not by you, I think."

"No."

"Because you're not from here. I've never seen you before."

"No. But Petrov's from here."

"What happened to your hands?"

Pasha decides to take a chance. "The gulag happened."

The priest grunts again. "Well, like I said, I've never heard of any Petrov."

"It's a common name. There must be a lot of Petrovs around."

"In Russia maybe. This isn't Russia."

Pasha turns the card over. It is a court card, a queen, with Irina's portrait.

"This queen wasn't drawn from memory," he tells the priest. "I'm the one who drew her—I could still draw then—and she was right there in front of me. She wasn't as finely dressed as this but she was very beautiful."

"Was?"

"She died. Give this to Petrov."

The priest looks at him for a time, then unfolds his arms and takes the card.

* * *

Pasha returns to the church in time to attend the evening service for the Blessed Virgin, to whom the church is dedicated. The same priest officiates, dressed this time in robes of white and gold.

Pasha's mind is not on the service. He observes the congregation to see if he himself is being watched by anyone. But no one seems to pay him any heed. All he sees is a gathering of devout men, women, and children.

Afterwards, as the church is emptying, he feels a touch on his arm. He looks around. A boy of about twelve is standing behind him. These people seem to make a habit of moving about unobserved. It takes him a moment to recognize the boy as the priest's altar server. He, too, was robed; now he is in normal clothes.

"Come with me," he says. Perfect Russian again.

He hurries ahead of Pasha, taking him through cobbled streets and along the edge of a small park, then over more cobbled streets enclosed by buildings of honey-colored stone. The route climbs steadily uphill in an easterly direction, eventually leading directly into woodland. When the path finally levels out, Pasha sees large sections of ruined masonry, overgrown and moldering, as if a great building, perhaps a castle, once stood on this elevated spot. The city is spread out far below. Rising above everything is the Korniakt Tower.

The boy enters a clearing from the far edge of which a flight of stone steps leads downwards. He descends, and, for the first time, waits for Pasha to catch up. He points to Pasha's left. Pasha sees that the staircase has followed the exterior contours of a stone archway flanked by a pair of stone lions, rampant as if on a heraldic crest.

Without a word, the boy dashes off down the lower path.

The woodland hush is shattered by a metallic sound. It is the unmistakable ratchet of firearms being primed. On the grassy bank above the archway, a man appears. He is carrying a pistol, held casually in front of him in clasped hands. He ignores Pasha, his attention on the clearing and the surrounding woodland.

Below him three men step from the archway. Two are also armed with pistols. These, however, are leveled at Pasha. The man standing between them is unarmed but carries himself with an air of confidence. No question who is the leader here.

"I'm Petrov," he says. "Who's looking for me?"

CHAPTER 51

THE TWO GUNMEN guide Pasha into the archway. Within is a deep grotto that might once have sheltered a statuary group or monument.

"Let's make sure our young comrade intends us no harm," Petrov tells his companions.

One man does an efficient job of checking Pasha for weapons while the other searches the fishing bag. He passes the passport and the last of Nina and Sofya's cash to Petrov but does not interfere with the other contents.

Petrov counts the money and returns it to the bag. He opens the passport.

Pasha watches. In terms of physical appearance he could see Viktor in Nina and Sofya, but he cannot see Irina in this solidly built man with his barrel chest. On the other hand, the curt and self-assured manner—yes, he can see Irina in that.

Petrov is looking at the address in Pasha's propiska.

"You're far from home," he says.

"Not as far as I once was. Not as far as Irina was."

"What was Irina to you? What were you to her?"

"We were friends. She was a very dear friend."

"Friend?"

"Only that. But she was a friend I loved."

"And now she's dead. My daughter. My child. That's what you're telling me. What you told the priest."

"Yes."

"In the gulag."

"Yes."

"Why should I believe you?"

"That's up to you. I can't make you."

"Where were you? Which camp?"

"Somewhere beyond Vorkuta, beyond the mining camp out there. I think our camp didn't exist before they sent us there. And it doesn't exist now. If it had a name, we never knew it." Pasha pauses. "Irina told me you'd be praying for her."

"Every day. Every night. Prayers don't always get answered. Did she keep her faith?"

"It was a hard place for faith."

Petrov has remained as inscrutable as the stone lions guarding the grotto. He produces from his shirt pocket the playing card that Pasha gave the priest, and looks at it, both sides, for a few moments.

"Who made these drawings?" His voice is thick, the first time he has shown any emotion. He clears his throat, as if to prevent repetition of such a display.

"Irina drew the Korniakt Tower. I did the portraits of Irina." Pasha sees Petrov's gaze flick to his hands. "And there are portraits on the other court cards in the deck. I did those, too. Here, look."

Conscious of the pistols trained on him and taking care to avoid any sudden movements that might provoke their use, he bends down to the fishing bag and finds the other playing cards. His fingers are clumsy as he tries to spread the cards out on a piece of broken wall. At Petrov's nod, one of the men steps forward and finishes the task for him.

"Irina made the actual cards," explains Pasha. "She used paper from the work we were doing."

"Paper. Strange kind of gulag work."

Petrov picks up the cards to examine them. He looks closely at their edges, apparently wondering how they were made. Some of the layers of paper are beginning to come apart. The cards seem fragile and vulnerable in his coarse hands. He focuses his attention on the court cards, spending the most time on the queens.

Throughout this inspection he keeps his head down. Pasha cannot see what effect the images on the cards are having. He wonders if the man senses some lingering presence of his daughter in these artifacts she created.

Petrov points to a jack. "This is you."

"Yes."

"And him?" He is pointing to a king.

"A man called Viktor."

Petrov nods slowly, as if he has already guessed how Viktor fitted into Irina's life.

He sets down one of the aces, carefully, like a man making the most of the moment when he plays a trump. Stalin stares out from the card.

"Well, at least we know this bastard's burning in hell. Some prayers do get answered."

He signals for the guns to be put away.

* * *

This time it is Irina's story that Pasha tells.

Afterwards Petrov leaves the grotto and walks some distance away. His back is turned but Pasha sees the swift gesture as he crosses himself.

The other men, now joined by the watcher from the grassy bank, roll cigarettes and light up.

"His wife got sick after Irina was arrested and taken away," one of them tells Pasha in a low voice. He has a flat, broken nose; his breathing wheezes when he speaks. "Sick in the head is what I'm talking about. All of us could see what was happening to her. It was like watching a flower wither. She won't be getting better. He'll have to decide what to tell her now. Frankly, I doubt if she's capable of understanding. Maybe that makes her the fortunate one."

After a few minutes, Petrov returns. His face reveals nothing.

"I apologize for the guns and other precautions," he tells Pasha. "There was no way to know who you might be. Like you, we're Russian—and that can be dangerous here. People think we're all Stalinists."

"People?"

Petrov shrugs. "Poles. Ukrainians. Jews. They all get a thirst for Russian blood now and then. Somebody always wants vengeance, some fool always thinks he has a reason. Memories are long here. You could have been one of those hotheads."

As he speaks, he is rolling a cigarette. Now he lights it. He looks at Pasha as he exhales.

"Or you might have been NKVD. In either case we'd have arranged things for you in keeping with the name of this little place."

"What name is that?"

"The Grotto of Suicide."

Pasha says nothing. Petrov the Pilgrim is not what he expected. He wonders why the man should have any more reason than anyone else to worry about the NKVD, why he thinks they might come looking for him.

"You'll accept my hospitality," Petrov is saying. "You've come a long way and it's the same long journey back. Rest up a few days before you set off for home."

Pasha shakes his head. "I'm not going home. There's no such place. I'm not going anywhere in Russia. I'm not going anywhere in the Soviet Union."

"You're not? Where then?"

"I intend to go to the West."

Petrov receives this with a skeptical smile. "It's an interesting aspiration. Admirable."

"It's not an aspiration. It's the truth."

"Big talk. How will you bring this about? Maybe it can be done if you have big money. Big talk needs big money. You don't even have the rail fare back to Moscow. So how exactly will you fulfill this lofty aspiration of yours?"

"I don't know."

"So it's cheap talk."

"I'll do it. Somehow."

For a long moment no one speaks. It falls to Petrov to break the spell. He looks at his companions, then at Pasha.

"Let's have dinner, you and me," he says. "Let's get some food into the dreamer's belly. You look like you could do with a square meal."

All five descend the hill together, but as they reach the streets, Petrov's companions go their separate ways. After half an hour, Pasha and Petrov come to an industrial zone, where the streets consist not of residential buildings but of workshops and small manufacturing units huddled together. The general area is badly lit but there are floodlights illuminating some kind of factory or warehouse area enclosed by a high brick wall. Pasha glimpses the roofs of an agglomeration of ugly industrial buildings and steel sheds. The wall stretches far ahead.

"This is where I work," says Petrov. "In here." He smacks the wall with the flat of his hand. The sound echoes in the long, deserted street.

"It's vast. What is it?"

"A bus factory. You're right, it's enormous, like a city in its own right. We're the biggest builder of buses in the Soviet Union—beautiful buses, too. Practically every bus you'll travel on in the USSR comes from here. More people work in this factory than in all the other places in Lvov put together."

In due course, wooden gates appear in the wall. Petrov stops. Pasha peers through the gaps along the edges. He sees lines of buses parked side by side, painted in various liveries. Behind them are wide, tall sheds and a ragtag assortment of other buildings, some linked by high-level metal walkways.

"What's your job here?" asks Pasha.

"Delivery scheduler."

"What does that mean?"

"All in good time."

CHAPTER 52

PETROV'S HOME IS well outside the city, another half hour beyond the bus factory. It turns out not to be an apartment, as Pasha expected, but is the middle housing unit in a row of three small dwellings surrounded by fields. In the light of the thin crescent of moon he sees a patch of vegetable garden. He hears a goat bleat.

Petrov is turning the key in the door.

"You'll have to make allowances for my wife," he says.

Pasha discovers that Irina's mother, Olga, is the source of her daughter's beauty. But in Olga it is a blighted beauty. She is small and slight, as Irina was. Her eyes are as green as Irina's but are vacant and unfocused. Although Petrov greets her tenderly and introduces Pasha to her, Pasha is not convinced she is really aware of his presence. If she is conscious of the world around her in any way at all, it is through the haze of a dislocated mind. She is very pale, not the sallow complexion of physical illness but a washed-out pallor that suggests she has not set foot outside the little house for a long time. Whoever the vegetable gardener is, it is not Olga. As Petrov prepares dinner, Pasha reflects that everything in this household is probably done by him.

Olga joins them at the meal, obediently taking her place at the table when Petrov tells her. She is able to eat without assistance.

Other than the supper grace that Petrov offers and to which only Pasha responds, there is no talk.

Pasha thinks about what Petrov's broken-nosed companion said; if Petrov plans to tell Olga about Irina, it will be when they are alone, not with this outsider present.

In the middle of the meal, Olga suddenly stands up.

"Olyushka?" says Petrov. "What's wrong? What do you need?"

She ignores him—or does not hear him—and goes to Pasha. She is staring at his hands. In fact, Pasha knows she has been staring at them for some time while he tried to cut his food. Now she takes both his hands and raises them from the table.

Petrov rises from his chair to stop her.

"It's all right," Pasha assures him. He looks at the man to emphasize that he means it, that he is not simply being polite. Petrov looks uncertain but sits down.

Pasha watches Olga as she examines what is left of his fingers. He cannot feel her touch but he sees that it is as gentle and light as a feather.

When she has satisfied whatever curiosity impelled her, she releases each hand. Then she takes his cutlery and carefully cuts up the syrniki pancakes and goat's cheese on his plate. She looks directly at him for the first time. Just for a moment her gaze is clear and lucid. Pasha feels a shiver run through him.

She goes to the icon of Christ on the wall and crosses herself, then returns to her chair. Her gaze clouds over again. The three of them finish the meal in the silence with which it began.

* * *

When Olga has gone to bed, Petrov pours vodka into two glass tumblers. He drains his in one gulp. Pasha takes only a sip. Petrov shrugs and refills his own tumbler.

Irina's bed is still there, near the stove, just as she described to Pasha. It is neatly made, awaiting her return. Above it is a shelf filled with books. There are also some long rolls of paper. Petrov hunts through these, extracts one, and pins it flat on the table. It is a large-scale map of Europe.

"Irina drew this and the other maps up there for me," he explains, without emotion. "I've always been interested in maps and what they tell us. It's time for a geography lesson. Drink up—we're in for a long night."

* * *

Two days later, shortly after dawn, Pasha goes back toward the city with Petrov. They do not walk together. Instead, Pasha follows at a distance, as if they have no connection with one another. They take the main road, a metaled highway, but well before they reach the bus factory, Pasha turns off the highway and onto a mud lane, its surface firm in the dry weather.

The few buildings in the lane are windowless sheds built of concrete blocks and roofed with corrugated iron. All look abandoned. Weeds and brambles grow undisturbed around their doorways. Some of the doors have rotted away entirely, leaving only a few staves of crumbling wood. After a hundred meters or so he finds the shed described by Petrov, distinguished from the others by the green tarpaulin stretched over its doorway.

He has been watching and listening for any signs of life in the lane, but all is still and quiet. He takes a final look around before pushing the tarpaulin aside and entering the dank, cool shelter.

Over an hour passes before he hears the sound of an engine and soon thereafter the crunch of heavy vehicle tires on the mud lane. He steps from behind the tarpaulin just as the bus comes to a stop beside him. It is gleaming and new; he can smell its fresh paintwork. The panels of the front door clunk open. He climbs aboard quickly. The driver is the man with the broken nose, whose name, according to Petrov, is Vasily. The door shuts immediately and the bus pulls away.

"Don't hang about," wheezes Vasily. "Check the seat. Make sure you know how it works before we get back on the highway. Stay there until we're out of Lvov."

Pasha goes to the back of the bus and raises the cushion of the long box seat. He drops his bag into the enclosed space beneath and climbs in after it. There is just room enough for him to stretch out full length if he keeps the bag beneath his head. As he pulls the seat cushion back in place above him, he is aware of the bus turning sharply as it doubles back to rejoin the highway.

Even this early in the day, it is hot in the narrow space, not only from the bright sun but also from the vehicle's engine, which seems to be directly beneath him. He reaches up and slides the seat cushion aside to let some air enter.

All he can do now is lie very still in order to keep his body temperature as low as possible. And replay Petrov's geography lesson of two nights ago.

Which turned out to be about more than geography.

* * *

"Here's Ukraine."

Petrov's hand descended on the map, as if he was an army general plotting his next conquest.

"Over here—Russia and the rest of the USSR." From there the hand swept in the opposite direction. "And here's the rest of Europe, some of it our beloved Comecon sister nations. And beyond them, the West." He paused for a gulp of vodka. "You know what Comecon is? You know who the Comecon countries are?"

Pasha thought back to his studies in the Leninka. "Our economic allies in Europe."

"Yes, but it's about more than economics. It's about politics. It's the countries whose leaders do what the man in the Kremlin tells them—Stalin or Khrushchev, makes no difference. He's the one who puts them in power and keeps them there. They're the countries that form a protective barrier between us and the West—Stalin's buffer zone that he demanded and got after the war with Nazi Germany. These days they're also the countries that buy Soviet-produced goods, including the beautiful buses we build in Lvov. Countries such as Poland and Hungary." The hand advanced across the map, hovered for a moment, and came to rest. "Countries such as Czechoslovakia." Another gulp of vodka. "Now, these buses of ours are great buses, but they don't have wings. So how do you suppose we get them to all those places, all those distant Soviet republics and the Comecon countries?"

"Someone drives them?"

"Correct. And it's my job to plan how that happens—who the driver will be and all the paperwork needed to cross country and republic borders."

He tipped the last of the vodka into his tumbler and sat back in his chair.

"In a couple of days I'll be sending a vehicle to Czechoslovakia—to the municipal transport authority in Bratislava." He looked at Pasha and raised his tumbler in a toast. "You'll be on that bus. You're going to Bratislava."

CHAPTER 53

GENNADY HAS AN uneasy feeling he should recognize the man standing in his doorway, but he cannot place him. There is nothing notable about his bland features, but his clothing provides uncomfortable clues: dark suit of good quality, the kind that can be purchased only in stores reserved for the nomenklatura and elite Party members; and stout city shoes with no dust on them, indicating that he travels by car.

Clues that are more than enough to cause Gennady's heart to sink.

The man is NKVD. He might as well have a sign about his neck. He knows it, too, for he does not even bother showing his ID.

"May I come in?" he asks, as if Gennady has a choice.

Gennady knows what is coming. Someone has reported Pasha.

"Nice apartment," says the man. He sits down, uninvited.

Gennady thinks about Valentina. She is at work. She will come home to find him gone.

"You don't remember me, do you?" says the man.

"I'm not sure." Gennady's mouth is dry; the words emerge as a whisper.

"You treated my mother. She'd be dead if it wasn't for you. She had a heart attack right outside your hospital. Coming up on six years ago. You saved her life and she's still going strong."

Dimly, Gennady remembers, though it no longer matters much now. As family of an NKVD officer, the woman had the right to be treated in a special clinic. But she collapsed practically on his hospital's doorstep. What else were he and his colleagues to do?

"Yes," he says. "I remember. I'm glad she's well."

The man nods slowly. His eyes narrow. "I understand you're looking for employment."

These people know everything. They will know all about Pasha, how long he was here, where he is now—in fact, they probably already have him in custody.

Gennady accepts that he is finished. There will be no amnesty from the gulag this time, no reprieve. Far worse, he has dragged Valentina down with him. It will not be a matter of her coming home to find him gone; they will take her, too—they may well be doing so at this very moment.

He thinks he is going to throw up.

The man is proffering a visiting card.

"Here," he says. "These are the contact details of the director of the Filatov Pediatric Hospital. You and I have a mutual friend there. That's who told me you're seeking a position. The director's expecting your call. He has a vacant post. He doesn't care that you've been away for a while. The job's yours."

He bids Gennady good day and departs.

CHAPTER 54

FROM LVOV, VASILY takes a route through lush countryside where cattle graze and wheat sways in the breeze. Pasha, released from his airless confinement beneath the back seat, now sits immediately behind Vasily. On the hillsides, rows of fruit trees stretch away on either side. Ukrainian land is rich land, Vasily tells him, more productive than much of Russia. There are collective farms, worked by armies of kolkhozniki, but there are also kulaki, known here in Ukraine as kurkuli, rich peasants who somehow survived or evaded the great collectivization of the land. It pleases Pasha that not even Josef Vissarionovich was able to subdue every Ukrainian.

The roads are poor, riddled with holes and cracks, some of them huge. Vasily is a careful driver who keeps to a moderate speed, but he cannot avoid every hazard. Sometimes a crack traps a wheel, so that he has to wrench the vehicle free with a determined lunge of the steering. Then he is obliged to stop and check the tire for damage.

Some of the road signs are in both Ukrainian and Russian. The script is almost the same, but the words are different. Sometimes the Russian versions have been defaced.

There is little other traffic, none of it private vehicles. All they encounter is the occasional lorry, sometimes military, or other buses; the buses are always fully laden with passengers. At these times, Pasha ducks out of sight in good time. Always he watches the road behind for vehicles catching up with them while Vasily watches ahead.

They pass roadside shrines and white-painted churches with golden domes. Occasionally, Vasily pulls in to buy fruit or vegetables from one of the stalls displaying racks of produce. As the bus slows, Pasha returns to his hiding place, where, if Vasily cuts the engine when he stops, he can hear him haggling with the seller. Vasily always uses Russian. Some of the sellers respond in Russian but some do not, either through ignorance of the language or on principle.

There is one occasion when Vasily does not haggle. Afterwards Pasha asks why.

"She was a gypsy. Never haggle with a gypsy. They put a curse on you. We don't want that, today of all days."

Sometime afterwards, Pasha is watching a lorry emerging from a dust cloud behind them when Vasily half turns and calls over his shoulder.

"It's time. Be quick."

It is the signal that they are approaching the border crossing from Ukraine into Czechoslovakia. Pasha retreats to the back seat and conceals himself. The bus continues for another ten or fifteen minutes, then slows down to what feels like walking pace.

He has been dreading this moment. It is all the worse for his entombment in this cramped space. He sees only darkness. It is afternoon now and the sun is high, turning the hollow seat into an oven. He does not dare move the cushion to let air in or heat out. All he can hear is the chug of the exhaust and the loud, throbbing beat of the engine, rising and falling as Vasily moves the vehicle forward by fits and starts, following what must be a queue of vehicles.

But what queue? With so little other road traffic in evidence, there cannot be many vehicles waiting to cross. In which case the delay can only be accounted for by the detailed level of inspection being given to each vehicle and its occupants and contents.

It is impossible to gauge time. Every minute stretches interminably. And in every minute Pasha waits for the abrupt removal of the seat cushion and the flood of daylight that will mean the worst has happened.

Suddenly he hears the clatter of the passenger door as it snaps open and the tramp of feet approaching along the aisle between the seats. He feels the vibration of each heavy footstep. They come closer and stop right beside him. He hears the seat cushion squeak as someone sits down. He hardly dares breathe. In a moment of panic he wonders if his sweat smells. Then he hears a reluctant sigh and the cushion squeaks again. A voice mutters something, as if its owner is complaining to himself about having to get back to work. The footsteps resume, growing fainter as they go away.

Pasha hears the clatter of the passenger door as it snaps shut.

The engine roars and the bus pulls sharply away. The uneven road surface jars his bones as the vehicle continues to accelerate through the gears, until, at last, it settles into a steady cruising speed.

His heart hammering, his body swimming in perspiration, he stares into the darkness, hardly able to believe what has happened.

He has left the Soviet Union.

CHAPTER 55

VASILY DRIVES FOR another few kilometers before taking the bus off the highway and into a stand of birch trees. He unpacks the fruit he bought along the way and shares it with Pasha, along with cheese and bread.

"Save your own food and eat this," he advises. "I'll get more, you can't. Keep what you have—you'll need it."

"Vasily, I'm not the first person you've taken on this kind of journey. Maybe Czechoslovakia, maybe somewhere else."

"You're not the first, no."

"How long have you been doing it?"

"About three years. Since Petrov got the idea."

"After Irina's arrest, then?"

"You might say that was what inspired him."

"What inspired you?"

"I'm Irina's godfather. I renounced evil on her behalf. I'm accountable to God for that. What happened to her—and Olga—is the work of the devil. He must be defeated. It's my duty." He scratches his misshapen nose. "You ask a lot of questions."

"What about the other men I met—are they involved, too?"

"Why would you want to know?"

"Are you armed today?"

"No. Too dangerous. If anything goes wrong, what use is one pistol? Better to be arrested than dead."

"There speaks a man who's never been to the gulag."

"At least it's only me who pays if I'm caught. And you, of course. You pay, too. But that's your choice."

"Why don't you and Petrov get yourselves out?"

"I have my family; he has Olga. You've seen how Olga is. She couldn't make a journey like this. My parents are old, they could never do it either. And my wife is too ill to travel—not ill like Olga, but ill in her blood. So what should we do—abandon them, leave them behind? That's why I'm allowed to do this delivery work—because I always come back. With family, I have no choice."

Pasha nods. It is a familiar story. It is the same as Viktor's warning to him and Irina in the camp.

He realizes that Vasily is still looking at him.

"It always feels like this for the ones like you," he tells Pasha. He bites into a plum.

"The ones like me? Meaning?"

"The ones who decide to escape. Russia never lets go of her children. She never lets go of your soul. That's why you're hurting."

"Am I hurting?"

"Naturally. Even if you don't know it yet. Or aren't admitting it, even to yourself." Vasily looks at his watch. "We should get going."

He spits out the plum stone, closes the door, and starts the engine.

Pasha turns away so that he can resume his scrutiny of the road behind them. And so that he does not have to meet Vasily's gaze in the driving mirror. He looks out the window but he sees the black river into which Viktor sank. He sees Irina, smiling like Leonardo's Mona Lisa.

Russia never lets go.

* * *

It is close to midnight when they reach the outskirts of Bratislava. The lights of scattered apartment blocks flicker through trees. The closer the bus comes to the city, the more dense becomes the housing and the nearer it marches to the highway. The road skirts a wooded hill and in the city proper divides into cobbled streets and a profusion of narrow, twisting lanes barely wide enough for the bus to negotiate. Here in the old town there are none of the ugly residential blocks, only steeply pitched tiled roofs and rows of four- and five-story buildings that watched many centuries pass before the tower blocks sprang up around them.

At this late hour the streets are almost deserted. No sign of any military patrols. Vasily lets Pasha sit behind him. They meet another bus and a tram in the same red and white livery, both vehicles almost empty of passengers.

They come to the river, a flat, sluggish expanse of muddy water.

"The Danube," says Vasily. They cross via a steel-framed bridge, a box-shaped structure of steel girders. Vasily flicks his cigarette butt out the window. "Some people call this the Stefanikov Bridge. It was destroyed by the retreating Germans at the end of the war, so the Red Army rebuilt it using German prisoners of war. As a result, the loyal socialists of Bratislava like to call it the Bridge of the Red Army."

On the south side of the river the character of the streets changes abruptly—the overbearing flat-faced apartment blocks are back; more are under construction. But gradually the buildings and the construction sites come to an end and the bus is passing through dark countryside again.

At last the vehicle begins to slow down.

"We're there," says Vasily.

The road is rough and narrow, formed of slabs of concrete, and little used, judging from the weeds sprouting between the slabs. On every side, Pasha sees only fields bordered by hedges. Nothing else, no lights, no sign of human habitation. He suspects that the waist-high vegetation in the fields is weeds, not crops.

Vasily stops at a junction where the road meets a graveled lane, maneuvering the bus to face back toward the city. He douses the headlights but keeps the engine running.

"This is as close as I can take you. Any closer and we'll attract the attention of a patrol. They might already have heard us, so watch your step out there. I have to get back to the municipal transport depot. The night shift will be waiting to check their new vehicle and sign it in." He points across the field beside which he has stopped. "The old railway track is just over there. You know what to do, right? Petrov explained everything? He showed you how it's done?" His gaze is gentle. "Good luck, my young comrade."

Pasha climbs down from the bus and watches its lights fade into the darkness. There is an emptiness in the pit of his stomach. His life seems to be a series of partings.

He finds a gap in the hedge and crosses into the field.

* * *

Petrov finished his vodka and eyed Pasha's tumbler.

"If you're not going to drink that, I'll have it before it evaporates."

Pasha slid the tumbler across to him. Petrov downed half of it.

"From Czechoslovakia you'll cross into Austria." He could have been outlining the itinerary of an afternoon stroll. "And this is where you need to understand the political geography of the place. Basically, Austria is a mess—for you, a helpful and advantageous mess. The country was carved up by the Allies, the four great powers, after the defeat of Germany. So there's an American zone, a British zone, a French zone, and a Soviet zone. Each power controls and administers its own zone. They're all stuck there, mired in the place. None of them wants to be there—all of them hate it; there's nothing they'd like better than to get out."

"I understand that—but which part do I enter?"

Petrov's gaze was slightly out of focus.

"The Soviet zone." He shrugged. "Where better?"

CHAPTER 56

Unlike the man who dropped in on Gennady, not all NKVD field operatives enjoy the luxury of performing their duties by car. The women who have been shadowing Nina and Sofya for the last few days must travel by foot, tram, and metro, like the targets of their surveillance.

There are at least six of these women, taking it in turn. They are there day and night, hurrying along behind their quarries in busy streets when their quarries hurry, strolling casually in Krasnaya Presnya Park when the sisters stroll, standing watch outside the dom. They never bother to conceal themselves, brazenly maintaining eye contact when either sister turns to look directly at them.

Even Alexei is aware of them.

"This happens to everyone sooner or later," Nina reassures him. "It means nothing. They'll stick around for a while, then they'll be off to pester someone else. Pay no heed."

"They want us to know they're there," she admits more truthfully to Sofya in private. "They're hoping to provoke us into doing something rash or careless. They want us to panic and give ourselves away. Or lead them to someone else."

"That only works if we have something to panic about, something to hide," argues Sofya.

"Well? Don't we?"

So that evening, once Alexei is asleep, the sisters comb through the apartment, looking for anything that could incriminate them or anyone linked to them, the obvious candidates being the more dubious of their late father's contacts. But they have always been careful in their dealings with these individuals. There is no evidence that could cause concern.

The same cannot be said in regard to Pasha Kalmenov.

"The remaining photographs of him," says Nina. "We can't take the risk. They'll want to know who he is."

It is a hard decision, for they both want to remember him, but she puts the prints and the negatives on the fire.

"We don't need photographs. We won't forget him."

Sofya sighs as she watches them burn. "What about the drawings of Viktor? They prove we had contact with someone from the camp."

An even harder decision, but the drawings go on the fire as well.

* * *

The knock on the apartment door the following night is so restrained that neither sister is confident it is there. Only when the knock comes again does Nina answer it. The two women she finds standing in the hallway are new faces to her, none of the ones she has seen before. Behind them loom two men, but it is the women who are in charge. Both present their NKVD badges for Nina's scrutiny.

The women and the sisters sit at the table. The men wander through the apartment. Nina warns them off Alexei's room. They shrug, unconcerned, as if they know they will get there in the end. Nina and Sofya hear the other rooms being searched.

To begin with, the NKVD women are as deferential as the gentle knock that announced their arrival. They verify Nina's and Sofya's identities and ask a few introductory questions. Then they get going in earnest.

"You have a brother," says the younger of the two, clearly the boss. "Where is he? Is he in this apartment at present?"

It is not what either sister was expecting. They look at each other in surprise.

"He's not here, he was arrested three years ago," says Nina quickly, anxious that Sofya might say he is dead—information they should not have.

"We have no record of any arrest."

"That's ridiculous," blurts Sofya.

Nina touches her sister's arm to prevent her saying any more.

"My sister doesn't mean to speak disrespectfully. It wasn't the Commissariat for Internal Affairs who arrested our brother. It was a militia unit. Perhaps if you check militia records?"

"We did. No militia unit made an arrest at this address. This means your brother is at large."

"That makes him sound like a criminal."

"If he was arrested as you say, then that's what he is. Is he a member of any underground or subversive organization?"

"What? Of course not."

"Certain people in this dom report that he hasn't been seen here for several years. There's no record of him applying for a change of residency. So either he relocated illegally or he's in hiding for some criminal purpose. After all, your father was a criminal. Perhaps criminality runs in the family."

"Kindly leave our father out of this. Our brother is no criminal. He was arrested for no reason, taken away from here, we don't know where. It's not our fault if the records are wrong."

"Who was the man you admitted to this dom and presumably to this apartment on two occasions recently? You brought him in through the service entrance under cover of darkness. Why did you feel the need to act in that clandestine manner? Was he your brother?"

Nina sees the danger. Sofya will be the weak link. If put under sufficient pressure, she will buckle and tell what she knows. And she knows a lot—everything there is to know about Pasha, for a start. She will tell about the forged passport and the man who supplied it; he in turn may give the names of his accomplices. Sofya will also tell about Irina's family in Lvov, endangering them if Pasha has found them and they have allowed him under their roof.

All these good people betrayed and sacrificed.

In that circumstance, both she and Sofya are lost. If they are lucky, they will end up in Lefortovo. Less lucky, and they will follow their father and Viktor to the gulag.

And Alexei?

He will be put into state care. An orphanage. God forbid. His life will be as good as over.

Nina steels herself. There is only one possible way out, one way that might save Sofya and Alexei and the others. If it works.

"Very well," she says, speaking over the NKVD woman.

Sofya stares at her sister in alarm. Nina responds with a warning glance. The young NKVD woman smiles coldly, sensing victory.

"You're right," says Nina. "A man did come here. It was our brother. He came for money. We don't know where he's gone now. We've disowned him. I gave him money and said we don't want to see him again."

"So you admit helping a criminal who's in hiding."

"I did it on my own. My sister was against it, she tried to stop me, but I carried on. She took no part in my crime."

"She failed to report it."

"I coerced her to remain silent. The crime is mine and mine alone."

The two men have returned, mysteriously detecting that matters have come to a head.

"Take this one to the van," commands the NKVD woman, indicating Nina. "As for the other one, I have no interest in wasting our time on her, even though she failed to report the crime. Let her take care of the boy. That will do for her. Why should the state have to clothe and feed the child of a criminal?"

Now she turns to Sofya. "This is a privilege apartment. The three of you should never have been permitted to remain here, and you and the boy will certainly not be allowed to stay on. More appropriate accommodation will be arranged for you."

Sofya bursts into tears. She pleads for Nina not to be arrested and taken from Andrei; she begs to be allowed to keep the apartment.

But Nina does not plead. She does not beg. Nina is silent. A glance passes between her and the NKVD woman. Only a glance, nothing more, but it is enough.

Nina recognizes mercy when she sees it, even thin, miserly mercy. It is still mercy.

CHAPTER 57

Pasha comes to the railway line after five or six minutes. Its rails are rusted and weeds have spread through the stony clinker. According to Vasily, like the Stefanikov Bridge, the line was destroyed by the routed Germans. Unlike the bridge, however, it has never been repaired.

He follows the line by walking beside it rather than on the track, to avoid the noise of the clinker and because the track's elevation would make him more visible. His only light is the thin moon. He cannot help thinking back to a railway line far distant from this one that also determined the path of his life.

When the fence comes into view, he crouches down among the high grass and tangled weeds. There are Czech army bunkers in these fields, but he does not know where; Petrov admitted that his information is imperfect, incomplete. "Like life itself," he jested, but Pasha did not see the joke. There are watchtowers, too, at intervals along the fence—but none close to here, Petrov insisted.

"They think the railway line makes this part of the fence impregnable because it's impossible to dig beneath it. But you won't be doing that. There's a better way."

Pasha stays very still; he watches and listens. He knows there are armed guards who patrol on foot. Sometimes they can be relied on to pass at regular intervals; sometimes their timing is erratic. He could waste time waiting for one that never appears or he could begin work and be forced to abort, with the panic of trying to leave no clues to his presence. His one advantage is that a trooper in heavy boots and encumbered by weaponry and equipment does not move silently.

Somewhere in the distance a dog is barking. Crickets click in the long grass. He moves closer to the fence. On this, Petrov's information is good—the fence is exactly as he described. It stands almost four meters high, consisting of timber uprights linked by horizontal stretches of barbed wire and with crosspieces also linked with wire. The wire is electrified. The brambles and tough grass that grow abundantly in the field have been cropped along the line of the fence, to ensure that its five thousand volts meet no obstacle to their killing power.

He decides not to delay any longer. Still crouching, he goes on the railway line and right up to the fence. He opens the fishing bag and takes out the gauntlets that Petrov gave him and the two lengths of wood that the man prepared. Each length has two short slats screwed securely into one end in a V shape. He hooks one of the lengths under the lowest stretch of barbed wire and slowly begins to raise the wire. Here where the fence crosses the railway the wire is set slightly higher than in the field, to allow clearance above the metal rails—because a wandering deer or dog, if electrocuted, might bring the wire into contact with a rail and cause a short circuit. The extra height is only about ten centimeters, but Pasha is glad to have the benefit of it.

As ever, his hands are a problem. Matters are made worse by the gauntlets. They have come from the bus factory and are made from some kind of heavy rubber. The idea is that they might provide a degree of insulation in the event of a mishap—though he is skeptical as to whether anything could mitigate those five thousand volts—but their stiffness makes it almost impossible for him to grip the wood firmly. He has to use both hands, and even then he still has to contend with the tremble that has seized him, for now fear has been joined by anxiety that the wire will snap and spring back at him, delivering its lethal voltage.

But the wire does not break. At last it is high enough for him to embed the bottom of the wooden prop firmly in the clinker. It is vital that the prop is vertical; he needs every centimeter. He sits back to steady himself and wipes his eyes on his sleeve; inside his clothing his body is slick with sweat.

He uses the second length of wood to prop up the wire where it passes above the other rail. He pauses to bring his breathing under control, all the time watching and listening for any movement in the darkness around him.

When he feels ready for the next stage, he pushes the fishing bag through the opening and slides it to one side. He follows it with his jacket and cap. He moves back from the fence and lies flat on his stomach in the center of the track, stretching his arms toward the fence and keeping them close together, as if he is a swimmer about to dive. He turns his head to the side. The height provided by the wooden props was checked and double-checked by Petrov; Pasha tells himself there will be no mistake: he should pass through safely without ever touching the deadly wire; he should be unharmed.

Should be.

He is sweating even more now. He digs his toes into the clinker and begins to push himself forward, raising his body the minimum necessary. Any other man would pull strongly with his fingers at the same time. He scrabbles at the stones; even though he has kept the gauntlets on to provide more grip, his efforts are feeble.

And yet he *is* moving. The world has been reduced to this single rusty rail before his eyes and these sharp stones beneath his cheek, and each of these things tells him that he is moving. He blinks sweat from his eyes, feels a railway sleeper against his cheek; now he is passing over it; now it is gone and the stones are there against his face again, the weeds folding as he moves over them.

The worst time is when his chest is under the wire, because now he feels trapped. He will be helpless, unable to save himself, if a guard arrives. He resists the temptation to speed up, to rush.

At last he is safely through. He wants to rest, but this is not the time. He turns back to the fence and carefully removes the two props while whispering a word of thanks to Petrov. He gathers everything together and descends from the rail line into the long grass, where he resumes walking.

For a while, until his nerves settle, his steps are shaky, uncertain. He has counted almost three hundred paces when the second fence comes into view. Somewhere between the first fence and this one is the actual border.

He squats low among the crabgrass and velvety weeds, and listens and watches as he did before. He is about to straighten up when he hears the crunch of a boot on a pebble or rock. He sinks deeper into the grass, until he is almost prone. There is a short burst of male laughter, close now, then a male voice, speaking in Russian.

"That's what I told him, but you know he's a fool. He'll never learn."

There is the sound of a match striking. A light flares briefly. A second voice says something, but now it is more distant and too faint for Pasha to make out the words. He smells cigarette smoke. Footsteps recede.

He stays there, listening, until he is sure the troopers have departed.

They were Russian: NKVD because borders are NKVD business. NKVD with their Kalashnikovs.

The first fence was Czechoslovakia's; this one is the USSR's. Beyond it is the Soviet zone of Austria.

He hunkers forward to the railway line, sets out the wooden props and the gauntlets, and gets to work again.

* * *

"Once you're in Austria, stay away from the Austrians," cautioned Petrov. "Don't make the mistake of thinking any of them will help you. They hate Russians. The Red Army lost tens of thousands of men in Austria. When they finally got rid of the Germans, they took what they considered their due reward—they raped and plundered their way through the country. Stalin did nothing to stop it, said it was only to be expected, that was just how war was—and since most Austrians had supported Hitler, why be surprised? The result? Austrians hate us."

"Everybody seems to hate us."

Petrov shrugged and knocked back the last of Pasha's vodka.

* * *

An hour later, the fences and the border are behind him, and he is deep within the Austrian countryside—a patchwork of fields that must once have been good farmland but are now overrun by scrubby undergrowth.

He has not forgotten his navigational skills. With the moon as his guide, he is heading west to begin with. He sticks to the margins of fields instead of cutting through them so that there is no broken vegetation as evidence of his passing. He avoids lanes and existing trails where he might meet troops or local people. When he sees the silhouettes of barns or buildings of any kind, he steers well clear.

A steep escarpment rises before him against the night sky. As he comes nearer, he sees that it is forested. The trees might provide good cover, but they could also conceal troops. He turns north.

He hears the river before he sees it. He has returned to the Danube. The sluggish water he glimpsed from Vasily's bus is here flowing smoothly and is so broad that the other bank is invisible.

He turns west again, still keeping to the fields instead of the track running beside the river. He is on course. He will follow the river upstream. He will rest along the way and remain out of sight. He has plenty of time, for daybreak is still a couple of hours away, the land is flat and the going easy, and he will have the whole of the new day in which to reach his destination.

Vienna.

CHAPTER 58

WITH THE VODKA gone, Petrov resorted to beer, a dark brew with a vinegary smell. He rolled a cigarette and lit it with a spill from the stove. The geography lesson continued.

"Vienna sits right in the middle of Austria's Soviet zone—an island in a Soviet sea. But in the same way as the country has been divided by the four Allied powers, so, too, Vienna has been sliced into zones that each of them controls, district by district. The Soviet zone of Austria takes you straight to a district of Vienna called Simmering."

"And which of the four powers controls Simmering?"

Petrov managed a lopsided grin. "The British."

* * *

It is early evening when Pasha comes to a shallow ditch between two fields. In front of him is a noticeboard advising him in Russian that he is leaving the Soviet zone of Austria and entering British-administered territory of Vienna. There are other languages on the board; he assumes they say the same thing.

He has reached Simmering.

He looks at the land around him, at this marshy field in which he is standing, a field as unexceptional as every other he has come through today, and completely indistinguishable from the field it adjoins, the field beyond the noticeboard. Apart from that single noticeboard, there is no other marker in sight. Above all, there is no electrified fence. In fact, there is no fence at all. There is no line in the ground saying one side is Soviet and the other British. There is no British frontier post to keep him out. On the Soviet side there are no NKVD troopers to keep him in. There is only a solitary Soviet checkpoint in the distance, which he spotted well in advance and avoided by an easy detour. He was not even convinced that the checkpoint was manned.

So simple. After everything else he has been through, it is all so simple.

He takes a breath, steps across the ditch, drops the fishing bag, and sits beside it on the damp earth. He is trembling. The tall blue thistles and tough grass grow as thickly on this side of the noticeboard as on the side he has just left. They look just the same on either side, as do the gulls circling above the river in the last of the light, and the rabbits foraging outside their burrows.

But he is sitting on the earth of Western Europe.

* * *

The evening is advanced and darkness has fallen by the time he reaches Landstrasse district, an uninterrupted walk from Simmering. This, too, is British territory, abutting the Inner Stadt where the four powers each have their headquarters.

His route takes him alongside the Donaukanal, its water malodorous and dark, the surface broken by ripples to the sound of soft splashes that make his skin crawl. On the other side of the canal is

Soviet-controlled Leopoldstadt. Here in the center of the city, the security presence is more evident and more alert, with Soviet checkpoints on every bridge. In the streets beyond them, he sees armed troops patrolling in twos and threes, military personnel carriers with the red star on their doors, and street signs in Russian.

He brings his attention back to his own side of the canal. Landstrasse is a place of ill-lit streets, ponderous buildings half destroyed by war and still unrepaired, and waste areas filled with rubble. Yet every ruined street corner seems to have its bar or nightclub with raucous laughter spilling into the night and its own parade of whores—unfussy enough to call out even to him—and every putrid alleyway has its drunks and beggars. He loops the fishing bag across his chest and holds it close. There will be thieves here.

The sound of a motor engine makes him swing around sharply, but it is not a military vehicle. A large black saloon car zigzags from the road onto the curb. Its windows are open, a woman is nuzzling the neck of the man who is driving. The car barely misses an old woman wearing footwear woven from basketwork and stuffed with rags. She spits on the vehicle as it pulls away. Its occupants are oblivious to her ire and her phlegm.

A man picks through rubble in the uncertain light of a street lamp that flickers on and off. On a burned-out building there are lurid advertising hoardings in languages Pasha does not understand, with illustrations of products whose purposes he cannot grasp. Above the hoardings, he sees faces in the frameless windows of smoke-streaked rooms he thought at first glance were uninhabited.

He wanders past everything in a daze. There was a time when he would have captured these sights on paper, a time when he would have closed his eyes and seen everything all the better.

But he does not close his eyes. Another vehicle is approaching. This time an open-topped military police jeep has rounded the corner and is coming in his direction, bouncing over the broken cobbles of the road. On its radiator grill is a badge showing the distinctive red and white crosses and deep blue background of the British flag.

Pasha steps into the vehicle's path and raises his arms.

CHAPTER 59

"BLOODY HELL," GASPS the British corporal as he slams on the brakes. His partner flips open his holster and rests his hand on his pistol.

Before them in the headlight beams stands a tattered figure remarkable even by the standards of this mutilated city. The man lowers his arms and stares straight at them, unblinking despite the harsh beams. The soldiers see a thin face beneath a leather cap, a grubby and shapeless jacket with at least one elbow out, and frayed trousers above boots caked in dirt. A shabby bag hangs over his chest.

The corporal applies the handbrake and both men vault from the jeep, hands on pistols.

"Can we help you, sir? Not a good idea to step into the road like that."

The man replies, but they have no idea what he is saying.

"Russian," declares the corporal, who has been here long enough to recognize the sound of the language.

The man allows himself half a smile. "Da—Russki."

"Sir, if you're a Soviet citizen, what are you doing here? Are you aware this is the British sector?"

It is not clear if the Russian understands. He does not attempt a reply. Nor does he seem particularly bothered.

The corporal looks him over. He has seen many types in his tour of duty here, but there is something different about this character. He looks like a hobo but he stands here as cool and composed as if he owns the city.

"May I see your papers, sir?" says the corporal crisply, feeling an instinctive need to assert his authority, though he is not sure why he should feel it has been diminished in any way. Still, the feeling is there, so for good measure he clicks his fingers and opens his palm in the universally understood gesture.

The Russian begins to undo the bag.

"Nice and slow," warns the corporal. He tightens his grip on the pistol.

Again the Russian gets the message. Again the half smile. He raises the flap of the bag slowly, keeping an eye on the corporal. He seems to find the procedure amusing. His eyes are pale, almost colorless.

With some difficulty, because something is wrong with his hands, he eventually produces a small, green-backed booklet like a passport and passes it over. He waits calmly as the corporal opens it and compares the photograph with the man before him.

The corporal does not read Russian, so cannot make out the man's name. But judging from what looks like a date of birth, he and the Russian are about the same age. Exhaustion and hunger age a person.

But neither exhaustion nor hunger could account for the mangled hands that fumbled to open the bag.

The corporal returns the passport.

"So how can we help you, sir? Would you like us to escort you back to the Soviet zone?"

The Russian seems to understand this well enough. He shakes his head slowly but firmly.

"Sovietskaya zona? Nyet."

"So what do you want, sir?" The corporal mentally searches his few words of Russian, then adds, stumbling on the pronunciation, "Chto khochesh?"

The reply is immediate and unambiguous. "Angliya."

"England?"

"Da."

The corporal pauses. "Sir, are you telling me you want to go to England?"

The Russian gives a decisive nod.

The corporal raises his eyebrows and exhales a long breath.

"Is he saying he wants to defect?" mutters his partner, new to this strange posting and finding it stranger by the minute. "What the hell do we do now?"

The corporal is in no doubt. He knows when a decision is above his pay grade. Knows it a mile off.

"We take him to HQ. If he's significant—like high-ranking military—there'll be a fuss. HQ will need to have a good hard think. If he's Comrade Ivan Nobody, there's a good chance we'll quietly let him in. Just another refugee. We take all sorts. We're all strays from somewhere. So, what do you reckon? Does he look to you like a major player? Does he strike you as a senior NKVD officer? Secret agent? Somebody who'll set diplomatic alarm bells ringing?"

His partner grins as he eyes the ragged stranger. "Nope."

"Well, then. Could be his lucky day."

The Russian raises no objection when the corporal pats him down to ensure he is unarmed. The grubby shoulder bag contains nothing but paper and sketch pads, a hank of black cloth that may be a woman's shawl, with tiny blue flowers embroidered on it, some ruble banknotes, worthless here, and a religious icon. As that last item appears, the corporal, a Methodist long lapsed, grunts. He replaces everything and returns the bag to the Russian, then sweeps his arm theatrically toward the jeep.

"Your carriage awaits, sir."

A minute later, with the three of them aboard, he throws the vehicle into gear and accelerates back toward the Inner Stadt and headquarters.

In the back seat his unexpected passenger sits very still, his head bent over his precious old bag. His eyes are tightly shut, his brow furrowed. It occurs to the corporal, who remembers such a look of deep concentration on the faces of those around him in his long-ago days in chapel, that the man might actually be praying.

PART THREE

CHAPTER 60

1979. Central London

It is one of those November days when London is at her best. Autumn leaves are falling along Whitehall. Their gold and ochre mingle with the wreaths of blood-red poppies that were placed around the Cenotaph on Remembrance Day. The scarlet of the poppies is there again in the buses lumbering along Whitehall and into Parliament Square—scarlet for the dead but scarlet also for those still busy with life.

In Parliament, the Commons Chamber is hushed and expectant as the Prime Minister rises to her feet. Her voice strong and clear, she tells the House that the individual whose name has been supplied to her in relation to the security of the United Kingdom—that being the parliamentary question to which she is responding—is Sir Anthony Blunt.

She describes how he was recruited as an agent and talent spotter by Russian intelligence while he was at Cambridge University. He joined Britain's security service, even though he was known to have been a Marxist, and over the ensuing years passed to his Soviet handlers whatever intelligence material came his way. She relates how he finally confessed to his crimes, but only after the security service granted him immunity from prosecution.

She provides many details, most of them to do with the security aspects of the case, and she refers also, though only briefly, to Blunt's appointments as Surveyor of the King's Pictures and later of the Queen's Pictures. She does not say that in these capacities he looked Her Majesty in the eye, and before that her father, on an almost daily basis for over thirty years while being fully aware of the treachery he had perpetrated against his country and them.

She says nothing about forged Leonardo artworks.

The man watching and listening in the public gallery is not surprised by that omission. Even a Russian like him can see how the acknowledgement of such a mishap would stick in a British throat.

Pasha Kalmenov, himself a British citizen these many years, sighs. Anthony Frederick Blunt is finished. That will have to be enough to satisfy him.

CHAPTER 61

THE LITTLE FLAT, Blunt's spartan refuge on the top floor of Home House, is long gone. It was a perk that came with the Courtauld directorship, and that ended five years ago. So these days the elegance of Portman Square has been exchanged for this uninspired and uninspiring blockhouse in Portsea Place, behind Edgware Road. What a difference a few hundred yards can make. And to think that in order to pay for the privilege, he had to sell a gorgeous Poussin. The unkindest cut.

No, not the unkindest. That cut was delivered today by that dreadful woman. That horrid, petty-minded person with her petit bourgeois mentality. Her statement to the House—there was no need for that. It served no purpose other than pandering to her own anti-Establishment leanings. It was simple spite—a kick at privileged ankles.

But he will not be bowed. The hounds may have brought the great pretender down, run him to ground all those years ago, just as she said, but the glorious game remains his, not theirs. He gave nothing—no names, nothing. Honor is unequivocally his, the honor of never giving up one single friend.

And, of course, there is the matter of the Leonardos. His last hurrah, his final flourish. He still has that. The dullard hounds will never even know of that glorious blow.

He turns the television off—it is the set the Courtauld staff presented to him as a leaving gift, the only one he has ever owned, and he treasures it to this day—and goes to the window. Yes, the press rabble are down on the forecourt, hovering like vultures. God, so many. They lost no time. They were tipped off, of course. The street is clogged with huge pantechnicons. That means television as well. The road is narrow; the traffic can scarcely pass. Electrical cables everywhere, floodlights—a circus, the only word for it. Crass, like that frightful woman.

Horrified residents, among them neighbors he recognizes, hurry past the horde, shaking their heads at the questions bawled at them, appalled to realize they may see themselves on the evening news or in tomorrow's papers.

He will not be popular.

* * *

Popular. He admits it is an odd thought to have in relation to himself. Popularity was never something he craved or sought. A cold fish, he has been called in his time; distant, standoffish.

Yet he is sure he has been loved. Not only by the staff at the Courtauld but by the students, too—oh, not sexual love, but the pure, devoted love of scholars for the master who flings open for them the doors of learning, who shows them how to weave gold from the arid dust of their studies.

And his lectures—how they always loved his lectures.

But there is one uncomfortable memory that surfaces. He used to give public lectures as well as those reserved for his students. Anyone could come to the public ones; that was their raison d'être. Cultural democracy, art history for the great unwashed: that was the idea. They were always a success, invariably well attended. The incident that comes to mind now must be over twenty years ago, but he has never been able to forget it. It involved that strange man who always stood at the back of the room. Never sat down, even when there were plenty of chairs. Never spoke to a soul. Walked off if anyone tried to engage him in conversation. Always left as soon as the lecture ended. No one had the foggiest idea who he was. This went on for about a year.

Then came the day when he did not leave at once. Waited for everyone else to go, then came right to the front of the lecture hall. Stood himself only inches away. Peculiar detail—it was the height of summer, a sweltering day, but he was wearing gloves.

"I know what you did," he said, without introduction. He spoke softly, one might even say gently, although his pale eyes were cold. "I have tracked you down. The Leninka was very helpful. Where are the originals? That was what I wanted to know—in which collection? I knew that these things are always a matter of record. The trail led to you, to your monarch's Royal Collection. There was even the little crown that used to puzzle me. You had control, you could remove the originals and prevent anyone knowing. It had to be you. So here I am. I should kill you, but I will not do that. I believe in life, not death. Your soul is black and thick with death but I will not put such a sin on my soul. There will be a judgment for you. Deuteronomy 32:35."

Then he turned on his heel and left. Thankfully, he never showed up again.

Report it to the police? Absolutely not. No one else heard what the man said. No direct threat was made. Quite the reverse, arguably.

One other detail—he spoke with a distinct Russian accent.

So no, it was best not to involve the police.

Later the clergyman's son unearthed his father's Bible and checked the reference.

"To me belongeth vengeance . . . the day of their calamity is at hand."

* * *

He realizes that the phone is ringing. He almost decides not to answer it—some reporter has winkled out his number—but he relents and lifts the receiver.

"Hello?" he says tentatively. He does not permit the instrument to touch his ear, as if it might be infectious.

He listens for a moment.

"Yes, this is he."

He listens again, but not for long. A knife to the heart does not take long.

"I see." There is a quiver in his voice. He does his best to master it. "Thank you for informing me. I'm so very sorry. So very, very sorry."

Courtesy in all things, in all circumstances. That was his mother's way, and it is his, too. Courtesy even when it is all we have left—above all, perhaps, when it is all we have left.

He replaces the receiver. He is shaking like a leaf. He can feel the right side of his face freezing and locking as the palsy strikes. A river of tears streams from the right eye—just another little affliction he has added to his growing list.

They have taken the knighthood away.

The unkindest cut of all.

CHAPTER 62

It is a pleasant street, tucked away between Shoreditch and Bethnal Green. It is leafy and dappled with sunshine in spring and summer, and in autumn and winter cozy with its warm red brick, as it is today. The residents and shopkeepers have always been friendly, even to a Russian, and there is a small park at one end where Pasha's daughters, Victoria and Irina, used to play when they were very little.

The locals were surprised when Studio Kalmenov arrived among them. Hardly the place for an art gallery, surely. A modest little street like theirs, with no airs and graces? Who would come here to buy fine art?

But plenty did, and they still do—because Pasha Kalmenov has an eye for talent and knows how to nurture it. And word spreads quickly among both artists and buyers.

So Studio Kalmenov is still here. As are the newsagent and the greengrocer, the launderette and the hardware store, the café and the bookshop, all of which were here before Studio Kalmenov but now enjoy the spillover from its success. Other small enterprises have joined them, so that the street is more alive than ever. There is a little cluster of garment shops, very chic, catering to the city people who have moved in. There are potted plants on the pavements, and benches outside every shop front, encouraging shoppers to linger and allow themselves to be tempted into making another purchase. On some days the street is given over to a lively open-air market, attracting outsiders who return when the street is back to its everyday self.

Today, Pasha is not in the gallery showroom where he is usually to be found. Today, he is in the workshop at the rear, working on one of his own paintings. He does not wear his gloves when he paints.

He is alone. The girls are at school, and his wife, Katya, is at her surgery. Winter is a busy time for doctors.

Like all Pasha's own work, the painting he is working on today will never be offered for sale; it is for him and him alone. It depicts a street filled with people—this street, in fact, bathed in warm summer sunshine.

He changes brushes and colors as he works, occasionally stepping back to see how things are looking. He still cannot draw, cannot do fine line work or be precise. Those gifts will never be his again. So instead, he seeks to capture feeling without detail, mood without precision. Here on his canvas are trees in leaf, and summer light on faces. Color and life. People bustle and weave through the sunlit scene. So much movement—yes, he decides, he has caught the flow of movement. He can still do that. No need of detail to do that.

In his painting the open-air market is underway. Multicolored awnings ripple beneath the trees in a soft breeze. The traders and the shops are busy with customers. So much going on, such energy, everywhere something fresh for the eye to discover.

Here is a tall young man, lanky, all elbows and so tall he has to duck as he passes beneath one of the awnings. Swift strokes of the brush suggest his thinning hair and a skimpy beard. He has his arm around the young woman by his side. She is petite and slender. The two of them are laughing, faces close together as he bends toward her, their gazes locked fast on one another, as if they will never part.

And they never will. They are safe within the painting's little world. Nothing can harm them here. There are tiny hints of green in her eyes—only hints, for the brushwork is imprecise. Impressions, suggestions, nothing exact.

On the other side of the street is another man with a beard—but a great hedge of a beard this time—and a mane of flowing dark hair. His tan-colored cape swings behind him as he strides along, upright and confident. He seems to have slipped into the scene from another era. A flourish of the brush creates a lazy trail of cigarette smoke.

Here is a woman with a black shawl fixed snugly over her shoulders despite the sunshine. Sprinkles of cornflower blue here and there in the shawl catch the eye.

There are many other people in the busy scene—among them two sisters, tall and graceful, a barrel-chested man, a little old man with distrustful eyes, and someone with oversized spectacles and an owlish gaze.

And down here, in the corner, is another intriguing figure, another young man. He is sitting on the bench outside Studio Kalmenov and has a sketch pad on his lap. He is sketching the scene before him. He draws with his left hand. The hand of an angel, perhaps.

A touch of Pasha's brush, and the young man's eyes close. There—he can see more clearly now.

Pasha puts his brush down and looks at his work. It is finished. He has conferred life on all of them in the only way he can.

It is a pleasant street, a good street. It is his street. It is home.

AUTHOR'S NOTE

THE ORIGINS OF THE LEONARDO GULAG

With my wife, Roz, and our three sons, I visited the Château du Clos Lucé in the French city of Amboise, where Leonardo da Vinci spent his last years. The château is now a museum dedicated to Leonardo, with working models of many of his inventions. During that visit a seed was planted in my mind, to write a novel in which Leonardo or his work would be central. But life and other novels intervened—until one day Roz said: "You should go back to *Leonardo*." So I did.

HISTORICAL NOTE

I have set *The Leonardo Gulag* firmly within the framework and timing of actual historical events and political circumstances. Thus, Stalin's gulag regime and his dictatorial leadership of the USSR are fact, not fiction. So are the timing and the mysterious manner of his death as presented in the novel, and the way in which his death was finally announced. Anthony Blunt's treachery over many decades is a matter of historical fact. He was Surveyor of the King's Pictures and then of the Queen's Pictures from 1945 until 1972, after which he continued as Adviser until 1979, when he was exposed and denounced by the then Prime Minister, Margaret Thatcher. The Royal Collection really does hold hundreds of Leonardo da Vinci's priceless drawings, and Blunt had complete control over the Collection during his tenure as Surveyor.

But, of course, *The Leonardo Gulag* is a work of fiction, an act of the imagination. So even though some of the characters are actual historical figures, their actions and thoughts remain entirely my own fabrication.

As for the question of whether some of the Leonardo drawings held by The Royal Collection may indeed be forgeries—well, I must leave that for the reader to decide.

MOSCOW STREET NAMES

Moscow street names can be confusing. After the Revolution of 1917, names with religious or imperial connections were changed in favor of names honoring revolutionary, military, or cultural figures. After the dissolution of the USSR in 1991, names were changed again, sometimes reverting to their previous names. For example, Malaya Nikitskaya Ulitsa (Little Nikitsky Street), the location of Beria's mansion, was known as Ulitsa Kachalova (Kachalov Street) during his time, and has now reverted to its old name.

I have used today's names in the novel. Hopefully this will assist any readers who wish to follow Pasha's wanderings through Moscow.

More information about *The Leonardo Gulag* and
my other novels can be found at www.kevindoherty.com